As the Cards Fall

As the Cards Fall

Christina Green

ROBERT HALE • LONDON

ISBN 978 0 7198 0935 4

Robert Hale Limited
Clerkenwell House
Clerkenwell Green
London EC1R 0HT

www.halebooks.com

2 4 6 8 10 9 7 5 3 1

Typeset in Georgia
Printed by MPG Printgroup, UK

Acknowledgements

I want to acknowledge the Dartmoor historians who helped me with research, and all my writing friends who listened, commented and encouraged.

CHAPTER 1

Abworthy, 1870

*T*he gunshot echoes around the yard, rippling through the hills surrounding the farm and then dying into silence, broken only by the dog barking, by rooks shouting in the elms and William's breath whistling through his teeth as he collapses. He falls heavily on one side, hand clutching the wound, which slowly begins to bleed.

Marianne, watching from the bedroom window, rushes downstairs, knocking into Mrs May, who was making her way to the kitchen door. 'Oh dear Lord, those brothers, always fighting. What trouble've we got now?'

Ned, eyes like cold stones and still holding the gun, stands staring at the large body on the ground. His lips are hard, his voice vehement. 'You took her to bed, you took my little wife, and I didn't know—'

William raises his head, sets his mouth and says quietly, pain in every hard-spoken word, 'You were drunk, boy. She deserved better than that. So yes, I took her, gave her quietness on her wedding night. You've got no reason to do this – here, help me up.'

All around, hands reach out for him; the yard men are at his side, leaning down, heaving him upright. The blood flows freely from his left arm. He looks down at it, dark humour in *his voice, mutters, 'Thanks for not hitting me heart. You were always a bad shot.' He turns, hand clasped to the wound just above his elbow and orders, 'Get me a drink. And a knife or something to get the shot out. And Mrs May, some of your herbs and a bandage.'*

Movement now in the yard and Marianne steps away, into the shadow of the stone house, hand pressed to her mouth, staring at the small procession shuffling towards the open door. When it disappears inside she looks towards Ned, standing with the gun couched on his arm. He has a shocked look, something that sends prickles through her. He hates his brother; suddenly it's clear and terrible. Ned is her husband. His ring is on her finger and she still wears the new dress she bought especially for the wedding yesterday. She is his wife. And now she knows that he wants to kill his brother. But William was kind to her last night, taking her out of the cider fumes and bawdy laughter, away from Ned, who had seemed too drunk to even stand.

She tries to sort out her thoughts. Yes, she must stand by Ned. And then another thought makes her flinch. She must forget William.

Abworthy, 1891

Isabella Reed climbed out of the trap, staring up at the granite-stoned house in front of her. They had arrived by way of a rough, sloping track where flint and mud coated them as the trap pushed along. High hedges scratched the side of the vehicle, and wandering branches fingered her as they drove along. And now here was what she imagined must be Abworthy Farm.

Looking around she saw a dirty courtyard, collapsing wooden sheds and dilapidated buildings forming a rough square. The grey house stretched the length of the yard, its granite shining in the misty rain that dampened the air. It looked old – centuries, perhaps. Bella had never seen such a house before. She was used to suburban Exeter, the residential area of set-back Victorian villas full of comfort and privacy.

Now, despite her continual longing for a different sort of life, here she felt suddenly and with a twinge of something akin to fear, that the house was a power in itself. And then, raising her eyes to look at the tall chimney, she saw something behind it gleaming through the mist. A rocky eminence, formed out of tangled slabs of stone, thrusting high into the cloudy skies, dominating and dwarfing the farm and its outbuildings. She sensed that it had a presence, and a shiver ran down her. Quickly, she climbed out of the trap. Lizzie Wharton reached for the valise and then stood beside her.

Stepping towards the huge black timber door, Bella looked down at her feet, feeling a sudden dampness. Her shoes were covered in something brown and disgusting. The smell drifted up to her and she frowned, mind chasing circles. What was she doing here? Why had she come? Surely the letter had been a hoax? What had Miss Carpenter said?

'Someone's idea of a joke, no doubt.' Miss Carpenter's short-sighted eyes had scanned the letter and then replaced it in the envelope. 'No scholar writing this, terrible scribble and the spelling – well, really....' Sitting opposite Bella at the breakfast table, Miss Carpenter had removed her spectacles, replaced them in the case and then poured more coffee. 'My advice, Bella, is to ignore it. So let us consider what we are doing today.'

Bella, now standing in the mire and wishing, for all the routine dullness, that she was back in that tidy and comfortable house where she lived as companion to elderly Miss Carpenter, wondered if she were dreaming. She couldn't possibly be here, in the remoteness of Dartmoor, with a stranger driving her in a trap to this ancient farm, where curiosity had forced her to meet an uncle she had never known she had. And the rough woman, who had met her at the station in Bovey Tracey, had actually said she was a cousin.

'Lizzie Wharton, that's me.' Shabbily dressed, face weathered into deep lines, she had smiled happily. 'We're cousins, Miss Reed. Your dad's sister, Alice, married Roger Wharton and they had me, see? Yes, cousins.' Lizzie passed the cob's reins to a boy emerging from a shed at the other side of the yard, and led the way towards the doorway ahead of them.

Bella followed, her mind clearing. She had taken the exciting step of coming here, so she couldn't stand in this filthy yard for ever and besides, Lizzie was carrying her valise towards the house; she must follow, and meet this uncle, who, so Lizzie had written, was ill and wanted to meet her before he died.

Uncle? But she had no family.

Ahead of her, Lizzie raised her free hand and pounded on the oak-planked door. A moment and then it opened, a young face staring out at them. Lizzie's voice was sharp. 'Take this, Sarah, and put it in the room we've got ready for Miss Reed. Where's Uncle William? Up or down?'

Sarah nodded sullenly, turned away into a door off the long passage ahead of them, saying over her shoulder, 'He's here. Come down just now. Said he'll wait by the fire.'

She led the way into a large room, Lizzie following, Bella looking around, taking in old dark furniture, damp-stained plaster walls and a huge fireplace. And sitting upright on a settle in front of the fire, was a large, heavy man, whose dark eyes met hers, staring and unblinking.

Silence for a moment that she felt too unsettled to break. She heard Sarah pounding up invisible stairs, felt Lizzie pushing her forward and then, finally, knew she must speak to this man who stared so intently.

'I am Isabella Reed,' she said clearly, straightening her shoulders and ordering her nerves to settle. 'Mrs Wharton —'

she nodded over her shoulder to the woman standing behind her, adding quickly, '– Lizzie, that is, wrote to me saying that my Uncle William wanted to see me.'

The man nodded slowly but his expression didn't alter and Bella knew she must go on. 'I was surprised, as I thought I had no family.' Silence, heavy and oppressive. But she kept her voice steady as she went on, 'So please tell me who you are and why you think you're my uncle.'

He didn't answer at once, but with obvious discomfort stood up, right arm pushing at the settle to help. She saw his left hand hanging loose beside his shabby jacket. Then he picked up the stick leaning against the settle with his right hand, carefully stepping away from the fire, looking down at his feet in their black boots to avoid tripping over the rug surrounding the hearth. He came towards her, deep-set eyes fixed on hers. Heavy breathing, and then a spate of coughing, and as he neared, the smell of unwashed clothes. Fumes of drink and tobacco. She wanted to run, but knew the woman standing so close behind her was an inescapable barrier.

And then, the man's low voice, hoarse and quiet, saying in a rough Devon voice, 'Welcome to Abworthy, maid. Yes, I'm your Uncle William. Your father, Edmund – Ned we called him – was my brother. Come to the fire, it's cold today and you look scrammed. Lizzie –' he coughed, cleared his throat, raised his head, looking around, '– bring us some tea. But now, Miss Reed.' His thin mouth lifted slightly, and beneath the heavy lines wreathing his weathered face, Bella saw the remains of what must have been a handsome younger man.

She found herself saying, 'Everyone calls me Bella,' and then, like a child, waited to be told what to do. Holding out his right hand, he gripped hers, drawing her towards the settle. She found herself seated in the corner nearest the fire, while he sank down beside her, stick safe between his knees, eyes steadily watching her.

At the fire, Lizzie pushed the humming kettle into the middle of the range. She smiled at Bella as she stepped back. 'You and Uncle want to talk. I'll go and see what Sarah's about.'

She crossed the room to the door through which the girl had gone and then disappeared. Alone with the silent man, Bella felt nervous and full of foreboding. She shouldn't have come. She should be at home, accepting the dullness of doing whatever Miss Carpenter asked, waiting, with thoughts of Jack Courtney, who might call on his way home from his chambers in town. Jack who was her friend. Jack who might one day soon ask her to marry him.

Uncle William's breathing creaked slowly and bored into her mind. He turned, eyes holding hers and said slowly, 'We got things to tell one another. You first, maid. Tell about your father and your mother.' A pause and a slight lift of the bloodless lips. 'Marianne, she was called, wasn't she?'

'Yes,' said Bella, and saw his eyes light up.

Where should she start? Her mother, her father ... she saw how Uncle William was watching her and felt her confidence grow. 'My mother, Marianne, died before my father. She had a weak chest and one freezing winter was too much for her. About ten years ago now. She went to hospital with pneumonia.' Those cold crowded wards with beds full of still, pale figures, her mother in the last one, by the window. She held Mother's hand while she opened her eyes, managed a last few words. 'Look ... after ... your...' a painful pause, a rattle of struggling breath and then, '... your father.'

Bella's eyes swam, remembering, until William's wheezy cough returned her to the present. Peat on the fire shifted, breaking the silence, and after a moment he said, 'She said that, did she?' and Bella nodded. 'Yes,' she whispered. 'I've never forgotten.'

Now she had to find courage to go on but her voice was unsteady. 'I wasn't able to look after Father for long – he had a heart attack at work and died before I got to the hospital.'

The old man sighed and Bella wondered what age he was. For all his cough, and wheezy breathing, William Reed didn't look old; lines on his long face, but thick hair without a trace of grey, and alert, aware eyes. She thought that living a hard life here on relentless Dartmoor must age a man, but Uncle William seemed almost ageless.

Turning, he looked at her and nodded. 'Go on, maid. Tell me your story. Without your ma and pa, what did you do?'

She blinked, remembering. 'Mother's friends, the Westerns, took me in and I lived with them in Exeter until their neighbour, Miss Carpenter, asked if I would become her companion. So I moved into her house and I've been there ever since.' She thought back. Dull years, they'd been, but safe and cheerful. 'It's a good situation and better than going into service, which seemed the only thing for me as I grew up.'

The old man nodded, then, 'Ned was a Dartmoor lad; our family always farmers. Your mother worked in a shop. Sold clothes. But you speak more like a lady – learned a bit, did you, with your Miss Carpenter?'

'Yes.' Going about in the busy city, meeting people at tea parties and other social events. And among them, Jack Courtney, her solicitor. Jack with his warm smile. Jack who had seen her off on the train this morning. As he closed the compartment door, she had said 'Goodbye, and don't bother to meet me, Jack, I can manage by myself,' only to hear him say quickly, 'But of course I'll meet you. Monday, you said, and the train gets in at noon.'

She remembered the way he looked at her, and knew he thought of taking her in his arms, but other passengers were watching. So they had smiled at each other, and now ... she caught her breath.

Now she was sitting here in this ancient house, relating the story of her life. William coughed, fumbling in his pocket for a handkerchief. She wished she could sit somewhere else, but there was only one hard brown chair and a couple of stools beside the long bare table in the middle of the room.

Lizzie reappeared, with Sarah, who looked curiously at Bella and said roughly, without smiling, 'I put your case in the room at the top of the stairs. Bed's made up and scullery's over there.' She nodded towards the corner, where a half-open doorway led into another room.

Bella felt that this ancient house was enclosing her, the eyes watching her becoming fetters. She stumbled to her feet, and said in a high, unnatural voice, 'I shouldn't have come.' She looked at Lizzie. 'You shouldn't have written to me. He's not my uncle. I don't know who he is, or who you are, but you're nothing to do with me. I don't want to be here. I'm going.'

CHAPTER 2

William watched her pull open the heavy door, disappear into the misty yard, and then sighed. 'She must come back,' he muttered. 'She needs to know 'bout the family. Get her back, Lizzie.'

Closing the door, Lizzie turned around. 'No need, I just seen Mrs May come home from market. She'll take her in, I dare say. Now, Sarah, get up and help me with the tea.'

William watched the girl reluctantly leave her stool. A useless maid, he thought. Lizzie's daughter, just like her idle father, Dan. Now, Bella – already she was Bella – belonged here at Abworthy Farm. His thoughts delved into the past. She looked like her mother, Marianne, with the slender body and thick chestnut hair. He remembered magical bright flashes under candle and lamp light. Marianne, twenty, twenty-one years ago? November of 1870. His right hand moved to stroke the wound that had never really healed. Ned's shot had hit the bone and although black bits of metal were dug out, the wound didn't heal properly. In damp weather it ached. Hurt when his fingers pressed too hard.

A shocking reminder of Ned. The younger brother, always unloving and envious of the elder William. The memory of that gun aimed at him. And, then, softening his hard thoughts, a picture of Marianne, hands pressed to her face, watching as he was helped into the house. So long ago.

Mrs May stopped at her cottage door, looking at the young woman running towards her. Distress, plain on the face staring down at the potholed ground, made her frown. Running from Abworthy – not more trouble? Ah, but that card dealt last night had foretold it. So she caught at the girl's arm as she passed and brought her to a stumbling halt. 'Careful, maid, ground's bad and those pretty shoes are not right for running in. Where you going, and in such a hurry?'

Bella stood quite still, breathing quickly, face tense. She must get back to Bovey Tracey station. Back to the safe life with Miss Carpenter and Jack in Exeter. This old woman, standing beside a crammed market basket, dressed roughly, and clearly another farm inhabitant, mustn't stop her. Another Abworthy woman? She snatched away her arm. 'Let me be! I've got to go—' She looked over her shoulder, for by now Lizzie Wharton could have harnessed the pony and the trap, already catching her up. But her shoes were wet through, coat clinging to her legs, hat slipping backwards, releasing a lock of hair that swept across her face. She needed safety, warmth, perhaps even a cup of tea....

'Come in, maid,' said the woman. Staring, Bella saw a smile of reassurance, the lined face crinkling around sunken eyes. 'Dry off a bit and then we'll think how to get you where you want to go. Come on, my lover.' And then she was in the cottage, part, she saw, of the hamlet which surrounded Abworthy. Inside it was dry, with a scent of cooking and something else, unfamiliar, but it was warm, a fire humming and a kettle singing on the hearth top. A tabby cat jumped down from the cane chair, arched its back and stood, watching, as she followed the old woman. They stood before the fire, which had a small black pot simmering at the back of the range, and the woman said in her easy, Devon voice, 'Take off your wet things and sit down.' She took the dripping coat and draped it over a chair beside the plain, scrubbed table in the centre of the room.

The chair creaked beneath Bella as it took her weight, and the cat leaped onto her lap. Green eyes looked at her and the animal started to purr. Emotions raged – it was all too much. She lowered her head, covered her face with her hands and couldn't stop the tears.

A hand touched her shoulder and the old voice said gently, 'Take your time, lover. I'll get us a mug of tea and then you can tell me what it's all about. You been to Abworthy, I dare say?'

Slowly, emotions settled. Here was a kind woman, the cottage was warm, the cat a pleasant lump on her lap. She looked at the mug handed to her and gratefully had a long drink of hot, bitter tea. Then she could smile. 'Thank you,' she said, her voice steady. 'I'm trying to get to Bovey station. I need to get home to Exeter, you see.'

The woman, sitting opposite her on a lumpy armchair, warming her hands around the mug of tea, nodded. 'So you been to see William Reed at Abworthy? I knew he was expecting to see his niece. That you, is it?'

Bella's smile faded. 'He says he's my uncle. I didn't know I had one.'

The woman thought, and then, 'Ned was your father, and Marianne your mother. I was there at the wedding. And back at the farm afterwards.'

'You knew them?' Bella felt disquiet fading away. 'You know we lived in Exeter? That Mother died first and then Father two years later? And you know I'm their daughter?' Thoughts rampaged. 'So who are you?'

'Ellen May, that's me. Mrs May they always called me 'cos I was more like a nursemaid and a friend. I looked after the family, see, when the old folks died.'

'William and Ned's parents?' Lizzie's voice echoed. 'Oh, and there was a sister in the family, too – Alice, Lizzie said.'

'That's right. William, Ned and Alice. Her daughter, Lizzie, married Dan, useless lump o'rubbish, he is, an' their daughter Sarah's not much better. Lizzie has her hands full, but she looks after her poor Uncle William best's she can.'

In Bella's mind a pattern was forming. The family at Abworthy, two generations ago; then her father who had died, while Uncle William still lived there now; Alice and her Wharton family, and now she, herself, running away from them. She tried to understand. She was the next generation, refusing to take any responsibility or interest. Uneasy guilt swept through her and she put down the half-empty mug on the hearth beside her feet. And then, there came back into her mind, the memory of the one visit she had made to Dartmoor, years ago. A day trip, but one which had given her pictures to remember and a strange feeling of wanting to return. They had haunted her ever since, beautiful, mysterious ... and now she was actually here. Need grew inside her.

Now she felt Mrs May's eyes on her and looked across the space. 'I've been very selfish,' she said quietly, and with a break in her voice. 'I didn't understand. The farm is so old. It seemed – unfriendly. Not what I'm used to. I – I just wanted to run.'

Mrs May nodded, and Bella thought there was understanding in her wrinkled face. She felt able to go on. 'But now that I know about the family, I think I might go back and apologize to ... to....' She couldn't bring herself to say the name.

'To your uncle?' A smile, a movement to poke the fire, the cat stretching and looking up with slit eyes, and suddenly Bella knew what she must do.

'Yes, to my uncle. I must apologize.' She smiled gratefully. 'You've helped me understand. He and my cousin Lizzie must be thinking badly of me. I'll go back.' New strength energized her body, and the old feeling of curiosity grew in her. No more fear.

Mrs May stood and looked down at her. 'Not tonight, lover.

You can stay 'ere with me. I'll go tell them at the farm. You be safe enough, and tomorrow things will look better. Just sit there with Jessie while I unpack my basket.'

The fire sang, Jessie rearranged herself and slept and Bella watched Mrs May take packets and jars from the basket and put them into a cupboard and onto shelves around the stone sink in the far corner. A bunch of some sort of dried plant was hung from the big beam, already decorated with what Bella saw were dead leaves and withered flowers.

Wondering about life lived in this small space, her eyes closed and her head nodded. So much excitement, and that uneasy atmosphere in the old stone house. Now she slept, restfully and without dreams, until a knock at the door woke her.

Immediately panic flew back. This would be Lizzie come to fetch her, to berate her for such bad and childish behaviour, or even Sarah, glad to have the chance of telling off the town girl. But it was neither of them. It was a man; she could just see him behind Mrs May, standing in the open doorway. He took off his hat and his voice reached her, low and rather slow as if each word must be thought out. Deep and with a hint of a different accent from the Devon burr of all the Abworthy people.

'Afternoon, Mrs May. Thought I'd say hallo now I'm back. Good to see you again.'

'My soul! Robert Verney! But there, I been expecting you. Come in, boy.' Mrs May sounded pleased.

Bella watched the man, who now entered the cottage, bringing with him a sense of power. He shut the door, smiling as Mrs May pulled out a chair and asked 'When did you get back, Robert? Haven't heard news of you for many a year. Where've you been, then?'

As he sat down, Bella had a good view of him. Tall, with heavy shoulders, wearing a shabby tweed jacket, breeches and expensive, scuffed boots. Very dark blue eyes met her and she could do nothing but smile. The smile was not returned, yet she saw a gleam of interest in those brilliant, penetrating eyes. Guessing that this was a complex man, she waited in silence for information to emerge.

But Mrs May was smiling and this told Bella a lot. Robert Verney must be a friend for she guessed that the old woman would not invite anyone into her home whom she had no time for. The introduction came casually as Mrs May went to the cupboard to produce another mug. 'Robert, this is Miss Reed.'

A moment's silence. He looked at her, nodded his head. 'Good day to you, Miss Reed.'

Mrs May poured boiling water into the teapot, eyes watchful as she did so. 'Miss Reed been visiting William at Abworthy. You remember William, Robert?'

'I remember him.' A sort of finality in the few words. And then, more casually, 'He must be getting on a bit now.'

Bella sensed a note of something secretive in the deep voice. She watched Robert Verney stretch his legs to the hearth and then take the mug handed to him.

Mrs May sank back into her chair. 'No, William's not that old. In his sixties, but looks older. My soul, he does. It's that old farmer's lung he suffers from like so many farmers round here. Something from hay and wheat that makes 'em cough, upsets the breathing. And of course, that wounded left arm of his don't help. He lives a quiet life now, can't do much. Relies on Joel James, his farm manager, and the stable lad.'

Robert Verney nodded, drank his tea in a series of large gulps and returned the mug to the table behind him. He looked at Bella. His eyes were dark. 'So, you've been visiting the farm.'

It wasn't a question but she felt an answer was needed. 'Yes, I have.' She paused, but realized that the truth must out. 'William Reed is my uncle. I didn't know until Lizzie, my cousin, wrote and said he wanted to see me, so I came.

This morning. Already she was ashamed of the panic she had felt at the farm. Suddenly it was important that this stranger didn't see her as a helpless young woman who couldn't meet a few strange events without flinching and running away. She was, after all, independent, with a will of her own. So she sat up straighter and, Jessie, on her lap, stirred at the abrupt movement.

'Your uncle, William Reed? Of Abworthy Farm? Well, that's news to me.' The narrowed deep-set eyes were fixed on her face and the slow words seemed almost threatening.

Mrs May interrupted. 'Robert, you been away for six or seven years. And Miss Reed didn't know anything of her family 'til Lizzie wrote.'

'Didn't know your family history? Nothing of it? Extraordinary.' His voice rose, sounding as if he didn't believe her.

Bella's cheeks grew hot. She said sharply, 'Not extraordinary at all. Not every family knows everything. And now Mrs May has told me things I never knew, which has been helpful.'

'Things you never knew.' That long unblinking stare, and then, 'And so now you're part of your family again. You must be pleased.'

'Yes,' she said, disliking the way he looked at her. 'And I'm on my way up to the farm now, as I'm staying there before I go back to Exeter on Monday.' The words had unexpectedly ordered themselves but she knew they were the right ones. Of course she must go back to Abworthy, apologize for her rude flight and spend the evening with Uncle William, doing what she could to ease his slow and painful existence.

Mrs May said quietly, 'You sure, maid? That what you need to do, is it?'

'I'm quite sure. Thank you, Mrs May for taking me in, but I shall go back to the farm before it gets too dark. I can find my way quite safely.'

'I'm going to Abworthy; you can come with me.' Robert's

words were casual.

She stared. Out in the unsettling darkness of the moor with this stranger? Something stirred uneasily, but it wasn't fear. The old familiar curiosity again. She glanced back at Mrs May, who was on her feet, pulling the black pan to the front of the hearth, stirring it and now pouring its contents into a small earthenware pot. Bella knew Mrs May wouldn't let her go with this man if she wasn't sure of his integrity.

'Thank you. That's very kind.' She rose, took her coat from the chair behind the table, felt a large hand offering help and, looking around, met the dark blue, intent gaze. He was smiling, but not with pleasure. Almost, she thought, as if somehow she was doing exactly what he wanted.

And then, even as she buttoned her coat and reached for her hat, Mrs May came close, holding the little pot, wrapped in a bit of rag. 'This is medicine for your uncle, maid. I make it for him every week. Careful now, it's warm.'

'Your old ways still keeping you busy then, Mrs May?' Robert's voice was suddenly full of amusement, and Bella, staring, saw the old woman nodding, smiling. 'I may be old, Master Robert, but I still know a thing or two. And one is that it's high time you come back home from wherever you've been.'

'Australia. But I've had enough of it. Missed Dartmoor.' His eyes were suddenly brighter and full of something that made Bella's interest grow. He turned to her, the smile waning. 'So if you're ready, Miss Reed, we'll go. It's only a short walk, or would you like to ride? My horse's waiting outside, I'll help you mount and then I'll lead him.' He went to the door and opened it, looked back, smiled at Mrs May, ever watchful by the fire, and then at Bella. A dark brow lifted. 'You do ride, of course?'

It hurt her pride to answer *No* but her voice was clear and steady, and she thought his expression changed slightly as they went out into the cool, darkling night, and one thing became very certain as they walked the sodden path back to the farm – he leading the horse, she a step behind – this Robert Verney, whoever he was, should not be allowed to see inside her churning mind.

They didn't speak as they journeyed on and it was only as the farm house loomed up through the mist that he said anything. And then, 'Abworthy Farm,' he announced. That was all, but his deep voice had a new strength to it that made her wonder.

CHAPTER 3

Robert Verney halted as they entered the farm yard. 'Go in,' he said, 'I'll stable the horse and then join you.'

She hesitated. What would Lizzie say? What must Uncle William be thinking of her? To go in to that hostile house alone ... yet Robert Verney must not see her fears. Slowly she walked towards the door, and then stopped, his voice turning her to look back at him as he approached her.

'What're you waiting for? It's your home, isn't it?' The unexpected words made her stand straighter, take a big breath and knock at the door.

Sarah opened it. 'You're back! We thought you'd gone ... Ma said she'd better drive to the station, make sure you were safe, but Uncle said for sure Mrs May would take you in. But you're so wet.' Sarah stepped back, pretty face tight with dislike. 'Don't bring all that muck in here – I've done enough cleaning today – take your shoes off.' And then, with a sudden wide eyed smile, 'Who's this, then? Brought a friend, have you?' She giggled, ignoring Bella's attempts to remove her shoes, and moving aside to get a better look at Robert Verney.

'I've brought Miss Reed home,' he said casually. 'And I'm going see William Reed. Want me to remove my boots, too, do you?'

Bella heard a note of quick amusement in the last words

and looked over her shoulder. Yes, he was grinning at Sarah as he took off his hat and then scraped his boots on the metal scraper on the doorstep. A complex man, she thought again, and then followed Sarah along the cross passage and into the big room leading from it.

Again, the shadowy presence of the big, lamp-lit room. The smells of woodsmoke and tobacco, of cooking, unwashed clothes and bodies. Of something that disturbed her once more, but now, with Robert Verney behind her, she braced her courage and refused to give in to weakness. She walked towards the settle at the fireside where William Reed sat, a small table by his knee, with a newspaper spread out on it. Lizzie sat beside him and was looking at her with a smile that seemed to suggest welcome and friendliness. Bella blinked, and felt that Lizzie would understand. She was able then to say, confidently, 'Mr Verney accompanied me from Mrs May's cottage where I – ' she cleared her throat, then pushed herself on, '– where she invited me in and gave me some tea. And dried my clothes.' A pause, and she felt sharp expectancy bolstering the shadows filling the room with something that made her heart pound. But now was the moment to apologize. 'Uncle William—' She met his gaze, those deep-set, eyes looking at her across the small space between them and then, suddenly, saw them leave her, and fix, narrowed and focused, on the man behind her.

'Robert Verney. God save us, what do you want, then?'

Silence lingered for a long moment. Bella heard Lizzie draw a quick breath, sensed Robert Verney move nearer, finding a stool and then felt him draw her down onto it. He stood, looking at the man on the settle.

'Just come to see how you are, Mr Reed. I've been away – a long time.' His voice was quiet. Again, silence.

Bella felt her blood pounding. What was happening? Had she unexpectedly stepped into some sort of age-old quarrel?

Again, she longed to get away. But she sat there and waited.

'You can see how I am,' muttered William. 'Good for nought. My life's slipping past with every day. And now you've come back to worry me.' The husky voice slid into a cough. He fumbled for a red handkerchief, glared over it. Coughing fit over, he said sharply, 'So tell me what you want, Verney. Going on again about losing that card game so long ago, are you?'

Robert took a step nearer the settle, bent down and said quietly, 'I'm not making trouble. Just that I've come home, Mr Reed. Home to Dartmoor where I was born. Like you, I'm not a young chap any more. Thirty next year. I've got a need to settle down, make myself a home. Foreign countries are interesting and I learned a lot about cattle when I was away and now I want to start farming. I only came to see how you are.'

He stood up straight, and continued to look at William's tight face. He laughed, almost casually. 'P'raps I hoped you might give me your blessing. After all, we go back a long time, we Verneys and Reeds; just you an' Alice an' me now.'

'And my niece.' The quick words cut in like a knife. 'Forgotten her, have you? She's all I got left to carry on the Reed name, so you must think about her, boy. Bella'll get Abworthy when I'm gone. She's my heir, see?'

'*What?*' Robert's deep voice was alive with disbelief. They stared at each other and Bella watched how William's grey face grew patchy red with pleasure, while Robert's remained expressionless, save for his set jaw. And then, she began to understand why she was here, why Uncle William had sent for her. He was dying and she – Isabella Reed, shortly to become engaged to Jack Courtney and settle happily in Exeter in a warm, comfortable suburban villa – would inherit this ancient stone house.

What an extraordinary idea. Was it really possible? But how? And why should the Verney man be so clearly surprised and enraged? Thank goodness she was sitting down. Suddenly her head began to spin, and she sensed the room's memories come to life.

Beneath the wavering light of the oil lamp and the tallow dip, cards are dealt, handled, stared at, and both men's minds centre on the pictures facing them. After midnight now, the peat fire crumbling to a mere glow in the open hearth and the servants long gone to their beds. Just the two of them here in the shadowy room, playing out the tricks of destiny.

Dick Reed sits back on his chair, feels sweat trickling down his face and allows a smile to lift his lips. So far, so good. The old fool sitting opposite is leaning forward, pale eyes staring at the cards he holds as if he could make them change their values by sheer willpower.

Hah! thinks Dick. No chance there, boy. Probably just a knave, a ten, an eight.... The smile becomes a grim one. Clearly old Verney holds no kings or queens, no aces. Whereas he – hah! again.

He lifts his cards half an inch nearer his face. Keep them hidden. He feels a strike of new excitement, a sense of potential power. One more trick and it'll be over. His game, their stakes lost regretfully by Peter Verney. His authority growing over the old friend and neighbour who had so longed to win.

And then ... Pete's long, horsey face lifting into a smile. His calloused fingers caressing the cards as he lays them down. Dick Reed gasps. Horror! All the royals. And that ace of diamonds putting the hex on the whole hand. The wicked ace grinning at him as he sits, open-mouthed, not believing.

So, after all, Pete has won. Has he cheated? Was that ace up his jacket sleeve all the time? By the Lord, if it were so, then Pete must answer for it....

Slowly, Dick Reed drops his cards to the table. His eyes meet Pete's and as he sees the pride, and hardly believing the power in them, so an idea comes to him. He will win back his losses by putting everything on one last hand. He can't lose. Shuffling the cards together, his self control in an iron grip, he says, 'You did well there. But I'd like one more go – what d'you say, then?'

Pete sniffs. Feels for his tobacco tin, fills his pipe, lights it with a taper from the dying tallow dip, then nods his greying head. 'Better be a good stake....'

Dick Reed takes a deep breath. A quick nod of the head and then, voice steady and full of self belief, he says, 'Abworthy. House and lands. Can't offer better than that, can I?'

A disbelieving stare and a mumbled, 'But, but ....' and Dick Reed tightens his mouth and grins.

'Mug o'cider, and then we'll see, eh?'

Pete nods. Blows a smoke ring and starts to dream of becoming more than just a hill farmer living in a damp hovel; why, maybe with Abworthy and its rich pasture lands, he could become ... anything he wanted. A smile on his long face, a straightening of heavy shoulders and a new will filling him. 'I'm your man, Dick. Abworthy it is, then.'

Ten minutes gone by and the cards are dealt again. Both men lean forward, forgetting everything; old age, the need for sleep, everything save a silent prayer for the cards to bless one of them. For one to win, and the other to lose.

The room is tense, the fire slips further into greying ash, and the tallow dip ends its short life. This one night will never be forgotten, the room always to remember, even as the years press on and generations change.

One to win; one to lose. The cards fall. Reed the winner, Verney the loser. And both families entangled in hatred instead of the old neighbourliness. But life goes on.

Bella started as the heavy door slammed to behind Robert Verney. She had caught a last glance of his furious face, hard and resolute. Dismay filled her for what might happen next. She looked at Lizzie as if for help.

Lizzie was up, folding the crumpled newspaper and moving the table away from the settle. She put her hand on Uncle William's shoulder. 'Don't take any notice of him, Uncle – they Verneys always were bad tempered. Don't worry, I'll make us some supper and then you can go up to bed and forget him.' She went to the big dresser, and Sarah came to her side, setting out plates on the table.

Unsure, Bella got up. Then, seeing the expression on her uncle's face she took Lizzie's place on the settle beside him, saying quietly, 'Uncle, I've come back to apologize. I was very rude, and I'm sorry. I hope....' Her voice faded. He looked grim, but she managed to finish, mumbling, 'I hope I didn't upset you too much, running off like that.' There, she had done her duty and apologized. But she was bewildered remembering those extraordinary words: 'Bella will have Abworthy when I'm gone.' It wasn't possible. He was confused; the Verney man had disturbed him. It was all a fantasy he had dreamed up. And yet, Robert Verney hadn't argued, plainly accepting what he said, so what was she to think?

William's stare was almost hypnotic. She watched his mouth purse, saw sagging flesh around his jaw tighten and was afraid she had angered him. But his voice was quiet as, after a pause, he nodded slowly, and said, unblinking eyes focused on her, 'Never mind being sorry. It's your duty to come to Abworthy.' Shifting painfully, he kept looking at her. 'You must understand about family being important. Family, land and inheritance – that's why you're here, why I sent for you. To inherit after I've gone.' Then he sighed, stared beyond her into the spaces of the big room. 'No Verney can make claim to Abworthy.' Another pause and then his expression loosened, his face easier. His voice softened. 'Those two old men, my father and Robert's grandfather, Pete Verney, playing cards.

They do say Pete was winning, but then....' A bout of coughing. 'The tale's been told often enough, that last final hand of cards, and Abworthy staying with us. And even though that young whippersnapper's come home, probably thinking he can get a hold on the house and its land, he's too late. Suppose he thinks he can get the law to work on his side, but he's wrong, see. He has no legal claim to our house because we Reeds have got an entail.' Looking at Bella again, there was triumph in his face. 'No, b'God, he won't get Abworthy and that's why he's gone off like that. Raging, but he'll be scheming, I shouldn't wonder.'

Bella's mind ran in circles, trying to make sense of all that William had said. What was an entail? She frowned. 'I don't understand – he wasn't saying anything about the house. Only that he was hoping to start farming.'

Lizzie was at her elbow. 'His ma, old Pete's daughter, died a year ago. Robert's the only one in the family, and the land beyond his cottage is his. He'll work that.' Her cheerful smile broke out and she nodded at the places laid at the table. 'Supper's ready. Come and sit down, Bella – and Uncle, give me your arm, I'll help you.'

But Uncle William shook his head, and looked up at Bella with a grin. 'Lend me your shoulder, maid. We'll go along together, eh?' He picked up his stick and began edging himself off the settle. At once she did as he asked, feeling his right hand strong on her shoulder, and both of them moving slowly, as one, until he was seated at the top of the table, with Bella on his left hand side, and Sarah sliding her stool to a place in front of the settle.

For all her bewilderment, Bella found she was hungry, and the stew, with its lumps of bacon and vegetable, was tasty. Big slices of heavy bread lay beside each plate, and they ate in silence. William let Lizzie cut his meat and then motioned her away. 'I'll manage,' he muttered and, one-handed, cleared his plate.

Sarah got up and brewed a big pot of tea, then disappeared to fetch milk. Bella, by now, with warmth in her stomach, and a more settled feeling spreading through her, thought about this ancient house. Looking around, she started to appraise the room they sat in. It was spacious, with walls a yard thick, granite stones showing through stained lime wash. On the hearth, peat lay in piles, to be thrown onto the bed of huge logs burning beneath, glowing as it burned and wafting out an earthy smell.

As she drank her tea, she looked at the faces around the table. Lizzie, seemingly contented, was smiling at something Uncle William said. There was a suspicion of a smile on his grey face as he nodded at her quiet words. But Sarah, huddled on her stool, eyes downcast, looked as if she were sunk in her own miserable dreams. With a return of confusion, Bella felt that she was caught in a spider's web of invisible, yet restraining threads.

The meal finished, Lizzie started clearing plates, and when Bella offered to help, she hesitated, then said, 'Not tonight, maid. I'll do the dishes before we go home while Sarah shows you your room. We live in the cottage at the end of the track.' She moved towards the door at the far end of the room, and finding a candle, called to Sarah, 'Show Cousin Bella her room, will you? Take a taper and light the lamp I put there, and then we'll be off. I'll make sure Uncle William doesn't want nothing before we go. It's getting late; your dad will wonder where we are.'

Sarah pouted, stared at Bella with a cold expression, but did as she was told. Taper in hand, she opened the door and said over her shoulder, 'Mind the stairs. Wood's rotten in places.'

Bella's alarm grew. If Lizzie and Sarah were leaving, then she would be alone with Uncle William. Momentarily fear struck but then common sense returned and she chided herself. *He's an old man. He can't hurt you.* Picking up her coat and hat, she followed Sarah. Yes, the wooden stairs were rough and it would be easy to trip. Sarah's taper fluttered in the sudden draught, giving off hardly enough light to see where she was going. At the top of the stairs, a dark passage loomed off in one direction, while at this end Sarah pushed open a creaking, obstinate door and led her into a room, which was dark and smelled of damp and musty furnishings.

'Your bag's there, on the chair.' Sarah put the taper to the small lamp standing on a chest beneath the window, and then a faint glow illuminated the shadowy room. 'Bed's had a hot brick all day,' she said. 'G'night.'

At the door, she stopped with obvious annoyance as Bella stared around her, seeing the washstand against the far wall, and said, 'Is there any hot water?'

The girl laughed raucously. 'Not unless you go and heat it up on the fire! What's wrong with cold? Plenty in the scullery downstairs.'

'No, nothing wrong, of course.' Bella smiled resolutely. 'Thank you, Sarah,' and watched the girl leave the room, heard the door squeaking as she banged it behind her. She stood, silently, in the middle of the dimly lit space, feeling her breath grow fast and shallow, wondering what she should do. How could she possibly spend the night here in this huge, cold room, so full of threatening shadows and almost invisible furniture? She couldn't stay here. The fear swirling around in her mind took action. She found a chair, carried it to the door and then, on its legs, pushed it firmly in place. No one could come in without her knowing.

And then Uncle William's voice echoed around her mind. 'Family, land and inheritance,' and slowly she realized he was right. The things that truly mattered. It was a dark thought but she was family, so she must accept that Abworthy could be her future home. Then images of Jack, of marriage and a busy urban life flashed through her mind and she tightened her lips, coming to a vital decision. She took a deep breath and found a redeeming certainty fill her mind.

No, she could not stay here. Tomorrow she would leave.

CHAPTER 4

The bed was lumpy and musty as, reluctantly, Bella laid her head on the one pillow, thoughts running around in a bewildering race. Leave Abworthy? Yes, but not until tomorrow. Now she must sleep.

The coldness of the room had stopped her removing her underclothes and so, shivering, and giving up the idea of going downstairs to heat up water and then stripping to wash, she slid between surprisingly warmed sheets, with the brick at her feet, and drifted away, worries dissolving as sleep overcame her.

She awoke to a pale light probing through faded curtains at the window opposite the bed. Outside, a rooster crowed. A dog barked. Dawn, she thought, pulling the coverlet closer around her shoulders. A cold day. But a new one.

That hope and the brightness of the morning allowed her to lie there for a few more minutes, thinking about yesterday, wondering about today. About Lizzie and Sarah, who lived somewhere close by, with Dan, Lizzie's husband. A no-good, Mrs May had told her. And a boy in the yard when she first arrived, and a man disappearing into a shed. So there were other people here, at Abworthy. For a moment she wondered about them all. Until the Verney man forced himself into her thoughts. Robert. Someone Uncle William disliked and was suspicious of. Why? And yet Robert had seemed polite at first, at least until he knew that Abworthy was to be left to her. Again, why? And Uncle saying something about an entail. A law, wasn't it? Her busy mind struggled to understand.

She sighed. If only Jack were here to explain ... and then it was Jack whose smile filled her thoughts. He would be meeting her train on Monday. But today was Saturday, and there was tomorrow to get through, too. Did they go to church on a Sunday? Where was the church? She began to want to know more about the place.

Out of bed, she went to the window, wiped bleary stains from it with a corner of creased curtain and looked out, then gasped. The rising sun was starting to colour the sky, a warm peachy glow appearing in the eastern sky, falling on the buildings grouped around the house. Everything looked so very different from yesterday's mist and rain. And she could see something coming to life in the distance. Huge hills covered in mysterious drifts of shifting colours – purple-brown, yellow and a sort of bleached white. Flowers, maybe? What would grow in this wild region? She must find out. She smiled wryly, knowing curiosity had returned. Last night she had been foolish. Today things were different.

Dressing, she felt a new confidence and resolution. She would return to Exeter on Monday, as planned. But now – and tomorrow – she wanted to explore this strange new land; a brief adventure that she could tell Miss Carpenter and Jack about. And – her face grew determined – somehow she must tell Uncle William that she couldn't accept his wish for her to inherit the old place. Just for a few seconds, she flinched. He would be hurt. Angry? She imagined what a scene it would be.... Just then, she saw someone moving across the yard, followed by a black and white dog. Someone going into a shed, carrying a bucket. Hens foraged in the yard, and a cow was lowing. She was suddenly intrigued. The life of the farm had begun, so she must dress, go down and find out about it, and if she hurried, she could perhaps explore before either Uncle William appeared, or Lizzie and Sarah arrived to look after him.

Very soon she was downstairs, going through the cobbled cross passage leading to the heavy door, pulling at it, struggling with the iron bar that latched it. And then she was outside, a blast of cold wind brought her up short and she stared about her.

She saw that the world had changed since yesterday. Even her thoughts were different, straying in new directions. A feeling of unexpected excitement compelled her to pull her coat tighter, tug her hat lower against the wind, and then step out across the yard, ignoring the dung heap and the damp mess leaking from it, making every footstep slippery, towards the shed into which she had seen the man with the bucket disappear.

And then voices halted her. Lizzie and Sarah were coming into the yard, muffled up against the cold and carrying baskets and – Bella's eyes widened – Sarah was carrying a pair of black boots. Her voice was sharp and quick. 'Here, these are for you. Ma said as you can't walk in those things you got.'

Bella took the boots – a size too big, she guessed, and smelling of grease and manure – but hid her distaste. 'Thank you.' She gave Sarah a tight smile. 'I shan't be going anywhere, so I don't suppose I shall wear them.'

But Lizzie cut in, walking towards the door, and putting down her basket. 'But it's harvest festival tomorrow. There's lots for us to do to get ready for it and you can help. So you can keep your feet dry in those boots. They're Sarah's second best pair, not up to much, but all we could find.'

Bella was ashamed of herself. She joined Lizzie in the doorway and smiled. 'It's kind of you. Of course I shall wear them, only –' she paused, wondering what Lizzie had meant, exactly, '– what can I do to help the harvest festival?'

The door was pushed open and Lizzie and her basket disappeared, her voice carrying back to Bella, who followed behind. 'We've got to decorate the church, see. And that means finding flowers and stuff. I've got the baking to do, but maybe you and Sarah can go and pick some bunches of what you can find.' In the kitchen, taking off her coat and going to the hearth, she said, 'It's cold today. Uncle won't want to come down till we get this going. Sarah, get the kindling, and be quick about it.'

Briskly, she took the blackened kettle to the larder, where a crock of water stood on the slated floor, filled it and put it on the hob. She bent to find old newspaper in the bottom of the cupboard and some dried furze, which she laid at the bottom of the range. When Sarah appeared with a basket of bundled twigs and pieces of chopped wood, she added them to the crumpled newspaper. From the mantel above the hearth she took a tinderbox and struck a flame and at once the fire was alive, crackling as it attacked the stems and paper, and then devouring the sticks. She looked back at Bella, standing watching, and gave her a smile. 'Not what you're used to, I s'pose, Cousin Bella. But it's how we live here on the moor. Now, try on those boots and see how they feel. Kettle'll be a while before it boils, so I'll tell you about harvest festival.'

Bella's mind expanded. She was learning facts and ideas that she'd never thought about before. This was how Dartmoor people lived; with patience and repetitive daily physical labour. She unbuttoned her coat, and pulled out a stool, sat on it and took off her stained shoes, thinking that the great black boots on the floor beside her were a passport to a different universe. Her small feet slipped easily into them and she felt spaces where her toes were. Too big, but she must make an effort to wear them, for it was kind of Lizzie to have brought them. With cold fingers she tied up the leather laces, stood up, feeling her feet were encased in heavy weights.

But she smiled and said, 'Thank you. I'm sure I shall be very warm and dry in these.'

Lizzie was busy with pans and food produced from the big cupboard beside the hearth. 'Harvest festival – well, I'll be making some loaves, someone's sure to bring a sheaf of wheat to put up by the altar and we'll put the vegetable and fruit we got round the steps. And then there's the wild flowers.'

Bella nodded, trying to reconcile the neat and tidy harvest festivals she had attended in Exeter with these new ideas. Sheaves of wheat? Loaves of homemade bread? Wild flowers? No, it had been beautiful floral decorations, elegantly displayed in tall vases, with certain ladies being very possessive of those they had arranged. She smiled with amusement, imagining what those urban pillars of society would say if they could see a Dartmoor harvest festival. Yes, she would have so much to tell Miss Carpenter and Jack when she returned on Monday.

They breakfasted on mugs of thick tea and chunks of yesterday's bread spread with lard and chopped rosemary leaves. Bella felt she had eaten more than enough and was glad when Lizzie suggested she and Sarah went out to pick some flowers, 'Whatever you can find,' before disappearing upstairs to help William Reed get dressed. Her smile was cheerful, but there was a note of sadness in her voice as she went. 'Says he can manage, but only one hand – it's hard.' In the empty kitchen, Bella wondered about working with Sarah, especially outside, in that wilderness.

With their coats buttoned tight and hats skewered on because of the wind, baskets in their hands, they left the farm, turning into the rough track and then passing Mrs May's cottage. Sarah stepped aside, crossed her fingers and put her head down as they did so. Bella looked at her. 'Why did you do that?'

Sarah's green eyes met hers with an expression of

amazement. 'She's a witch, that's why. You were lucky to get away last night.'

Bella stared. 'That's ridiculous! There aren't such things as witches ... and anyway, Mrs May was very kind to me.'

'You were lucky, like I said. Didn't you see her cat? And herbs everywhere? She brews up potions, everybody knows she's a witch.'

They trudged on in silence, Bella's mind thrown into shock. That kindly woman with the warm smile – what was Sarah talking about? Doubtfully, she asked, 'What proof have you got that she's a witch?'

Sarah turned off the path and began climbing the big hill behind the farm. 'She stops bleeding and ringworm. And she charms for warts – it's only a white witch that do that, see. But I expect she can do bad things too, like overlooking and curses.' She turned her head and stared at Bella struggling with her heavy boots over the rough turf. 'You'll see, when we go to church tomorrow.'

'What will I see?'

Sarah grinned, set down her basket and wrapped her hands in rags pulled from her pocket before starting to pick branches of furze. 'Something that the vicar doesn't like. But he daren't stop her – she'd get at him, if he did. Now, we got to pick this stuff, so make sure you only pick what's still flowering.' She frowned at Bella. 'You got soft hands, so you better cut the heather – no prickles, like this.'

Slowly, they filled their baskets. But soon, as Bella straightened her back, she realized she was a stranger to physical labour. She saw Sarah grinning at her, clearly thinking her a weakling, but took no notice for the landscape was slowly and wonderfully revealing itself. Through the flying clouds shafts of brilliant sun fell upon the land beneath. Things changed into a new perspective and she realized that the hill they were climbing was the huge rocky pile she had seen behind the house when she arrived yesterday. It had been misted over then, grey and rather sinister in its wet immensity, but this morning, suddenly the granite rocks at the apex were becoming gleaming flashes of light and the hill itself had become a monarch surveying its kingdom below.

Bella looked up, her eyes dazzled by the shifting sun, thrilled by all that she saw. And then, turning, she looked outward, down into the valley where Abworthy and its surrounding cottages stood, its irregular-shaped courtyard grey and, no doubt, still covered with manure and rubbish, though now it was being worked. She watched as a man herded a cow from the barn and followed it out of the yard, through a gate leading into fields beyond, and then she lost sight of them. Back in the yard a boy carried a bucket to a fenced space at the further side of the barn, and she heard the snorts of pigs. And the dog, barking, as someone brought a horse from the stable and spoke to a visitor, standing by the big door of the old house. Abworthy, she thought; busy and full of life; no longer the frightening, empty place she had thought it when she arrived yesterday. Yesterday – was it only then that she had come here? But so much had happened; she had met so many people, and she felt differently about a lot of things. Again she looked around the moorland enclosing the land, and saw the sun suddenly sweep down a distant hillside, like a caressing hand, bringing into vivid colour its purple coverlet. The same heather that she had picked with such difficulty here in her basket; there, in its natural state. Dartmoor, she thought with a wild, new feeling, was a very special place, and one that she was already wishing she knew better.

But Sarah was there, nudging her, her voice rough, 'Come on, stop dreaming. We got to get back and do up the church.'

Bella nodded, followed the girl down the hill and then stopped as a horse and rider appeared around the side of the hill, putting all her thoughts into a new rush of panic.

'Morning,' said Robert Verney, nodding at Sarah, and then looking down at Bella with intent dark eyes. 'Come to inspect your inheritance from up here, have you? A good view. Pleases you, I daresay.'

Inside her, anger suddenly reared. This rude man could not be allowed to treat her like this. She met his penetrating gaze and smiled coolly, saying, 'And if it does, Mr Verney, then it's nothing to do with you.' And then, 'Let us pass, if you please.' She stood quite still, waiting for him to move on, but he stayed there, looking down at her, and she felt her anger grow. This man was insufferable. Thinking to walk around the horse, she sidestepped and then twisted her ankle on an invisible thick stem of heather. She fell clumsily, trying to get up at once, grabbing at the basket which had thrown all the flowers onto the ground beside her and feeling a fool.

Sarah was guffawing as she helped retrieve the fallen heather, but Robert dismounted and, still holding the horse's reins, took a hold of her arm, helping her to stand upright again. He looked at her and said, with obvious amusement, 'They say pride goes before a fall, don't they? Well, Miss Reed, let me advise you to watch your step in future.'

She glared at him, breathing heavily, furious at herself, furious with him, with Sarah still giggling behind her. But no words came to mind and she stood silently, watching as he finished filling the basket before handing it to her. He thought her a fool, of course he did, and perhaps he was right. But whatever he thought, she was as good as he was, and in no way would she accept his patronizing remarks. 'Thank you, Mr Verney,' she said tightly, and tried to move away, but his arm came across, barring her way.

'Robert,' he said, with a brief smile that lit up his tanned face. 'That is, if you can bring yourself to let me become your friend.'

Call him Robert? Never. Straightening her back she said

curtly, 'I see no reason for us to be friends, Mr Verney. And now, please allow me to pass. Sarah and I have to help decorate the church.'

He nodded, 'Harvest festival, of course. Can I offer you a lift back to Abworthy, Miss Reed? Justice won't mind the extra weight.'

'No, thank you. I can walk perfectly well. It's not far.'

'But you could take me – I'd like a ride. Help me up, eh?' Sarah's voice was suddenly sweet and childish. Bella watched as Robert Verney grinned, nodded, put his arms around her and swung her up into the saddle. Then he mounted behind her, and, holding her safely in front of him, told the pony to walk on, down the rough path. He turned once to smile at Bella before trotting away down the track at the bottom of the hill, and called out, 'See you in church, Miss Reed. And watch out for hidden surprises.'

Bella felt her cheeks flame as she tightened her lips and carefully descended the hill, the basket heavy against her body. She hadn't been prepared for this meeting, which left an unpleasant memory in her mind. Her head lifted. Now she would forget Robert Verney, and ignore him, should they ever meet again.

It was only as she reached the farmyard and saw Sarah waving goodbye to the mounted figure who rode out of the far gate that it dawned on her that it was difficult to forget him completely. He was part of Abworthy, and, as she reminded herself, shadows in her mind darkening, Abworthy would one day be her home.

CHAPTER 5

Robert Verney's cob trotted down the track leading to Abworthy, his left arm around Sarah's waist. She kept turning, trying to see his face. 'What you doing, now you're back on the moor?' Her voice was lively.

'Earning my living, of course,' he said casually. 'Seeing to my cattle. What're you doing in the Reed house?'

'Waiting for someone to come along who'll fancy me and ...' she giggled.

'Marry you? Is that what you want?'

'Of course. Get me away from Abworthy. Dirty old place.'

He thought for a moment. 'How long has Miss Reed been here?'

'Came yesterday, 'cos Uncle William wanted her. Ma wrote, said as he was dying an' she must come quick. But she'll be going on Monday.' Sarah's voice was hard and Robert heard a note of resentment.

The pony halted inside the yard, but Sarah stayed where she was, looking at Robert with a hopeful smile. He dismissed the invitation, not needing to play that game. Steadying his hold on her waist, he lifted her from the cob's back. Easy girls like Sarah were all over the place and he could have his pick if he wanted, but another face was already imprinting itself in his mind and Sarah could usefully tell him what he wanted to know. Leaning down from the saddle, he said, 'So where does

Miss Reed come from?'

Sarah's smile vanished; she was sullen-faced again. 'Ma says she's a cousin, from Exeter.' Her dreams died. Clearly he had no use for her, but she tried one last time. 'See you at church, will I? Tomorrow's harvest festival – everyone goes.'

'I'll be there.' He turned the pony, nodded thoughtfully and then rode out of the yard without looking back.

Sarah pushed open the farm door, her face twisting. Same old smells, same old jobs; it'd be peeling potatoes and then down to the church with Ma's loaves and the heather. She had to get away. She went into the kitchen, wondering where she could find a man to take her somewhere else. Could it be Robert Verney?

Bella took her time returning from the tor with her basket of heather, for she felt herself reacting in a new and exciting way to the wonderful landscape. No more smells of town dirt and humanity. No more rushing bodies crowding the pavements, racing off to work, and, she guessed, thinking only of what the present day held.

Leaving behind her the rough turf and brown-stemmed heather bushes, she reached the track and paused as new thoughts filled her expanding mind. The wind soughed in a small copse of trees bordering the track, and a bird called. Looking up she saw it, wide-winged, soaring, giving a mewing call. She must ask Lizzie what this was. So much to learn. So much she wanted to know.

She reached the house, forgetful now of that awkward meeting with Robert Verney and instead concentrating on the idea of helping Sarah decorate the church. The kitchen was shadowy as usual, even though the fire flamed under the hob. Lizzie was busy, cheeks red and hands pushing and pulling at a roll of dough. On the table lay three small loaves, giving off an appetizing scent. Bella put down her basket, unbuttoned her coat and pulled a stool from beneath the table.

'What lovely shapes, Lizzie – how do you get them like that?' She stared admiringly, then looked at Lizzie, who raised a hand to wipe her brow, and smiled.

'It's a history lesson you're wanting, then? Well, I plait the loaves, before putting them in the oven. Made with the new wheat, cut back in August, they are. Used to be called Lammas loaves, but now we celebrate the harvest later, like now.' She returned to the dough, slapping it into a ball then putting it into a bowl with a cloth over it, setting it near the hearth, and then turning back to Bella.

'I see you got some heather and furze. Well, now you can both go and put them in the church afore dinner. Loaves can go later, when they're cold.' She went to the door leading upstairs, opened it and shouted, 'Sarah, where are you? Come down, maid, your cousin Bella's waiting for you.' Back at the table, she smiled at Bella. 'Don't know what she gets up to; she's never here when she's wanted.'

Bella smiled back. She also wondered what Sarah was doing upstairs, which took her thoughts to Uncle William, who hadn't appeared yet. 'Will Uncle William be down for dinner, Lizzie? Is there anything I can do for him, before going to the church?'

Lizzie straightened her back, smiling across the table. 'You're a good maid. No, the old man's dressing himself; won't be helped if he can do without. I'll give him a hand downstairs later on. Now, maid, do your coat up, sounds like it's breezy out there. You got that knife I give you for the heather? And here's some string. Heather's a strong thing to try and arrange.'

Sarah appeared, looking mutinous. 'What you want, Ma?'

Lizzie frowned. 'What do you think? Church needs decorating, and Cousin Bella's here waiting. And what were you doing upstairs?'

Just for a second Sarah paused. Then, smiling, 'I been making her bed. Like you say, Ma, I got to help out with the work.'

Sarah, in her room? Bella pushed away a suddenly unpleasant thought. 'I'm ready, Sarah, are you? I've got my basket and the knife and some string.' Sarah pulled her coat around her and yanked her old hat down over her brown curly hair. Her eyes locked on Bella who thought she saw ... could it be jealousy? But outside, walking down the track to the road, aware of the landscape touching her senses, filling her mind, the thought died. The wind blew leaves from the trees, and small mauve flowers growing at the bottom of the scrubby bank beside them made her pause and pick a tiny bunch. And there was the church tower in the distance.

They walked for what, to Bella, used to catching an omnibus in town, was a very long way. Because going to the church had seemed an occasion, she had left the black boots behind and changed into her usual leather shoes. But now it was clear that they were not hardy enough to cope with the flints littering the narrow lane, and already they were covered in mud. She tried to dismiss the discomfort of her dampened feet by talking to Sarah.

'What do you do, all day?' she asked. 'Except for helping your mother and Uncle William?'

Sarah scowled. 'Help in the yard – feed the chickens, and the pigs, and sometimes Mr James gives me things to do.'

'Mr James? I don't think I know who—'

Sarah sighed impatiently. 'Who do you think! He's the farm manager! He works for the old man now he can't get around no more.'

Of course. She should have known that someone would be in charge. 'Yes, of course.' She glanced at Sarah's sullen face. Clearly, she wasn't interested in answering questions. Perhaps she should offer some of her own information? Anything to break the cold and unfriendly atmosphere she felt growing between them.

'My work is quite different,' she said brightly. 'I am a

companion – that is to say, I live with an elderly lady and help her with all sorts of things.' She looked hopefully at Sarah and thought she saw a thawing of the dull expression. 'We live in Exeter – it's a busy city, with lots of shops and people. We visit friends, and entertain them, too.'

'But what do you do as a – a – companion?'

Bella thought quickly. What would interest the girl? Clothes? 'Well, among other things, I look after my employer's wardrobe. I make sure all her gowns are ready to be worn, and sometimes I repair any little tears in the hem. Long skirts so often get caught in things. And then there's her hats, and her jewellery to look after.'

She chased around her mind for enough information to continue this hopeful conversation. 'And sometimes I play the piano. Do you have someone in the church who plays a harmonium or reed organ to accompany the hymns?'

'Yes. Mrs James plays the old harmonium.' Sarah stopped, and Bella saw interest in her green eyes. 'Go on. Tell us about the clothes.'

'Well....' Clearly the girl's interest was caught. Bella, returning to St Leonard's Road in Exeter, looked into her wardrobe. 'This winter I'm wearing my old grey wool – this one – with a tiny check in it, because a new one would be expensive and I earn very little.'

'But your coat's lovely. Warm, and soft....' Sarah put a hand on Bella's sleeve and her face was suddenly wistful.

Bella took a chance, but she was learning that Sarah might be far less difficult than she appeared. 'I expect Cousin Lizzie takes you into Bovey Tracey for new clothes, doesn't she?'

Sarah's laugh was raucous. Then she scowled. 'No, she don't. We go into Moreton market sometimes and buy things from the old clothes stall. They're worn, see, so don't cost much.' Her voice grew soft. 'I'd like something new, really new ... nice clothes like you got. Like that warm nightdress on your bed, and the shawl you hung on the chair....' She stopped, plainly aghast at what she'd said.

Bella was instantly annoyed. So that was what the girl got up to when she wasn't in the kitchen. Prying, putting dirty hands all over her clothes, so neatly arranged in the big, cold bedroom. And then, instead, she felt the dawn of sympathy. Poor girl. How awful, to always wear other people's cast-off clothes. And have a longing for something new. She remembered the black leather boots, with their scuffed toes. Glancing very quickly at Sarah, striding along beside her, she saw with dismay and understanding that beneath the ancient coat and holey shawl, pulled tight around her shoulders, the girl wore a faded print dress of some sort of mauve check material, patched in several places, while the hat covering her thick thatch of hair was weather-stained and had lost its shape.

Sarah was a pretty girl. Surely she deserved something better than second-hand rags? Bella decided that back in Exeter she would buy something nice for Sarah, and send it to her. After all, the girl was a relative, daughter of Cousin Lizzie, so she must also be a cousin, if a more distant one. A present for Sarah, yes. Something important to do when she got home.

Sarah sighed, her face reverting to its normal sullenness. 'Here we are,' she said and Bella understood that the conversation was over.

Now they were in a village, passing cottages and some shops, heading for the grey church, which stood on the edge of a large green. Sarah pushed ahead of the groups of villagers walking up the churchyard path and went into the porch, not waiting for Bella, who followed slowly behind, feeling more of an outsider than ever. Suddenly doubt struck her; she felt that she could never become a member of this community. And then, a strong decision, pushing away the doubts: once she returned to Exeter she must forget Dartmoor completely.

*

Mrs May had seen them go, walking through the Abworthy hamlet, heading in the direction of the village, heavy baskets slowing their steps, walking in silence. She shut her door, stroked Jessie, and then sat down in the creaking armchair, thoughts busy. So this was the girl the cards had forecast. A queen of hearts indeed; tall, very slender, just like her mother, Marianne. That same chestnut hair that turned to gold under the summer sun. The warm, welcoming smile and, yes, she remembered clearly, the very same look on her pretty face, an awareness of life, an intent to learn and do things.

Bella Reed was definitely one of the Reed family. But did she share the same unpleasant ideas and attitudes of her masculine forebears? Edmund, or Ned as she thought of him, and William. And Lord knows how many others before them. Men with strong feelings about ownership and possession of their boundaries – and their women. Men who laboured to keep their farms going, to maintain their meagre Dartmoor lands in good heart, to make a living that took them just that bit beyond ordinary farm labourers. Yeomen farmers, the Reeds, thought Mrs May, nodding to herself.

The queen of hearts flashed into her mind again and she frowned. A good card, but put it next to that black spade knave and things could become nasty. She made a decision; when the right moment came, she would invite Bella back and spread out the cards before her. A day and a night could make a difference. The girl might have learned something and – Mrs May chuckled – she wouldn't mind betting that the black knave was already making plans to take advantage of his nearness to the queen card.

But back to work. She reached down a small bundle of dried corn hanging at the end of the beam above and put it on the table in front of her. Scissors from the drawer. Red ribbon from a bundle of pieces in a basket beside the fire.

Jessie's green eyes opened in a knowing slit, and before slipping back to sleep, the cat watched Mrs May's gnarled fingers creating the sacred offering that would be taken to the church for harvest festival the next day. Of course, the vicar would make his usual efforts not to accept it, but, she smiled; it was too strong for him.

It would be there, as near to the altar as she could manage, and everybody would understand that the old ways never changed.

CHAPTER 6

The church was busy with people. Two men were stacking tall sheaves of wheat against the altar rails; a woman stood on a ladder to tie bunches of cottage flowers around the window frames. Bella recognized marigolds, past their best but still bright and eye-catching, and bundles of lavender and faded green leaves already turning golden. She thought she could smell the country in the cold, grey church and looked around with amazement, leaving Sarah to sit down in an empty pew and gather bunches of furze from her basket.

Two women in the sanctuary carried tall vases up the steps. One of them paused, looking down at Bella. 'You Miss Reed?' she called and Bella said *Yes,* wondering how her name was known here in the village. Sarah whispered, 'That's Mrs James. She wants our flowers – c'mon, help me get the bunches done.'

Bella sat beside her and they started manhandling the thick and awkward flowers into two huge arrangements, Bella setting her small bunch of blue flowers in between the heather stems. Sarah wiped her prickled fingers and sighed with relief. 'Thank goodness that's done. Go on, take 'em up to her.'

Bella made her way up the altar steps, where Mrs James turned, took the offering, looking at her with critical eyes. 'You're from town, so I hear. What do you think of all this, then?'

Aware of heads turning to stare, Bella said carefully, 'I

think it's looking lovely already. How hard you're all working, bringing the wheat here and putting those flowers up there by the windows.' She had hardly finished when a man and young woman came in from the porch, carrying a big basket between them. It was full of apples, red and shining, some green monsters that were probably as sharp as they looked and a heap of tiny golden fruit, crab apples so small Bella thought they were plums. Heads were nodding all over the church, and she saw smiles directed at the newcomers

'Kept a few cider apples back, I hope, Joe?' called a man at the back, busy sorting out prayer books.

'Don't you worry – we got some sacks ready at the farm,' answered the apple owner with a chuckle and a ripple of laughter swept through the onlookers. Then the door opened again, and a man entered, carrying a sack on his shoulder. He looked around, caught Bella's eye and nodded without smiling. Instead he called, to no one in particular, 'Where do you want these?'

Bella stiffened. Robert Verney, here in the church, and paying her no attention. Well, she didn't expect him to. Didn't want him to. And yet.... She watched Mrs James come down from the sanctuary, screw up her eyes and ask, 'What you got?'

'Beetroot, parsnips, turnips, potatoes, all scrubbed.' Robert Verney grinned at the small, plump woman, brought his sack into the nave and let it fall with a bang on the floor. 'Where shall I put them, then? What about piling them up by the rood-screen? Congregation'll see them there. Is that what you want?'

Mrs James was beside him, looking at him with short-sighted, yet keen eyes, and half laughing. 'That's what I want, Robert Verney. It's good to see you back, and we're grateful for all these roots.' She turned her head, looked around her. 'Why, Miss Reed, you're not doing nothing, maybe you can help? Men are useless arranging things.' Someone shouted from high above, on the window beam, and she was off again.

Robert looked at Bella, in the pew, clearly unsure of what was expected of her. But now he smiled and she felt the abrupt and completely unexpected attraction of that smile. How could such an aggressive man, with untidy, near-black hair curling behind his ears, and mud stains on his worn tweed jacket, suddenly have such an allure? But he had long legs in brown breeches, and an upright stature. And eyes that caught hers, made her feel that she must keep looking at him. Almost without knowing what she was doing, she approached the sack he had left lying on the floor. 'Let me help you,' she murmured, and then stepped away because he was too close, too personable, too charismatic. What on earth was happening to her?

But he seemed in no way aware of her nervousness. He nodded at the sack. 'If I take them out, you can pretty them up. You ladies are good with decorations.' Already his big hands were tipping out the roots and Bella quickly tucked her skirt out of the way and knelt down on the stone floor beside the panels of the roodscreen.

In no time at all they were arranged. Small piles of different vegetables, colours enhancing the dark wood with its painted images, and making the entrance to the sanctuary look less forbidding. Bella worked in silence, aware of the man standing close by. She heard him chatting to someone up there on a ladder working at the flower-decorated window, and then stopped what she was doing as a shout came from outside the big door. 'Verney? You in there? Come out 'ere.'

She stared at Robert as he turned his head to the door. 'What the hell—' His deep voice was sharp and he strode out of the church, leaving an atmosphere of startled expectation behind him.

Bella got up from her knees and saw Sarah, eyes wide and excitement written all over her face. She glanced at Bella. 'It's Mr James. He got something to say to Robert Verney – I'm going to see what's happening.' And she almost ran out of the church.

Bella waited; no one said anything, but she thought she sensed a deep breath being let out by people who had momentarily ceased their work, and then all was normal again. Flowers, vegetables and a newcomer bringing in some berries from the hedges. Whatever happened out there was no business of hers, but even so, a tiny flash of interest lingered in her mind.

Robert Verney strode out of the porch, coming face to face with Joel James standing in the churchyard, legs akimbo. They stared at each other and Robert said sharply, 'What do you want, James?'

The smaller man hunched his shoulders, twisted his red face into a hard expression and said, 'Your beasts've got into our fields. Mixing with our cattle. Get 'em out, Verney. You know the rules – keep to your own pastures and leave us to ours. That's all I got to say.' He marched away, down to the green where his pony was grazing, looking behind him once before trotting out of the village.

Robert Verney stood outside the porch door, watching. So Joel James was on the lookout for broken rules, was he? He nodded to himself. He knew the rules, even after seven years away. William Reed's pastures were the holy grail to the Abworthy men, who wouldn't even allow a tearaway hen or duck to invade their land. And his beasts, those new Scotch cattle, with their wandering instincts, had made little of the neglected walls between the few Verney lands and those belonging to William Reed. He smiled grimly, ignoring Sarah, leaning against the porch entrance, eyes wide and a smile ready to break out. He didn't even see her, as he walked towards his own cob, harnessed nearby, mind focused on more important matters than a dreamy young girl. Of course, earlier today he'd wondered if the cattle would seek richer pasture beyond those broken-down walls. Perhaps he'd even hoped they would. Mounting the cob, he grinned more easily. Yes, he had. It had been the first small pinprick into the lethargic Reed family mindset. Just a small jab to force Joel James – and his master, old William – to understand that he, Robert Verney was on his way, renewing the old plans of his family over the past years to get back the land and the house that by rights should be his.

Abworthy estate, which his grandfather Pete had almost won at a game of nap, and then lost – by one card, so went the old tale – but which William had now entailed and therefore kept in the Reed family. For ever, so said the law. Not even a will could change it. Which was why, Robert thought, as he trotted slowly away to his cottage just down the road from Abworthy, his only chance of getting back his rights was by perhaps marrying William's heiress. He opened his eyes wider. Was it possible? Amused at the workings of his mind, he thought wryly, well at least she was attractive; a slender young woman with shining hair, pretty enough, he supposed, but who looked as if she had nothing much to say for herself. The idea grew. He imagined her as a woman he could dominate and force into a marriage, which would bring him all he wanted.

Reaching his cottage with its small yard, two derelict sheds, and a muddy path leading out to thinly grassed fields, Robert Verney lifted his head, narrowed his dark eyes and looked around him. England. Dartmoor. Good to be back where he belonged. And the plan was already becoming workable. Once old William was gone, Abworthy, and its timid new mistress, could become his. He set about gathering his beasts from the far fields, and allowed himself a huge grin. Life was improving.

Bella found Sarah standing beside the big cross outside the church, moodily staring down the road. She didn't reply when

Bella said, 'If we've finished here, shall we go back to the farm? I'd like to see my uncle.'

Sarah nodded, started walking away from the church, and Bella followed, mind full of unanswered questions. Why had Robert Verney been called out? And who by? She wanted to ask her companion, but, seeing her gloomy expression, kept silent. Then, after a few yards Sarah glanced round at her. 'They're always fighting, Verneys and Reeds,' she said, dully. 'An' Mr James does it for Uncle William nowadays. I s'pose now Robert Verney's back, the old troubles are here again. My ma's told me about those quarrels. All to do with Abworthy House and its land.'

She kicked a pebble and pouted, looking again at Bella. 'You'll have to get used to it, those rows, when you're here.' Her face grew ugly. 'When the old man's gone an' you're mistress at Abworthy; when you got to see to the farm and the market, and the work in the house and everything. Think you can do it, do you?'

Bella read the expression right. The girl envied her, thought she was a useless town creature, imagined that she couldn't run a house, keep a farm going. But she felt determination and knowledge thrusting inside her, and said firmly, almost without further thought, and with a new steeliness that surprised and pleased her, 'When that happens I shall make arrangements for Abworthy to be sold. I have no intention of running a farm, or of living here in the wilderness.'

Sarah's gasp told Bella she had taken a step in the right direction. In due course, and it might be years away, but certainly she would sell the awful old house, and its lands, get rid of it. *Get rid of Abworthy*. Continuing their walk she began to plan. But just as they came into sight of the hamlet, with Mrs May's cottage ahead of them, she began to wonder. Abworthy was the home of generations of Reeds, she herself latest in a long line.

Family, land, inheritance, Uncle William had said. If he knew she was planning to sell her inheritance, he would die unhappy, angry that he had ever tried to find her. She couldn't live with that. She must help Uncle William in his last days. *Don't even think of selling Abworthy.* Her mind was running in circles, but when Mrs May appeared in her cottage doorway, beckoning, Bella smiled gratefully and turned aside.

'Where you going?' Sarah's voice was rough.

'To see Mrs May. I'll be back before very long.'

Sarah frowned, striding on down the track, and Bella entered the cottage, Mrs May's welcoming smile sending new light into her confused thoughts.

'Thought as you'd like a drink before you go back to Abworthy.' The old woman went to the fire where a kettle hummed. 'Sit you down. We're glad to see you.'

Bella felt strangely at home. How stupid of Sarah to think Mrs May was a witch. 'The church is looking lovely,' she said. 'I'm looking forward to the service tomorrow.'

Mrs May sank into her chair opposite. 'Been helping with the flowers? Working already, are you? You'll be busy when you get Abworthy, I can tell you.' Her eyes were bright, and Bella wondered if Mrs May knew about her plan to sell the farm. She looked down into the mug of tea handed her, and wondered how she could suggest that she might not be staying.

Slowly, she said, 'But it's possible I may not come here, after all. I have a good situation in Exeter, and I might be thinking of marriage soon.' Jack's remembered smile brought returned confidence. She looked steadily into Mrs May's unblinking eyes. 'After all, Uncle William might live for a long time yet.'

'He'll be buried before the turn o' the year.' The words were quiet, but the shock of them sent a shiver down Bella's back.

She stared at the old face, suddenly almost mask-like, and, into her shocked mind, Sarah's words echoed.

She's a witch.

For a long moment they looked at each other, Bella pale and tense, and Mrs May still as a statue. Jessie awoke, green eyes blinking, and then leaped into her waiting lap.

'Good puss,' said Mrs May, and then she was looking as friendly as ever, sipping her tea and inviting Bella to have a refill. Bella smiled to herself – of course Mrs May was no witch. She felt glad to be here.

Indeed, she thought she might tell the old woman what she really planned to do with Abworthy.

CHAPTER 7

'You want to hear about your parents?' Mrs May said, smiling over the hearth. 'I'm remembering all sorts about them.'

Bella allowed her mind to settle. Yes, Mrs May had things to tell her. She wondered about the old woman's age; she had been nursemaid to both Ned and William, so she had said yesterday. So, with Uncle William somewhere in his late sixties, Mrs May must be over seventy. Bella smiled at the lined, weather-beaten face regarding her. No doubt some of the tales would be muddled, even embroidered. But it was pleasant enough, sitting here in the warm, so she relaxed and waited.

'Long time ago, now,' began Mrs May, pausing now and then for memories to clear, 'Ned and William were small when I came to look after them and always fighting, they were. Neddie was younger, see, and delicate, so he had to be given into more than big, rough William. I recall....'

The room was still, the fire a soft breath in the background and Bella's imagination took hold. She was back at Abworthy, long ago....

Mrs May thought for a moment, and then, 'Marianne and Ned stayed for three weeks before their marriage and I saw it all. It was like all the old, earlier quarrels come back. William didn't like Ned being given into more'n him. I saw him

59

watching Ned acting as if he owned the farm, instead of being just the younger son.' She paused and Bella could see it was all there in her mind. 'When Marianne comes – an orphan, so she stays here when the banns are read – Ned takes her out in the trap, tells the village as how they'll be master and mistress of Abworthy, even though they'll rent a house in Exeter 'cos he has a job in a gents' outfitter's.' A smile, a chuckle. 'Ned, he did tell such lies. Yes, always come back to Abworthy, they will he said.'

Another stop as she stared across at Bella. 'Marianne was a good maid but she didn't take to the place, even though William tried to entertain her, 'cos Ned would go up to the inn of an evening, see, and leave Marianne alone. I saw how she grew to like William, doing things to help when she could.' She nodded, and her voice deepened, words coming more slowly, lengthening into something that brought darkness to Bella's mind.

'It was a funny time. A real strange feeling round us. Not happy. And then it comes to a head that night after the wedding when Ned comes home roaring drunk.'

Bella stiffened. She could see it happening. She almost didn't want Mrs May to continue. But of course, she did.

'He comes in only just standing up, and shouts at William, sitting on the settle with Marianne beside him. 'You rogue! Leave her alone – she's my wife, not yours. I'll teach you to make up to her.'

Silence, then Mrs May frowned and her voice grew unsteady. 'There was a fight. Marianne screamed, little hands over her mouth. I saw William's arm sweeping round and flooring Ned. Between us, we took Ned up to bed. I heard William talking quietly to Marianne, and then I went home, but I knew things weren't finished. And then next morning – well, Ned and his gun. I heard the shot echoing round and got my things together – reckoned blood had been spilt, see.'

Mrs May stopped and said nothing for a long moment. Then she went on. 'Ned and Marianne packed their things, and they went, William, with his arm bandaged, driving them to Bovey to take the omnibus to Exeter. When they left, Marianne sat beside William in the trap with Ned in the back. He frowned, but she smiled and waved. I remember as the sun was shining that morning. All the hillside aglow with light. Seemed so wrong that the family had broken up, but there, it had been coming for years.'

That last scene was almost visible, Bella thought; the trap bucketing down the track, brothers ignoring each other and Marianne sitting there, no doubt reliving all that had happened here at Abworthy. And Bella knew that she must have wondered what the future would bring.

The fire shifted and she sighed. 'And was that the last time you saw my mother and father?'

Mrs May stood up, put more peat on the fire and sat down again. She smiled with an expression, Bella thought abruptly, of tender amusement. 'No, no. They came back later that year – with you.'

'With *me*?' It was a shock. Bella had never imagined that she had been at Abworthy before. 'Are you sure, Mrs May?'

The smile became a chuckle. ''Course I'm sure. A pretty little babe, you were, good, too. I had care of you when Marianne and Ned went off in the trap. Stayed just a few days, they did. Ned was full of his job – getting on, he said, promotion soon – and Marianne told us about the rented house.'

Another silence, full of imagining and wondering. Until Mrs May said, quietly, and not looking at Bella, 'William was good with the babe – with you – he was. Carried you round the yard; "Look at the pigs," he'd say, "look, there's a new calf, and here's the old bull." 'Course, Ned told him he was daft; you were only a babe, couldn't understand all he said. But William said it was important for you to get to know Abworthy.' She stopped, then added, almost inaudibly, 'I see him now, you in his good arm, the bad one propped 'gainst it to hold you safe.'

The fire hummed and moved. Mrs May stood up, stretching out her hands to Bella. 'Time you was going home, maid. William'll be waiting, I don't doubt. Find your way, can you? Just mind the holes in the track.'

So the remembering was over. Bella was torn between astonishment at what had happened, and a new unhappy urgency pushing her away from the old house, full of its haunting memories. But she reached out to touch the offered hard, knuckly fingers in a gesture of some sort of gratitude, then pulled her coat around her and walked to the door. Turning, she saw Mrs May watching, a smile giving her lined face a comforting warmth.

'Come again, maid. More I can tell you. But we'll be at church tomorrow, won't we?'

As she opened the door, a blast of wind awakened Bella's confused mind. 'Yes,' she said, 'of course. Goodbye, Mrs May,' and began the rough walk home.

Home, she thought? And then – but it had been *her* word in *her* mind, not Mrs May's.

The rest of the day passed almost without Bella knowing. Lizzie and Sarah left soon after the meal, when Bella helped to dry the dishes. Then she joined Uncle William on the settle by the fire. She wanted to talk to him, to get to know him better, to let him find out what she was like; and if the idea of saying she would sell Abworthy once he was gone had flashed through her mind, she knew now that she could never be so cruel.

'Uncle William, tell me about the farm. I'm a town girl, but I'm interested in what you do.'

He grunted, fidgeted, rubbed his left arm. 'What I did, you mean. Can't do any more now.'

'But you have Mr James – Sarah told me. He does the work.

Where does he live?'

The old man half turned to look at her, eyes dark and narrowed, and she saw a gleam of amusement in them. 'Joel James is my farm manager, lives in a tied cottage up the road with his bossy little wife. He's worked for me for a long time. Dare say he hopes to get Abworthy when I'm gone. But he won't.' The hoarse voice deepened. ''Cos it must stay in the family. Yours to take over one day soon – not so long now.' He sighed and, sensing his sadness, Bella put her hand on his, words suddenly rushing out.

'But Uncle, I can't just come and live here. I belong in Exeter, you see. A good situation, with loyalty to my employer to consider. And I have a friend – Jack Courtney – who I think loves me. I expect we shall marry. He is a solicitor, so we will have to live in the city. And so ... so....' Then she saw the sudden blankness of his deep-set eyes, and wished she had kept her thoughts to herself. Why couldn't she have left him thinking that in the future all would be well at Abworthy? How could she possibly be so unkind? But she knew he had understood all that had remained unsaid.

He coughed, wiped his mouth, sighed and then patted her hand. 'I see,' he said quietly. A long pause; her heart was pounding, emotions raging, until he added, very slowly, 'So Abworthy has to wait, eh? The old house must keep itself going for a bit longer. 'Till you decide to come back.'

It wasn't possible now to say she would never come back, but perhaps he saw the pain in her eyes, saw her mouth working, trying to find words that refused to come, for he said, almost to himself, 'But you'll be here, maid, sometime. Don't think Abworthy will let you go, for it won't. You see, we're your family; it's your land, your inheritance. But you'll go back and you'll think 'bout us here p'raps ... and I'll wait to see you again.'

He had talked too much, and now he looked and sounded

exhausted. Bella stood up. 'Uncle William, let me get you a cup of tea and then you should go to bed and rest.'

He drank his mug of tea wearily and used her shoulder as a prop to get him up the staircase. Slowly they went along the passage, then Bella pushed open the door of his room. Lizzie had put the small oil lamp there, and told Bella a hot brick was in the bed. At the door she hesitated. Someone usually helped the old man to undress – should she offer? He must have read her thoughts, for he chuckled as he sat heavily on the edge of the bed. 'You're a good maid. Help me take off me boots and me coat and then I can manage. That's it.'

She knelt on the floor, unlacing his boots, and then helped to take off the tweed jacket smelling of smoke and humanity. She could never have believed what she was doing. Not Bella Reed, with her cleanliness and neat clothes, orderly mind and lack of disturbing thought. But this Bella was strangely different. Ready to do what she could for her old, suffering uncle. For the first time in her life, she became aware of the depths and demands of family. And then another thought thrust its way into her mind; tonight, when she went to bed, there would be no chair against the door, but she knew she would sleep with half an ear out in case Uncle William should need her.

There were no calls asking for help, and it was only when Lizzie's footsteps came up the stairs next morning that Bella awoke, aware of farm noises, her head full of memories. She dressed quickly, went down to the kitchen and put plates on the table, watched the fire and pushed sticks onto the embers. How extraordinary that she should do such things. In Miss Carpenter's house on a Sunday morning, the maid would serve breakfast, then they prepared for the important morning service, sometimes in the cathedral but more often at St Leonard's Church beside the busy river.

By the time Lizzie had helped William to get up and start dressing, Bella had found the pan that she had seen used to cook porridge yesterday and was finding her way to the dairy for milk. She paused in the doorway, meeting Lizzie's astonished eyes. 'I hope I've done it right.'

Lizzie laughed, and said, 'Not bad for a townie, well done. Now sit down and we'll have a cup o'tea while the porridge cooks. An' I'll show you what I got to take to the church.'

In the apple basket beside the table were three plaited loaves in the shape of flat fish. Lying on top of them were two pies, pastry golden brown, with fruit juice trickling from under the crisp lids. Lizzie re-arranged her goods. 'Outside I got a little basket of berries. Blackberries, some plums, sloes, rowan berries, too, still bright red and fresh. They'll go along the pews – make it all look pretty.'

Looking at the luscious, rich colours of the fruits, Bella learned something more about country life. Not plums bought from Exeter market, but what Lizzie had gathered from hedges and trees around the cottage where she and her family lived.

Words were lost for the moment, thoughts raging, and then William was coming down, his heavy steps on the wooden stairs bringing Lizzie to her feet, going to the door and offering her arm. 'Careful now, Uncle William – don't want you falling, do we – not with harvest festival waiting for us.'

Bella looked at the old man as he walked towards the settle. Whiskers trimmed, she saw, and a clean shirt showing up the tanned skin of his withered neck. The old jacket was replaced with a dark green corduroy coat which had once fitted him but now sagged over his shoulders. But it brought an air of old-fashioned elegance, which would make him stand out in the crowded church.

There was no time for conversation and once breakfast was over and the dishes washed, a message was shouted to Joel James to harness the pony and have the trap ready in five minutes' time. Lizzie pulled on her dark brown, rather rusty coat, skewered her hat into place and picked up the basket of offerings.

Waiting by the door, Bella said, 'Let me help,' and between them they stowed the basket in the back of the trap, then returned to the kitchen door. 'Come on, Uncle – trap's waiting,' said Lizzie, and William appeared, walking slowly but steadily into the yard. Joel James helped him into the driving seat, where he picked up the whip with his gloved right hand, and looked around.

Bella, climbing into the back of the trap, along with the baskets, watched the old man stare up at the sun-touched tor, saw narrowed, deep-set eyes blink in the bright daylight before William's head turned to inspect the sheds dotted around the yard. She knew he took in the filth of the midden, guessed he was imagining the cow in her pasture and hoping that cattle, pigs, sheep, chickens and yard dog were all being looked after. Instinct told her, too, that he wished that he was still working here.

Mrs May's voice rang in her head, then, and in her inner sight she saw him, taking her around the yard, showing her the farm animals. He had held her in his wounded arm, and ensured her safety with his other hand. They had been together. She knew, with intense finality, that it was a thought that would never leave her.

Lizzie's voice broke through her reverie, saying, 'Let's go, Uncle.' The whip flickered over the pony's back and the trap moved out of the yard. There was unexpected strength in William's right arm as he drove them along the rough track, then out onto the road and down, through the valley, towards the church, where the bells were already summoning the village to celebrate the harvest

CHAPTER 8

Bella watched Lizzie put the bread, bunches of rose hips and a bottle of cordial on the open pew ledges where Sarah was already sitting. Then she sat down next to Bella, halfway along the pew, and smiled a big grin of satisfaction, helping Bella to understand how important this harvest festival service was to Dartmoor people. She marvelled at how the church had been taken out of its cold greyness, new life and belief showing in the abundant bounty of the countryside.

She sat quietly, until she saw Uncle William slowly making his way up the nave, staring about him, nodding at the occasional smiles and low voices greeting him. He came to what she now realized was the Reed family pew, watched him sit, and then, painfully, kneel to pray.

A new disturbing sensitivity rose inside her. She hadn't been prepared for this; the decorated church, the hum of subdued voices around her, the fidgeting of bodies, and over it all the sonorous peal of the calling bell. Instinctively she slipped onto her knees, covering her face and waiting for calmness to return. At last, sitting down again, she looked around her.

There was the man she supposed to be Joel James – having only briefly seen him once before – on the other side of the nave, dressed in what looked like his Sunday best. There, too, was the prayer book sorter, on his knees now and finding it difficult to rise again. There the farmer, red-faced and puffing a bit, who had brought the basket of apples. And more villagers still entering, filling the pews.

And there was Robert Verney, sitting just across the aisle from her, looking unfamiliarly tidy and more than usually impressive, with shorter hair, a white shirt and a well-cut jacket that showed off heavy shoulders and strong frame. He looked across at her, and for a moment – obstinately storing itself in her memory – he smiled and nodded his head. Not the patronizing, amused smile of yesterday on the hill, but something truer, warmer, and a smile which Bella found friendly. Confusion clouded her mind for it was as if Robert Verney was no longer the aggressive charmer who she felt she must be careful of; this man looked sincere as he met her eyes.

Bewildered, she looked away at once, and then was thankful when a small stir in the church doorway made all heads turn to look at the latecomer. Mrs May entered, carrying a laden basket, her black coat billowing around her legs as she bustled up the aisle. She had no eyes for anyone, but stopped at the roodscreen, where she began emptying the basket. The congregation peered and shifted to see what was happening. Mrs May piled jars of what looked like jam and jelly against the panels of old wood, added a crusty pie and then bunches of rowan berries and sloes. A handful of dried herbs was the last to leave the basket, but Mrs May had not finished. From the depths of the almost empty basket, she carefully took out a long straw artefact.

Now the watchers' breath was collectively sucked in – someone muttered, 'Her old corn dolly' – and Bella was caught by the sudden silence in the church. The dolly was a long, plaited hanging decoration of straw, its rounded shape simple and familiar. A thread of straw at the top provided a hanging loop and at its other end ears of wheat spread out in a perfect flower shape.

Her amazement grew. Was this what Mrs May had been

making when she left the other day? Mrs May rose from her knees, took her time to go to the altar steps. There she placed the corn dolly, and bowing her head, knelt down, remaining there for a few moments. Eventually, the calling bell stopped pealing, the vestry door opened and a procession of choir members filed up the nave. The Reverend Dudley Greenstreet followed, his small pale eyes sweeping the congregation, and finally alighting on the pagan offering on the altar steps.

Bella's heart pounded. Surely something extraordinary must happen now. How could a Christian priest accept a pagan idol? He looked at Mrs May as he followed the choir through the church, finally taking his stance beside her. She sensed the church was alive with expectancy, and was taken aback as Mr Greenstreet bestowed a tight smile at his pagan parishioner, nodded to her, gestured that she should return to the body of the church and then, stepping forward, put his right hand on the straw dolly, lying there before him. Was it a blessing? Bella hoped it was; she felt the atmosphere change almost as if the congregation breathed heavily with relief.

Bella saw smiles relaxing the tension. She turned to Lizzie, beside her, and, under cover of hymn books being opened and people rising to their feet, whispered, 'So he accepts it? He won't order her to take it away?' and Lizzie whispered back, 'Reverend's too sensible. He doesn't like it, but he knows we still follow some of the old ways.'

A movement across the aisle and Bella saw Robert Verney looking at her again. This time there was no smile, just a keen inspection by those vivid storm-blue eyes; she thought the square jaw had never looked so strong and resolute, the weathered, angled face regarding her as if she were ... what? A prickle of uneasiness ran through her, but then, even as the harmonium wheezed to life under Mrs James's fingers, and voices were raised, singing lustily, 'All is safely gathered in,' she saw how he turned away, smiling at his neighbour, offering to share his hymn book, no longer bothering to look at her.

When the service ended, amid shuffling of feet and a hum of voices, the congregation filed out. Mr Greenstreet stood by the door, offering his hand to his parishioners. When he saw Bella with Lizzie and Sarah, he looked at her very intently. 'I welcome you to the village, Miss Reed. I noted your arrival at Abworthy.' Pale eyes gleamed. 'Village gossip, you understand. And I trust your stay will be a pleasant one.' He took her hand, nodding at her before releasing it.

Wondering exactly what he knew about her connection to Abworthy, Bella smiled politely. 'Thank you, Vicar. But I shan't be here much longer. I return to my home in Exeter tomorrow morning.' As she spoke, she saw Robert Verney arrive at the vicar's shoulder. She met his quick gaze before he saluted Mr Greenstreet and then he strode away, out to the village green where horses and traps waited. She wondered if he had heard her words, but because of his hurry, decided it was unlikely.

It was pleasant on the green, the sun shafting down between the chestnut trees, and Bella looked around the granite-stoned village, hearing slow voices discussing the vicar's sermon, Mrs May's corn dolly and the decorations around the church. She waited for Uncle William to appear, nodding when Lizzie and Sarah said they would make their own way back to Abworthy, where the midday meal needed a last heat up.

They ate a good meal of stew, thick with vegetables, and there was bread, cheese and apples to follow. Being a special occasion a bottle of farm cider was poured and the harvest toasted. Uncle William ate in silence while Lizzie asked Bella what she thought of Mrs May's corn dolly.

Bella thought, then, 'I don't understand what it's meant to be. Just a pretty decoration? But it seemed more important, the way Mr Greenstreet put his hand on it.'

'He blessed it. Always does. Doesn't like it being there, of course, but as it's the spirit of the corn god he can't do nothing about it.' Lizzie refilled Bella's mug, despite the shake of her head. 'See now, that sheaf of wheat is the last one that's cut at harvest time; the men make a big thing of it, calling it the neck, and then it goes up onto a beam to stay 'til we have harvest thanksgiving when it's made into the dolly and offered up in gratitude.'

'Thank you for telling me. I had never heard of it before. But then I know so little about Dartmoor. But why does it stay in Mrs May's cottage?'

Lizzie and Sarah exchanged glances. ''Cos she's a witch, that's why,' Sarah muttered.

'No,' exclaimed Lizzie, 'don't say such things. Mrs May's our wise woman. We go to her for remedies, and help when we have problems, all sorts – and the Reverend knows that.'

'Ah, she knows a thing or two, does Mrs May.' Uncle William's voice was sharp and he looked at Bella keenly. 'She's got our family's history in her head. Ask her anything 'bout the Reeds and she'll know. Found that out yet, maid, have you?'

Bella felt a sudden rise in the atmosphere of the old room of something that was frightening, almost as if a flash of the past was being repeated. But she met his unblinking gaze and said, 'Yes, Uncle. She's told me a bit about my mother, and my father.'

'Marianne. And Neddie.' The old man sighed, looked away. 'She's a good woman, is Ella May, so you can believe what she says. But look,' his frowning stare made her flinch, 'there's things must remain untold. So don't go bothering her any more. Understand?'

Silence; Lizzie and Sarah looked at each other, shaking their heads, and then they were quickly on their feet, clearing away plates and dishes. But Bella knew that she could not accept this dogmatic order. As a member of the Reed family, she needed to know everything about it, no matter what. She looked into William's pouched old eyes and said firmly, 'I'm sorry, Uncle, but I can't believe what you say, for surely a family must share everything, know everything? It must do. And although I won't ask Mrs May to tell me more, well, if she wants to, then I shan't stop her.'

They stared at each other, his old eyes becoming angry, misty, and even deeper set. But she felt a new strength, a growing sense of certainty and confidence. She smiled, and then, to heal whatever wound had opened between them, reached out her hand and laid it over his, squeezing tightly. 'Uncle William, don't let's fight,' she said quietly. 'I won't do anything that will hurt or shock you. But as your niece you must let me find my own way into our family.'

She waited, hoping he would reconsider. Very slowly, he did. Looking down at her small fingers, spread out on his calloused wrist, he allowed himself a smile that doused the fire in his eyes, then lifted his thin, dry mouth, and nodded his head. 'You're a good maid,' was all he said, but Bella felt it was enough. She left the table and then turned as the old man suddenly caught his breath, coughed noisily and almost fell over the table.

A flurry of skirts, and Lizzie was there. 'All right, Uncle, let me help....' She sent a demanding look at Bella, who went to the old man's other side, and between them they got him to the door and up the stairs, into his bedchamber and finally onto his bed.

He opened his eyes and stared at them. 'Just need to rest. Leave me be. I'm all right.'

Lizzie unlaced his boots and removed them. Then she covered him with the patchwork coverlet and looked down at his suddenly pale face, which Bella thought was even greyer and paler than usual. She glanced at Lizzie. 'Should we leave him? What if he wants us?'

But William Reed recovered a flash of his old spirit. 'Leave me, I said. B'God, a man can't get any rest with you women mothering on and fussing.' He closed his eyes and breathed heavily, and Lizzie nodded anxiously at Bella.

'I must go home to Dan – an' Sarah's going off somewhere. Well, let him sleep awhile, but will you bring him some tea? Make sure he's all right for the night? I'll be here first thing tomorrow.' At the door, she turned again, met Bella's eyes. 'You'll be off in the morning, so I'll tell Joel to harness the trap after breakfast.'

Bella had almost forgotten she was going home the next day. But now the thought was no longer the dream she had indulged in since her arrival. Now it seemed wrong that she should leave Uncle William, so clearly suffering another bout of his chest problems. And yet, Miss Carpenter must be missing her. Jack would meet the noonday train and what a lot she had to tell them both. A twist of conflicting thoughts. Yes, this evening, she must pack her valise and be ready for an early departure in the morning. But for now....

The house was quiet once the Whartons had left, and Bella heard snores drifting down from her uncle's room. She saw to the built-up fire, and then looked around the room. Everything was still and ordinary, yet there was a feeling, something like a stirring of old life and, ridiculously, she had the sudden urge to escape. She stood, immersed in a flurry of ideas. The afternoon was hers – she would go out, then come back for tea, to spend time with Uncle William and then to settle down for the evening and cook something simple for their supper, because it would be her last night here.

Leaving the house, she saw the autumn sun flashing bursts of fire as it glowed on the granite outcrop of the big tor. She would climb to the very top stones, stand there and look around. She might not see Dartmoor again, for, once back in Exeter surely this weekend would become just a memory, to be smiled at, even regretted at times, and then forgotten again. Abworthy being her inheritance was just an old man's fancy.

She reasoned that, apart from Mrs May, who said she had known the family in past years, there was no legal evidence of any connection. Most likely, William Reed, on the border-line of his second childhood, and longing for an heir, had just dreamed it all up.

As she climbed, she felt the cool, fresh invigorating air, energizing her; seeing the landscape stretching all around her, it allowed a last, probably never to be seen again, vision of the wilderness into her appreciative mind.

She felt soft turf, saw tiny four-petalled yellow flowers, realized that the heather was indeed going over, but that the nutty smelling furze was still in brilliant bloom, and pushed aside the fox-brown stalks of dying bracken as she went, ever upwards. A straggle of foraging ponies came around a clitter of rock as she climbed and watched her moving away from them.

By the time she reached the top of the piled granite, she was out of breath, ready to rest, and she sat down heavily, smiling because of all that she saw. Moorland stretched around – green, brown, pale, dark – sometimes lit up in soft dusky colours where cloud shadows rolled down its slopes; other great tors reared glittering, sunlit heads, encompassing the lowland pastures below with their straight walls; there was the occasional glint of a winding river or stream and half-hidden farmhouses, each remote in its own valley, sheltered by a ring of trees.

Bella felt she was in an enchanted world. Yet reality also came into her mind. Here, in early autumn, the sun still shone, the wind, although cool and capricious, was gentle in its intent, lifting the skirt of her coat and teasing her hair from beneath the well-skewered hat. But what might winter bring? Gales, snow. She couldn't take her eyes off the horizon, each view offering a precious memory that, with dismay, she knew she must hold onto and remember. It was as if the moor had cast a spell on her.

Directly below the tor was Abworthy, standing rock-like, small and lumpy in its awkwardly shaped courtyard, with tracks leading to the various cottages surrounding it. There was a path leading through a gate at the end of the yard into an orchard, and then on into small fields sloping down to a stream. Her land, if Uncle William could be believed.

Seduced, her eyes followed the views. After the Abworthy fields ended, there were smaller, stretching pastures, one of them enclosed by a copse of dark trees. She made out the shapes of sheep, white dots, in the last field. Knowledge came to her; this must be Robert Verney's land.

Even as she thought his name, she saw him, a fast-moving figure, his unmistakable dark hair and long stride, walking towards the flock of sheep. He carried a stick and beside him a farm dog ran. She heard a whistle rising in the air, faintly reaching her, saw how the dog rounded up the sheep into a tight circle and then saw the man walking amongst them. A hand lifted; he bent down to inspect a hoof, whacked an obstinate animal standing in his way.

So this was Robert Verney on his own patch of farmland. What might he think if he knew she was watching him? Unable to look away, she saw him leave the sheep, he and the dog moving onward, out of the fields towards the open moorland ahead of them, and even stranger thoughts came to her. She had a wild longing for new experiences. A sort of truth to be chased. To discover the moor, somehow, sometime. Robert Verney knew Dartmoor, for there he was, striding off, almost out of sight, enclosed by the heights of the waiting tors, hidden from view, but knowing every step he took and where he was going.

If only she could do that. With Robert Verney? Her wildness retreated. No! What a terrible idea! Reluctantly she returned to the present. A grey billowing mist was creeping up the valley, mercifully defeating all those self-indulgent thoughts and ordering her to go back to Uncle William. Descending the hill clumsily over the tussocks of dying heather, the big boots chafing her heels, Bella knew she would be glad to feel the warmth of the old kitchen, see the glow of the fire, make tea for herself and her uncle.

She felt that Abworthy welcomed her and, after taking off her coat and hat and thankfully putting on her own shoes, then becoming busy with the fire and the teapot, she found herself in charge of everything. There were still no sounds from the upstairs bedroom. She looked forward to taking the old man his tea, telling him what she had done, what she had seen – but, of course, nothing about Robert Verney.

Indeed, it was good to have other things to think about now and defiantly she clung to them. Soon she would be going home. And then the idea of packing her valise and getting ready to leave tomorrow morning began to glow more brightly. Returning to her proper life, and Jack, who would be meeting her train.

Not long now, she thought determinedly.

CHAPTER 9

In the morning, breakfast was over quickly and dishes washed and put away before Bella went up to say goodbye to Uncle William, who sat in his bed staring at her with his penetrating gaze.

'I'll wait for you to come home again, maid. Don't be too long, 'cos maybe I shan't last the winter.'

She forced a bright smile, brighter than she felt, and found hesitant words, which she hoped might comfort him. 'Perhaps at Christmas, Uncle William. I might come then.'

'You might. But remember me, maid. And remember that Abworthy'll come to you. You're family, see?'

With tears tightening her throat, she took his hand, leaned over the bed and kissed his leathery cheek. 'Yes, Uncle. Family. I won't forget.' She hurried from the room, with his last words, hoarse and full of meaning, in her ears. 'Family. You've got to come back, maid.'

Downstairs, her coat, hat and valise were waiting. Lizzie stood at the door. 'I told Joel to harness the pony – he'll be waiting. And ... come back soon, eh, Cousin Bella?'

Bella put down her case and hugged her cousin. 'I don't know,' she said unsteadily, 'but I'm grateful to you for everything. And please let me know how Uncle William gets on. Oh, and tell Sarah I shall be sending her a present.... Where is she?'

Lizzie returned the hug and then turned away, but Bella had

seen anger tighten her mouth. 'Gone off on her own – I don't know.' She opened the door and her voice changed. 'Here's the trap, but well, my goodness! What're you doing here?'

In the yard Bella met Robert Verney's amused smile. 'I have an errand in Bovey this morning, so thought I'd save Joel James a job by giving Miss Reed a lift.' He lent forward, hand outstretched. 'Let me take your valise.' Surprised, Bella saw his eyes light up with amusement, while the already charming smile grew. 'Don't look so shocked. I'm not planning to run off with you, just doing a good turn. Let me help you up. Mind your skirt on the step.'

Bella was outraged. He was too rude and autocratic for words. She would refuse to go with him. But already his arm held hers in a hard grip, she was being firmly persuaded to climb into the trap, where she had no option but to seat herself, watching helplessly as he came around to the other side and joined her. Laughter twinkled in his deep blue eyes and his voice was light. 'Nothing to say? No shocks or refusals? How sensible. And think how grateful Joel James must be. Now, say goodbye to your family, Miss Reed, and then we'll be off.'

Obediently she half turned, met Lizzie's grin, and waved. 'Goodbye ...' she called faintly. They were off, the cob walking smartly through the yard and then breaking into a trot as it reached the track leading to the road. Bella had no time for a last look behind her but in her mind one picture remained; Abworthy, its age-old stones agleam with the morning sun.

Slowly, reality returned. If Robert Verney expected her to talk to him, then he was mistaken; her thoughts were too busy, too private, to communicate. Here she was, on her way home, which was, of course, wonderful and what she wanted, but somewhere in the background of that pleasure lurked a dark shadow: Uncle William, frail and in his bed in that cold chamber. And then it was a warmer image of Lizzie stoking the fire, stirring broth, somehow making time in her busy life to care for the old man. And lastly she saw herself, selfish, wanting only her own future with Jack and disregarding all she had learned and experienced during this extraordinary weekend on Dartmoor.

As they drove along, the moorland unwinding itself around them, terrible doubts filled her mind and, panic-stricken, she looked at Robert, beside her. 'I can't go!' Hardly knowing what she was doing, she pulled at his arm.

He drew on the reins, and the cob halted. He looked at her keenly, and then said, frowning, 'Are you sure? Shall I take you back?'

'Yes! No! I don't know.' She bowed her head and felt her heart pounding. This was a terrible moment, breaking down like this, with Robert Verney, of all people, beside her. But when she looked up into his eyes, she thought she saw understanding there.

'What shall I do?' Her voice was uneven, and she pressed her hands together as if to fight off the uncertainty filling her.

He paused before answering, and then his voice was low and firm. 'Forget the train. Come with me into Bovey, and then I'll take you back to Abworthy.'

She stared at him, her mind in chaos. She had a return ticket. Jack would be waiting at Exeter. Miss Carpenter had probably missed her terribly and would have dozens of little jobs for her to do. But Uncle William was waiting at the old house. And now Robert Verney was looking at her with determination written all over his strongly featured face and she felt in the middle of a battle. What was she to do?

And then – help came. It was as if his low voice was moving her towards a decision. 'Look around you, Bella. This is Dartmoor, the place where you'll be living when old Mr Reed dies. What does it say to you? "Go away, I'm only an old piece of wasteland"? "Don't bother to come back"? Or has it already taken a place in your heart?' A smile lifted his straight lips. 'I know how Dartmoor holds on to one – it's the reason why I've come back from the other side of the world. Yes, you've only been here a few days, but surely you must have learned something about it?'

This was all so unexpected that Bella's mind began to resettle itself. He was talking sense, and he needed a sensible answer. She sat back on the hard seat, and turned to look at the road ahead snaking down the hillside. Yes, she had learned something. She knew that all the brown heather stalks were strong and easy to trip over. She had climbed her way up the tor, between the stalks of dying bracken. Those small blue flowers she had picked probably had a name and suddenly she longed to know what it was. And those tiny yellow, four-petalled blooms that covered the ground – what were they? If she ever came to live on Dartmoor, she must know them.

She knew, too, that Dartmoor people were strongly resolute, their hard, solitary lives making feelings for family and land equally strong. Did she have that same blood in her own body? The same feelings? The same obstinate strength?

Then the wind came blustering down the hill, and her hands went to her hat. It was, she knew, just another facet of moorland life. But it forced her thoughts back to an easier existence. In Exeter, winds were only gentle and transitory. Hats never blew off. Coats retained their warmth. Beds were softer and warmer, living rooms comfortable and tastefully furnished.

She heaved a huge sigh, and her circling mind unexpectedly decided. Turning back, she met interrogating blue eyes, and said, almost casually, 'My train leaves at 11.20. It gets to Exeter just after noon.' And then the final words: 'I mustn't miss it.' She was breathing more slowly now, thoughts looking forward. Jack would meet her. His smile warm, always the same. No complications with Jack, just understanding and strength. Exactly what she needed.

She smiled more easily, thinking what a fool she was.

There was no question of whether she stayed or went home. Another big breath, her body relaxed, and she said, 'Yes, I shall catch the train. And perhaps come back here sometime in the future.' No need to think any further. She paused while the anxious clouds loomed again, but now she had enough strength to disperse them. 'I don't know. It all depends on so many things.'

Robert was still looking at her. Silently, he nodded, flicked the reins, then said a word to the pony, and the trap continued on its way. But he said nothing. When they reached Bovey Tracey station, he hitched the reins to the waiting post, picked up Bella's valise, offering his other hand as she alighted from the trap, then walked with her to the station entrance. Her ticket clipped, she went onto the platform, aware of him just a step behind her.

Turning to face him, she gestured at the valise. 'Please put it down. I mustn't keep you any longer. A porter will help when the train comes. And thank you for bringing me here.' She stopped.

Those all-seeing vivid eyes were fixed on hers. Slowly, Robert Verney removed his gloves and stowed them in his jacket pocket. He looked at her, holding her gaze and finally nodding. 'Yes, I'll leave you now. You're safe enough here. Are you being met in Exeter?'

'Yes,' she said faintly. His expression surprised her. She had thought him arrogant, bold and not all that mannerly, but now his smile was warm, and even as she still gazed at him, he reached out and took her hand. 'Have you made up your mind, Bella? Are you sure you won't come back?'

The seemingly innocent question stirred up the troubled images filling her mind. She stared at him. 'I don't know.' But then again, she was back with Uncle William, old, lonely Uncle William, coughing himself to death in that icy bedroom. Of course she must return. But her thoughts were in chaos. 'I don't know. I can't decide.'

Robert's fingers were strong about hers. Again, surprise – but at her own feelings. Such a warm hand. Such a powerful man. And smiling at her. Unevenly, she said, 'About visiting Uncle William again? Yes. I will....'

'One more thing, Bella.' Robert's deep voice resonated in her head, and the final words surprised her even further. 'Remember that Mr Reed needs you to return – wants to see you back in your rightful place at Abworthy.' And then, slowly, holding her gaze, he unfurled the glove on her right hand, and lifted her arm towards his lips. Carefully, opening the curled fingers, he kissed the palm, then pulled the glove over her hand again, letting her arm drop to her side. His voice deepened even more, the words so soft she hardly heard them. 'And I want you to come back to Abworthy, too. Remember the old man's waiting for you – just as I shall be. Don't keep us waiting too long.'

She couldn't answer, just stared at him, the kiss warm on her hand, his last words singing in her head.

A distant puffing and steaming down the line and he stepped backwards. 'Here's your train, Miss Reed. I'll get you a porter. So, until you decide to come home, goodbye.' A last flash of glittering blue, another rapid smile as the train came and he was gone, striding up the platform and out of her sight.

Entering Exeter Bella picked up her valise, preparing for the train to stop. Jack's name rang around her head; he would be here and delighted to see her. They would take a cab back to St Leonard's Road, where Miss Carpenter would be awaiting her return and then he must return to chambers. But he would call again during the evening, or tomorrow at the latest, she was sure.

'Bella!' His voice carried down the crowded platform, his eyes found hers, and there he was, taking the valise, smiling at her, looking, thought Bella dizzily, as if he wanted to put his arms around her and kiss her a proper welcome. But not here. Not for Jack to unroll a glove and kiss a warm palm, in the middle of a station platform, with waiting travellers noticing and probably gossiping.

Instead, he put an arm around her shoulders for a single second, and then said firmly, 'I have a cab waiting. I'll take you home, Bella. My word, it's good to see you again.'

The house in St Leonard's Road was just as she had left it, only four days ago. Emmy opened the front door and beamed at her. 'Welcome back, Miss Reed. Shall I take your bag and your coat? Madam's waiting in the drawing room.' She looked at Jack. 'May I have your hat, sir? And will you be staying to luncheon?'

Jack stood by the door, impatient to go, thought Bella suddenly. 'No, thank you, Emmy, I'm not stopping, I've been away from my work for too long as it is. Bella, I'll call around tonight if I can, or tomorrow. I'm sure we have a lot to talk about. Give my compliments to Miss Carpenter, please, but for the present, my dear, goodbye.'

No kiss. Just a quick smile, a speedy retreat, the door closing and his rapid footsteps fading away into silence.

Bella met Emmy's smile, and took a hold of herself. She must go into the drawing room, where Miss Carpenter would welcome her. And then recount the strange tale of Uncle William, of Lizzie and Sarah, of Dartmoor and of Abworthy. Of Mrs May, perhaps, and certainly of the harvest festival. But not a word about Robert Verney. Bella stiffened her back and rearranged her thoughts as she opened the door in front of her – for goodness' sake forget that unexpected kiss. But it was still warm on her hand.

CHAPTER 10

'But, my dear child, you have no proof at all that this man – this Mr Reed – is your relative. It could be a trick of some sort.' Miss Carpenter resumed her knitting and Bella, sitting opposite in the warm, comfortable drawing room, picked up her embroidery frame, staring at the half-finished pink rose, surrounded by green leaves.

She said nothing, and then she looked at Miss Carpenter and said very firmly, 'But, if I had my birth certificate, that would be proof. Mr Reed is my father's brother – both he and Mrs May told me this.'

'Mrs May – who is she? A village woman? She could easily be mistaken, or even making up tales.' Miss Carpenter frowned at her knitting then said sharply, 'Why not ask Mr Courtney for his advice? He could send away for a copy of your birth certificate.'

Bella thought hard. Then she said, 'I'll ask Jack when he calls.'

Their eyes met. Miss Carpenter asked carefully, 'Do you expect him soon?' Bella nodded. Of course he would come, as he had said he would. This evening, perhaps, or tomorrow.

'Yes,' she said firmly. 'He'll probably call in when he leaves chambers tonight.'

Miss Carpenter laid her knitting in her lap and looked at Bella with lowered eyes. 'Of course, dear child, I wouldn't dream of intruding on your thoughts, or your plans, but—'

Bella hid a smile. 'Jack and I are growing fond of each other, Miss Carpenter,' she said quietly. 'He's a nice man, reliable, and – and – charming.'

And then, for no reason at all, Robert Verney's smile was in her mind, and she felt again his kiss on her palm. She blushed and bent again to the wretched pink rose, but she guessed that Miss Carpenter had noticed.

'Ah! So you have an affection for him, do you, my dear? And is this likely to grow further? Certainly, Jack Courtney is all you say, polite, reliable, strong-minded, and with a very good situation. When his father retires he will become senior partner, no doubt.'

Bella met the faded, questioning eyes, feeling that she must brazen out the fact of a possible marriage, both for her own sake and that of her employer. 'Yes, I believe Jack will propose to me soon,' she said calmly. 'He has hinted at finding a house, and is clearly very fond of me.' She stopped abruptly as all the necessary parts of a marriage flashed through her mind. A villa, in a quiet residential part of the city; elegant clothes, ordering servants, her part as a social partner to an important man, meeting new people, entertaining. Having a family....

Suddenly she let the embroidery frame fall to the floor. Reaching to pick it up, she caught her breath, and tried hard to push out of her mind's eye the vision of Abworthy, dull and wet, with the glinting tor high above it. Uncle William, coughing. Lizzie fussing around him. Sarah sulking, and Robert Verney inspecting his sheep.

Wildly, she got to her feet. 'It must be teatime. I'll carry a tray up for Emmy. I know her legs are painful.' Anything to escape and still the memories.

Outside the drawing room, she stood in the passageway,

trying to quieten her raging mind. Why was she caught by the haunting thoughts of Abworthy and the people who lived there? Why could she not settle down to the more pleasant dreams of marrying Jack and starting a new, easier, life?

She talked to Emmy about the freshly baked fairy cakes and then carried a tray into the drawing room, helping Miss Carpenter to put aside her knitting and sit up straighter in order to pour the tea.

Routine, she thought, desperately, will help me forget Abworthy. And I am looking forward to Jack coming tonight. Or tomorrow. Sometime soon. I must see him and ask his advice.

He arrived in a rain storm the next evening, leaving soaked outdoor clothes in the hall and giving his umbrella to Emmy to dry down in the kitchen. Hearing his voice, Bella at once left the drawing room to welcome him. He was in the hallway, eyes shining and smile warm. 'Bella,' he said quickly, 'it's so good to see you again.'

Unexpectedly, he opened his arms. 'Shut the door,' he murmured as he pulled her towards him. 'My dear, it's been such a long time.'

Bella lifted her face and closed her eyes, laughing. 'What, four days?' And then he kissed her, and this, she told herself was all she needed to return her to the familiar life here in Exeter.

But his lips were gentle, merely touching hers lightly before stepping away. 'We must behave ourselves. Miss Carpenter is waiting for us.... Shall we go in and see her?'

Bella nodded. She was surprised at his lack of passion. She had expected something more exciting. But she knew that Jack was always in command of his emotions. Now his hand was on her arm as they went in to meet Miss Carpenter's smiling welcome.

'My dears! Come along in. A glass of sherry, Mr Courtney?'

'Thank you, Miss Carpenter, but not at the moment. I can't stay long, but I am looking forward to hearing Bella's account of her visit to Dartmoor.' He guided her to the usual chair and then pulled up another, at her side. 'So tell us all about it.'

Bella sat up straight and wondered how to introduce the extraordinary and poor life she had been part of at Abworthy. But, whatever they thought, she decided that the truth was all that mattered and so began by saying, 'I've already told Miss Carpenter, so I hope she won't mind hearing it again.'

A nod and a smile. She took a breath and began. 'It was very wet when we got to the farm, my cousin Lizzie Wharton having met me at the station and driven me there.' She stopped. How to introduce Uncle William with his terrible cough, his piercing black eyes that never blinked, but who had treated her with warmth and, indeed, a sort of love? Would they understand?

Carefully, then, she poured out the words describing Abworthy and its inhabitants and found that she was enjoying going back to the shabby farm, to meeting her unknown relatives and introducing them now to the listeners around the fire.

But when she had finished, two pairs of eyes gazed at her in silence and she wondered whether she had said something terrible. Jack cleared his throat. 'You sound as if you enjoyed your stay there, but –' he stopped, glanced at Miss Carpenter, who nodded, and then continued, '– but, Bella, it all sounds very – well – poor. Run down. Impoverished.'

She breathed deeply. 'Yes, it is poor. They live a hard life on the moor, they don't have all the comforts we have here.' But she was floundering, could see from the expressions on their faces that they were not convinced about the propriety of her visit. She met those frowning eyes and waited.

Jack fidgeted, cleared his throat. 'Your – er – uncle—'

'Uncle William. My father's brother. He is very ill and Cousin

Lizzie thinks he is dying. It's a terrible moorland disease, something to do with wheat and corn affecting his chest.'

Miss Carpenter tutted. 'Has he seen a doctor?'

Bella shook her head. 'I don't know. There wouldn't be one near, you see. But Mrs May makes him a remedy each week.'

'Mrs May?' Jack's voice was sharp. Bella said nothing. Suddenly she couldn't tell them any more because clearly they had no opinion of Abworthy and of anyone who lived there and she knew it would be best to keep her thoughts to herself. Such – now she realized it – precious thoughts.

Miss Carpenter said, 'I think a copy of Bella's birth certificate is required, don't you, Mr Courtney? There are so many doubts in what she has told us – things need clearing up. I believe that the dear child is being taken advantage of, and we can't allow that.'

Jack stood up, stepped to the fireplace and turned around, facing them both. He rocked on his heels, his voice quick and firm. 'I agree, Miss Carpenter. I will put the matter in hand tomorrow morning. Yes, like you, I feel that Bella is being made a fool of, and, which is worse, is being forced into experiences which will do her no good and certainly not bring her happiness.'

Bella sucked in a huge breath and wished she could leave the room. This was worse than she had feared. Jack was planning to take over her life and Miss Carpenter was aiding him. Anger began to grow, but she pushed it away. Think of now – of events here which will change the subject....

'Coffee,' she said suddenly. 'I'll ask Emmy to bring some up.' She left the room.

After that, it was somehow easier to behave normally, hearing Jack talk about the latest building development in the city: 'A pleasant site down by the river,' he said, nodding at her and, she sensed, already planning their life together.

And then Miss Carpenter suggested a little music might end

the evening before he had to leave, and so Bella seated herself at the piano, with Jack ready to turn the music. She played one of Thomas Moore's melancholy Irish airs, and then Miss Carpenter said, 'My old favourite, *Home Sweet Home*, please, Bella.'

Bella found her mind wandering as she began to play. The word *home* was in the forefront of her mind and the verse rang through her head; homes all over the world. People in their little houses, their vast castles and draughty mansions. Dartmoor people like Uncle William, sitting in that old room at Abworthy, full of memories and atmospheres.

When the music finished she remained at the piano, eyes blind to the music on the stand, until Jack said, laughingly, 'Come along, Bella, where have you gone? I think you need a good rest after those difficult days on Dartmoor! Off to bed with you.' He put a hand on her shoulder and reality returned instantly, sharp and hard to accept. She rose, looked into his amused eyes and knew that he would never understand about Abworthy. But she knew that she had to tell him about the entail of the estate. And then, in the hall, calling down to Emmy to bring the dried umbrella, she accepted a new and bleak piece of personal information. She would marry Jack, of course she would, because it was clearly her future, but Dartmoor would always haunt her. The ancient house and the tor behind it, glinting in the late summer sun. The mysterious, solitary wilderness.

But, as he pulled on his coat, she was unable to stop the words churning in her mind. 'Jack, my uncle's estate has an entail on it and he is leaving it to me when he dies. I shall inherit Abworthy.'

'*What?*' He swung around, staring at her with shocked eyes.

Unsteadily, she said, 'I haven't told Miss Carpenter because I don't want to upset her, but – but I felt you had to know....' His face had tightened, lips hard and pressed together. 'Thank goodness you did. I shall go into this very thoroughly – and quickly. Abworthy, did you say? And this wretched man who is clearly trying to get something from you—'

'He's not like that. Uncle William is a good man, and I—' Her heart was racing. Why should Jack react in this hateful fashion? Determination grew. 'I shall be going to see him again very soon.'

'You certainly won't, I shall make sure of that. Now, my dear, don't worry.' Then the harshness died, the straight lips were smiling reassuringly. Putting on his coat, he picked up his hat and took the umbrella from where Emmy had left it. 'Leave the whole sordid business to me. I will sort it out for you. But Miss Carpenter must be wondering what we are doing out here....' He bent, pecked her cheek, nodded and, frowning again, said, 'Abworthy, on Dartmoor, you said. And what's his name?'

She stared at him. Now was the time to argue, but her mind was in rags, and Miss Carpenter would hear raised voices. Dismayed at her own weakness, she said very quietly, 'Reed, the same as mine.'

He left with a bright smile, the door closing like an impenetrable shutter behind him and Bella was left standing, hating herself, wondering what she could do to remedy the horrible mess into which she, poor Uncle William and the old house had fallen.

CHAPTER 11

Mrs May spread the cards on the table. The queen again, and the black knave. And – ah, a new one – another knave, diamonds this time, fiery but unreliable, running on the tail of the queen.

She sat listening to the hum of the fire and Jessie's breathing, half asleep on the opposite chair, and thought deeply. What could be done to help things along? Already the queen had met the black knave and that game was in hand, slow, but on its way. But this new spread foretold of the queen being used by a newcomer who boded no good. Perhaps it would be wise to bring the maid home to Abworthy, where she could be kept safe from unwanted forces. Yes, thought Mrs May, suddenly smiling and creaking up out of her chair. She would call the girl home.

After a night's sleep, she rose, seeing just a mere glow in the eastern sky, but enough to light her way. Dressed, leaving the fire made up, she left the cottage. She found the way unwinding easily before her slow footsteps. In the old days she would have walked to Scorhill stone circle to invoke her magic, but that was beyond her now. But she was creating her own circle, following the track down to the river, hearing its rippling music, seeing birds in and out of the water living their secret lives, and then walking on through wild moorland, where she kicked aside half-dead bracken and bent to pick a few blue sheep's bit flowers. Take them home, keep them with the other herbs; a touch of true blue always helped the potions.

Now the sky was lightening, pearly and wide, colours growing with every minute. Mrs May looked around her and smiled up at the morning star, fading as dawn diminished it.

The wind was rising, a swirl of cold air touching her cheeks, a dab at the skirt of her old coat. As she walked along, turning in an arc and heading back to the river, the start of her walk, her thoughts entered the magic realm. The circle was complete, air, water and earth all about her and fire at home. It was time to call back the little maid, one day soon to become mistress of Abworthy.

Bella Reed. Bella Reed. Come home, maid. Come along home.

Back at the door of her cottage, Mrs May felt the usual loss of energy and was thankful to stumble into the half-lit room, stretch cold hands out to the fire and tell Jessie, 'It's done. She'll be here, don't know when, but soon.' And then she settled down for a long morning in her chair, with the blessing of sleep returning her stamina and preparing her for the rest of her long and useful life.

Down the lane from Abworthy, Robert Verney opened the door. He stopped. Something was moving at the end of the yard. A blow of the morning wind, perhaps; a swirl of quick life and dull colour just out of his vision. Now, shrugging on his jacket, pulling his hat low down over his eyes, he walked to the pigsty and pushed himself into the brambly space beside it. Somewhere to wait and find out what was happening here.

A few minutes, and then she appeared, nervously flickering eyes, tight mouth, old patched shawl tied around bony shoulders: pretty Sarah Wharton, up to no good, he bet wryly. Stepping out in front of her he said her name and then stared at her.

'Oh my!' So great was her surprise that she almost

overbalanced. He thrust out his hand, pulled her back onto her feet, but didn't smile and they stood for a silent moment, eyeing each other, until she said unsteadily, 'I thought you were indoors.'

'And now you know I'm here. So you can just tell me what you're doing, hiding in my yard. What're you up to?'

Her thin face flamed bright red and she stared down at her feet. Her voice wavered. 'I – I – thought I'd help you. Somehow. Feed the pigs – collect the eggs. Whatever you want.'

Robert let her arm drop and his anger disappeared. Silly little maid, got an eye for him, hadn't she? Well, he could probably make use of her. 'Yes,' he said, as her eyes rose to meet his. 'Give me a hand, if you like. But on condition—'

'What? Oh, anything—'

'That you tell your ma where you are and what you're up to, and that you don't miss out on any of your work at Abworthy. All right?' That'd get her off his back, and, yes, she was an amusing little scrap. Just needed to grow up a bit and she'd make someone a useful wife.

A wife.

For an instant, an image of Bella Reed flashed through his mind. It softened his voice, produced a handsome smile, as he said cheerily, 'Pig swill's in the bucket in the shed, and there's corn for the hens in the barn. Off you go, then.' And then, abruptly, mind running on, 'Any news from Abworthy?'

'No. Old Uncle still coughing. An' Cousin Bella gone.'

He knew that. 'Any idea when she'll be coming back?'

'Never, she said. An' she's going to sell the house when she's got it. I dunno.' Then she ran off, a last delighted grin at him over her shoulder, shouting, 'I'll do it all!' before disappearing into the shed.

Robert Verney stood still. So, quiet, self-contained Bella Reed deciding to sell what he still thought of as his birthright? He hadn't thought she might do that. Slowly going towards the cowshed, he wondered; maybe she had more sense, more strength, than he had imagined. It was a new idea holding distinct possibilities and difficulties. He milked the cow, his mind stretching in different directions, considering potential benefits. He must get hold of Bella Reed and start working on his proposed courtship. He needed her to return to Abworthy – and very soon.

'Miss Carpenter, when I go into town this morning, would you mind if I took a few minutes to buy something for myself?' Bella's mind was busy with the need to find a present for Sarah.

'Very well, my dear. Something personal, is it?' Miss Carpenter's small world welcomed anything new. She wondered about possible articles of trousseau, her eyes marking Bella's appearance; slender, tallish, such a good posture, and a smile that would surely turn the hardest heart. What good fortune to have such an excellent companion – yes, small favours were willingly granted.

Bella left the house, walking quickly through the city and to the arcade where any of small shops might suit her needs. As she went, she thought of Abworthy and its people, for that slight altercation with Jack last night had brought the farm into clearer focus. Mrs May and Cousin Lizzie and Sarah were now suddenly important in her life. And Uncle William, of course, but this morning it was particularly Sarah, pretty, shabbily clothed, bored with her dull life, wanting smart clothes and a more interesting life. A present, perhaps a shawl, she thought, wandering down the arcade and looking in shop windows. Nothing too costly, for her savings were few, but something warm and pretty; a friendly gesture to her distant cousin whom she would like know better. Something that might improve Sarah's life.

It took her eye as soon as she pushed open the door of the last shop. A fine wool shawl, fringed at both ends, displayed hanging over the back of a chair. Bella handled it, thinking how its soft tones of autumn ochres, browns and faded greens in large checks reminded her of the moor, slowly folding itself towards winter. It was warm and she saw, in her mind's eye, how it would look over Sarah's thin shoulders, giving the girl something to be proud of and to show off.

It cost more than she had expected to pay, but it was the one thing that appealed to her. 'I'll take this, please,' she said. She asked the assistant to parcel it up and find a label. Waiting, she wrote a note to enclose, thinking hard and finally writing, *To Cousin Sarah, from Bella Reed.* Sarah would certainly be surprised – would she also be pleased? Bella hoped so. Wryly, she hoped also that Sarah would be more friendly when next they met. *When next they met.* When would that be? Confusion began to weave its web again; the urge to return to Abworthy, but common sense telling her that it would be foolish and wrong. Jack's cold words rang around her mind: *You certainly won't go* and, switching them off, she was glad to suddenly find herself, instead, thinking of Mrs May. Not just thinking but seeing – yes, she could see the old woman standing in her cottage doorway, smiling. And saying something. What was she saying?

Bella sat very straight, not noticing when the shop assistant held out the wrapped parcel, because it was important to hear Mrs May's words, but when they came they were unsaid, merely thoughts impressing themselves onto her alert mind.

Must go back to Abworthy. Must go back.

With the shawl parceled up and the bill paid, she addressed the label, then took the package to the Post Office, seeing it fall into a delivery bag. It was done. But, as she walked back to the quietness of St Leonard's Road, she found the confusion fading from her mind and, by the time Emmy opened the door, she knew she was thankful to be home.

For, yes, home was here, and she was Miss Carpenter's

companion. Nothing was going to change that and she must put Abworthy to the background. After all, she had other, far more important things to think about. And then again, Jack was in her mind, smiling at her now, so reassuring and strong that at once she began to look forward to his next visit.

Sarah couldn't believe it. 'For me?' she cried, pulling apart the brown paper parcel, holding up the scarf, loving its softness, admiring the colours and patterns. She bent, tucking the fallen note into her pocket.

Breakfast was finished and Lizzie was keen to clear up and then get Uncle William downstairs. She must get home and deal with the chores waiting there, for Dan was in bed again, his stomach this time, he said. 'Can't get up, can't work,' he moaned, pulling the coverlet over his head. So now she only looked at Sarah, fussing about with her parcel, out of the corner of her eyes while her hands dealt with the dishes.

'See to the fire, maid,' she ordered sharply. 'Got to get some hot water going for Uncle to wash.' Glancing over her shoulder, she realized Sarah had gone. The sound of laughter drifted back through the cross passage and the big door banged shut. Lizzie sighed. Down to the Verney farm, of course.

Dishes dried and put away, Lizzie wondered who had sent the parcel. She had anxious thoughts: Had Sarah met someone? Could it be an admirer? Was she behaving herself? And where was the dratted girl? Never there when she was wanted, but oh yes, gone to tell Robert Verney about it, she supposed. Stoically she heaped peat on the fire, pushed the pan of water closer to the centre of the glowing range and thought uneasily about her daughter, now dividing her time between here, home and the Verney farmstead. Really, with all this work of caring for Dan, and for Uncle William, she needed her daughter's help. Setting her lips into unaccustomed hardness, Lizzie went up the dogleg stairs, her mind making plans for bringing Sarah to heel.

*

'Isn't it lovely? Don't I look well in it? Feel how warm it is, and these colours are lovely with my dark hair.' Sarah prinked in Robert Verney's small kitchen, wriggling around in front of the small bleary mirror that hung on one wall. Excited and pleased, instinctively she knew that the shawl was a new step in her dull life. There were no mirrors at Abworthy, so here she was, hoping the shawl would make her look nice for Robert. Perhaps even make him think she would be a good wife. What *was* he thinking about her? She swirled around, eyes on his thoughtful face as he reached out for his coat, found his hat and staff and prepared to start his working day. He said nothing, so she softened her smile, and almost whispered, 'Don't I look nice, Mr Verney?'

Robert nodded. 'Yes, but the hens are waiting and the pig's grunting for his breakfast. And you're here to work, Sarah Wharton, or so you said, so put your new toy thing away and get on with it.' But he relented, seeing her smile die, watching the shawl being carefully folded up. 'Where did you get it? A present – not your birthday, is it?'

'No,' she said sullenly. 'My birthday's in the spring. Don't know where this has come from.' And then she remembered the scrap of paper she had pushed into her skirt pocket. 'There's this note.' A second's reading, and then, 'It's from Cousin Bella. She's sent it to me.'

She met his surprised eyes, and wondered at the expression on his face.

'Is there an address?' he asked, hand out, taking the paper and looking at it.

'Why? What d'you want to know for?'

Robert rammed his hat on his head and opened the door, looking at her over his shoulder. 'Because you'll have to write and thank her for it. That's all.' He stepped out into the yard, calling back, 'Do the usual things, Sarah, and then you can go. Don't leave your ma with so much to do, or she'll stop you coming.'

Unchaining the dog, he strode out of the yard, heading for the pasture where the cattle grazed, intending to work on the dilapidated walls. He wanted no more trouble with Joel James. As he walked, his eyes were as observant as ever, but his mind was busy, considering how to find Bella in Exeter. A good excuse, perhaps, to call on her and take Sarah's note of thanks?

As the morning wore on, the plan worked out. Lizzie Wharton would have the address. He would call on her to offer a few days' work to that useless hayseed, Dan and he would ask for the address. And then a trip to Exeter would be the next thing. A polite call on Miss Reed, where ever she lived – and all on Sarah's behalf, of course. No one could blame him for that, could they?

CHAPTER 12

Bella was tidying Miss Carpenter's wardrobe, when Emmy knocked at the door.

'Mr Verney to see you, Miss. He's in the drawing room with Madam.'

Putting down the embroidered jacket she was inspecting, Bella stared at the maid, surprise raising her voice. 'Mr Verney? Thank you, I'll be down at once.' But not quite at once. She put away the jacket, shut the wardrobe door, looked in the mirror – wide eyes, and a patch of pink on each cheek – before straightening her shoulders and then, with mounting self-control, went downstairs and into the drawing room. It was easy, then, to smile and say, 'Good morning, Mr Verney.' And then, before he replied, she turned to Miss Carpenter, who was watching from her chair by the fire. 'Miss Carpenter, this is Mr Verney whom I met at Abworthy. He is a neighbouring farmer and called on my uncle to see how he was.' She was aware of Robert's dark blue eyes watching every movement, guessed that he was amused at the way she was floundering with such polite conversation.

Miss Carpenter nodded, smiled, eyes slightly narrowed, and said, 'Mr Verney has already introduced himself. I understand he's come with a message for you, my dear.' And then, as if she saw Bella's awkwardness, 'Ask Emmy for coffee, will you? I'm sure Mr Verney could do with a cup. He tells me he has walked all the way from the market.' The final words were directed at him, and Bella saw a laugh light up his steady gaze.

'We farmers walk miles every day, Miss Carpenter, when our stock is out on the moor – so from the market to here was simply a stroll. But, thank you, coffee would be most welcome.'

Bella went to find Emmy, wondering if Robert was charming her employer into acceptance of his visit, and yet reminding herself that, despite her age, Miss Carpenter had a sharp mind. Had she accepted his excuse of a message? And then, what message, she wondered? Was it important? He would have told her at once had it been about Uncle William. Which left her wondering: What was the real reason for this call?

Returning to the drawing room, she felt again the old confusion. Abworthy calling her; Jack forbidding her to go ... and now Robert Verney had come, starting all this wretched disturbance again. In the room, she looked at him. He was sitting, clearly at his ease, booted legs stretched to the fire, entertaining Miss Carpenter with tales of his years in Australia. 'I learned a lot but there was always this call to come back. Dartmoor, you know, Miss Carpenter, puts a spell on anyone born there.' He rose, looked at Bella as she resumed her seat, and then sat again, saying, 'And I think Miss Reed herself has felt the pull of the Moor. In the few days she was with us she managed to see a bit of it. Well, there's a lot more waiting for her when she returns.'

A moment's silence; Miss Carpenter sat more upright in her chair, lifting her head and, Bella guessed, preparing to deal with the suggestion that she should return to Abworthy. It was difficult to avoid Robert's eyes, which seemed to question, almost challenge her. Quickly, she said, 'I don't know when I shall be visiting Uncle William again. Not for some while....' The words grew clumsy and confused. 'My situation here – I don't wish to leave Miss Carpenter – it's all rather difficult, you see.'

'Yes,' said Robert Verney, 'I see.' He stared at her and Bella realized that he did see; he did understand but that he had only one thing on his mind: to persuade her to return to Abworthy.

After coffee was poured, Miss Carpenter said, slowly, but very firmly, 'I do not think Miss Reed should return to the old farm, Mr Verney, until she has some proof of the family relationship that is being thrust at her. I'm sure you will agree that this would be a safeguard to any – well – underhand dealings, which may well be developing.'

Bella caught her breath and looked at Robert. He put down his cup, the expression on his face stern. 'Underhand?' The word was full of disbelief. 'You need have no worry on that account, Miss Carpenter. I can assure you that the Reed family is of long standing, and good repute. My own family has lived alongside them for generations and their reputation has always been blameless. I think you should consider that Bella –' he nodded towards her and she saw anger glinting in his eyes, '– that Miss Reed is fortunate to be reunited with her family. And I hope that, before much longer, she will indeed return to her old home.'

Silence. Miss Carpenter gave him a chilly smile, and then said, 'I understand all you say, Mr Verney, but my solicitor, Mr Jack Courtney, who practises in the city, is taking up the matter of the legal provenance of any such relationship. Perhaps we can talk about it later. And now – you said you had a message for Bella?'

Robert felt in his coat pocket and produced a folded paper. He gave it to Bella, his face dark with what she recognized as ironic amusement, and she imagined he had not been prepared for Miss Carpenter's unexpected attack. However, he smiled, as Bella took the paper, and said, 'Written with a lot of head scratching ... but much gratitude. I can tell you, she wears the shawl every day.'

The unsteady writing brought a sudden tenderness into

Bella's heart as she read:

Dear cousin beller, thank you for the shawl. Its luvely. Keeps me warm. From sarah.

It took her back to the kitchen at Abworthy, and then to the tor, in the cold wind and the brilliant sunshine, finally to Mrs May's cottage, listening to what the old woman was telling her. She tried to think herself back into the present, but instead found she was looking into Robert's watchful eyes, and saying very quietly, 'Please thank her and tell her I shall be coming back. Quite soon.'

Again the room was full of alarm, but the easier expression on his face, suddenly softer, warmer, brought her a feeling of reassurance. It was as if something had charmed her and she knew for certain now, that, despite Jack's and Miss Carpenter's worries about the legality of this new family relationship, she would be going back. And soon.

Abruptly, a shutter opened in her mind, and then, without further thought, she said rapidly, 'Miss Carpenter, please allow me to go and visit my uncle again. Could you spare me this weekend, when your sister is coming to stay? I will do all the necessary errands before I go.'

She saw Miss Carpenter's ageing face tense, eyes gleaming and knew her request was about to be refused. But she must go. Her voice even firmer, she said, 'I'm sorry, but it's important that I see him. He is so very ill.'

She sensed Robert's approval, heard him say, politely, 'I agree with Miss Reed; the old man is thought to be very near his end – and I will do what I can to make her journey easy. I can meet her train and take her to Abworthy, for Mrs Wharton has enough to do without getting out the trap.' He paused and Bella watched Miss Carpenter fighting to regain her shocked breath. And then, smiling, he added, 'Shall we name the day? And the expected arrival of her train? Then it will all be arranged and there'll be nothing else to worry about.'

Bella turned to him, said quickly, 'If Miss Carpenter agrees, I'll come on Friday, and catch the same train as I did before, which arrives at Bovey at 11.45 a.m.' Her smile broadened. 'Thank you, Mr Verney, for your offer of help, which I accept most gratefully.'

The looks they exchanged were, she thought, a step forward in the strange friendship forming between them. Robert nodded and looked at the old lady, who was still staring at him with disapproving eyes. 'Miss Carpenter, I will look after Miss Reed while she is on this short visit. Have no fears, she will be safe, and returned to you unharmed.' His smile was full of amusement, his voice light, and Bella watched Miss Carpenter struggling to recover her self-control.

'Unharmed!' she muttered and shook her head.

But it was Robert who brought the difficult conversation to an easy end. 'I must leave you now, Miss Carpenter, Miss Reed.' He stood up, bowed to them both, smiled that charismatic smile that Bella had found so alarming when first they met, and then walked to the door, which he opened, waiting for her to precede him into the hallway. She stopped by the front door, and at once he took her arm, saying very urgently, 'Come into the garden. I have to talk to you.'

'I can't! She will wonder—'

'Let her. Old ladies like something to wonder at. It's good for their failing brains.' With his free hand he unlocked the door, gripped her arm more tightly and led her out onto the brick path. A gust of wind met them and, even as she stepped back and shivered, his arm went around her. 'You'll have to get used to gales and cold weather when you're home at Abworthy.' His words were quick and light, almost whispered, his body very close, his face full of laughter and Bella felt, yet again, his charm. Unable to stop herself smiling, at once she saw the dark eyes narrow and grow sharp. 'Look,' he said rapidly, 'we'll talk when you come on Friday. I have a lot to say to you, but, in the meantime....'

He paused, looking into her eyes, and she breathed, 'Yes?' because she felt his power, and longed to understand it. How extraordinary to stand out here on the path, feeling cold yet excited, and talking so intimately. For a second her mind flashed to Jack, and what he would say about this shocking conversation ... but Robert was pulling her even closer, his eyes holding hers, as he said, 'Don't think any more about selling the old house. Understand? You've got to keep it going.'

Her breath caught as she remembered Uncle William's raspy voice telling her, 'Family, maid, land and inheritance, see?' and then she let her tight shoulders relax, smiled up into those interrogating eyes, and said simply, 'I know. It's going to be my home. Of course I shan't sell it.' And then, because of the expression on his face, surprise, relief, maybe, added, 'Whatever made you think I might do so?'

He shook his head, a smile lifting his straight lips; his voice was almost casual. 'Gossip. You don't know yet how Dartmoor folk love to gossip.'

'I expect I shall learn.' When he stepped away, clamped his hat on his head and half bowed, she said, 'So I shall be going to Abworthy on Friday.'

'I'll meet you at the station. I'll tell Lizzie you're coming.' He looked at her for a long moment, then walked down to the gate, turned and said, 'Go in, Bella, make your excuses for this private conversation, and don't let the old girl bully you. Remember you've got granite blood in you. You're strong. Goodbye, then – until Friday.' He unlatched the gate, stepped out onto the pavement and then was gone, away from her.

Bella went back to the house, entering the drawing room, inside which, she guessed, trouble awaited her. But she was strong. And Miss Carpenter – and Jack – must learn this. Taking a deep breath, she opened the door and went into the room.

*

As he walked, Robert replayed their conversation and smiled as he recalled Bella Reed's expression, changing from suspicion to acceptance of his offered help. It had been sensible, finding her and planting seeds of what the future might hold. Selling Abworthy had simply been an idea, easily forgotten; now she planned to make the old house her home – when William had died. It could be any day, Lizzie had said, according to Sarah's tittle-tattle. Then it struck him that he must tell the foolish girl to leave, didn't want her mooning about his cottage and yard any more. If he intended to court Bella, he wanted no gossip about the girl being so often with him. Courting Bella – Robert smiled wryly, decided he could put up with her straight-laced values and thoughts because, once he had married her – master of Abworthy at last, he thought with satisfaction – she would be just an ordinary moorland wife, so busy with all the household and farmyard duties that fell to her – not to mention having children – there would be no question of her bothering him. But it dawned on him then, uneasily, that Bella had a prettiness all her own, and a charm, which forced one to look twice at her, even to listen to her voice, full of music and quiet attraction.

The train came into the station and as he looked at the passing fields and copses, an unwanted thought came to him, strong and undeniable. He was finding Bella Reed far more attractive than he had imagined he would. A farmhouse wife, was that all she would be? And before he disembarked at Bovey Tracey station, he was aware that his plan was shadowed with an unknown, new, unpleasantly grating feeling of guilt.

CHAPTER 13

He was waiting on the platform, handsome head turned to scan the passengers leaving the train. Bella saw him as she prepared to get out, feeling a mixture of emotions. Guilt was uppermost, for this thrill of excitement should surely be kept for Jack Reliable, Jack, who would do anything for her. Yet she was longing to hear Robert's voice, see the gleam in those dark eyes when he looked at her, instinctively warning her that private thoughts were being kept private. Thoughts, she knew, which were important and which she must somehow try and seek out.

But quickly common sense returned. She was here to see Uncle William, to try and comfort him, certainly not to waste time over Robert Verney. So she held on to her self-control and said politely, 'Good morning, Mr Verney,' as he helped her from the train, taking the valise from her hand.

'Good day to you, Miss Reed. The trap's outside. I'll have you home at Abworthy before you know it.' His smile was pleasant, the words reassuring, and she felt some of the tension in her body relax as they walked out of the station. Helping her into the trap, he climbed up beside her, and took the reins, saying, 'Walk on, Justice.'

And then, abruptly, with the landscape magically opening out as the trap journeyed on, she knew the world had changed: she was in a special place. *Dartmoor*.

Now she sat more comfortably on the hard seat, forgetting

lingering anxiety about what Miss Carpenter was thinking, what Robert might be planning and even how poor Uncle William was suffering, for all that mattered was where she was. Head held high, eyes seeing everything, she felt she was somewhere that had been waiting for her. Absurd? Of course – but it was a steadily growing instinct, and she felt happy with it, so happy that at first she didn't realize the cob was taking an unfamiliar road.

Only as a vast hill that had once been far distant came ever nearer did she turn in her seat and stare around. 'Where are we? I don't remember any of this. Where is Abworthy?'

'Not far.' His sideways glance was steady. 'We'll turn back in a minute, but I thought we'd come this way – you haven't seen much of the moor, have you?'

'No. But—'

'Forget your buts. Old man Reed can wait another half hour for you to get to his bedside.' His voice was low, and then rose slightly as he smiled at her. 'I had the impression that you were eager to know the moor better, so this is a chance for you to do so. Am I right?' Bella felt at a loss. Yes, he was right, but bringing her here without asking permission, not even suggesting she wanted to come, brought a quick feeling of irritation, and her reply was sharp. 'Of course I want to explore the moor, but not now. I should be at Abworthy. Turn around, please, Mr Verney, and take me back.'

She expected exasperation, even anger, but Robert just nodded and said, 'In a minute, when you've seen a little more.'

Despite the need to turn back her mind was guiltily dancing with expectation. She stared at the huge hill steadily raising itself out of the green valley before them, mottled brown and vast and mysterious. 'Is that a tor?'

'Hameldon,' he said shortly. 'You'll enjoy walking along the top where the view is wonderful. We'll go, on a clear day.' He looked at her. 'When you come again.'

She nodded, now accepting the last words, knowing it was inevitable that she would return – of course she would. But the moment took over. Hameldon. A name to remember. A place to explore. With Robert Verney.

He turned to her and his smile was warm. 'Aren't you glad I brought you here, Bella? Forgive me for not asking your permission. I'm a rough man, you see – no manners, some would say.'

She heard the familiar wry amusement in his voice and could only smile back, thinking that maybe he wasn't the rude, too-forthright man she had imagined; perhaps, after all, he was quieter, nicer, friendlier. 'I forgive you, Mr Verney.'

'Robert.'

Breathing deeply, she pushed aside all the old doubts and allowed impatient new ones to replace them. 'Robert. Thank you for bringing me here. I shall remember all this.'

'And now I'll take you home.'

She imagined she heard a note of something deeper than usual in his low voice but her doubts were swept aside by the word *home*. Yes, time to go home, to Abworthy.

They drove back in silence, and when the pony turned down the rough track, Bella looked at Robert, her smile radiant. 'It's good to be back.'

The words were quiet but had a ring to them and he looked at her keenly. 'And it's good to have you back. I'm sure all the Reed family will be glad to see you.' Halting the trap in the courtyard, he jumped down. 'Stay there, I'll take your valise in and tell Lizzie you're here, then I'll help you across the yard.' A light, easy smile and Bella nodded. Of course, he meant she mustn't dirty her shoes in the over-flowing midden. Sarah's second-best boots came into her mind, and with them the girl herself. Would she be here? Would she be friendlier than before, after receiving the shawl? Her smile faded, remembering that at Abworthy many problems awaited her; resolutely she forced herself to accept that she must confront them and somehow find resolutions.

Robert came to her side of the trap, opened his arms and said, 'I'll carry you in. Mustn't get your town clothes in a mess.'

She didn't know what she had expected, but the idea of being in his arms was embarrassing. And particularly when, as he carried her through the doorway and up the stone passage, Sarah, standing by the kitchen door, eyes wide, said shrilly, 'Carrying her in? Oh no! Not married, are you?'

Bella stiffened. 'Put me down, please.' Her voice was sharp, and she avoided Robert's chuckle. She struggled as, despite her order, he carried her into the kitchen, before lowering her to the floor. 'There you are, safe from the dirt – and don't take any notice of *her*.' He gestured towards Sarah, watching from the doorway, adding lightly, 'She's a great one for imagining things.' Looking back at Bella, standing in the middle of the room and obviously feeling the atmosphere catching at her emotions, he said quietly, 'I'll be on my way home, but I'll be around again later – in time to let you catch the late train back. A bit earlier, perhaps, I want to talk to you. Give my best wishes to your uncle.'

His eyes, dark blue and unblinking, stayed on her longer than she expected, but she said steadily, 'Thank you for collecting me, and I enjoyed our drive. Very much.'

A casual salute, boots crunching on the old stones and off he went, leaving Sarah staring, and Bella becoming more and more aware of the disturbing impact of being back here, in this ancient and well lived-in room. Slowly, her senses focused on things other than what had just happened; never mind Sarah and her vulgar curiosity, or Robert's disturbing presence. She looked around, seeing, smelling, sensing. The fire gleaming and the peat piled on the hearthstone; a cauldron of something bubbling slowly; woodsmoke, and then the smell of something dark and thick – yes, that little pan of something at the back of the fire; the one she had seen Mrs May brewing up, a remedy, she had said, for Uncle William's cough.

She moved across the room very slowly and came to a halt in front of the settle.

The empty settle.

And then, at once, the absence of Uncle William returned her thoughts back to the reason for her return. At the door leading upstairs, she called as she climbed up, 'Lizzie? Are you there? It's Bella.' At the top she was confronted by Lizzie, looking at her, unsmiling, an expression on her face, which brought Bella to a sudden stop.

'What's wrong? Uncle William? How is he?'

Lizzie shrugged, shook her head slowly, but said nothing. She stepped backwards, opened the bedchamber door and stood aside as Bella entered.

The old man lay in his large bed, a small, still figure beneath the coverlet. His eyes were closed, breathing shallow and irregular. Bella knelt by the bedside, emotions raging. 'Uncle ... Uncle William. It's Bella. I've come back – you said you would be waiting for me....'

The words died as he moved his head slowly, stiffly, on the pillow, and then opened his eyes, looking into hers. Blackberry-dark, narrow and pouched, but alight with some-thing that helped Bella smile warmly at him.

'Marianne,' he whispered. 'And you, the little one....' A spasm of coughing overtook him, the bed shook and the coverlet twisted.

Bella turned to Lizzie. 'What can we do?' she said helplessly but Lizzie only shook her head.

Bella watched her help him into a half-sitting position and then offer the cup holding Mrs May's herbal drink. When he had sipped a mouthful, together they lowered him back onto the pillows, neatened the bed cover and then stood at his side, silent. Lizzie stepped away, gesturing Bella to do the same. They left the room, slowly shutting the door and outside, Lizzie whispered, 'It's a matter of time. Doctor come out yesterday and said so. Nought he can do. So we just wait.' Her face was stiff, but then she managed a smile, taking Bella's hand in hers. 'Good of you to come, maid. He's been asking about you and now he knows you're here maybe he'll die easier.'

Bella saw tears in her cousin's eyes, and pressed her hand, her own emotions rising to the surface. 'You've been wonderful with him, Lizzie – all this time before I knew Uncle William, when I could have helped.'

Lizzie sighed, found a handkerchief and wiped her eyes. She smiled weakly. 'Never mind what's gone, maid, you're here now and that's what matters.' Her voice grew more cheerful. 'Now he'll sleep; that old brew Mrs May makes takes him off for an hour or so. We'll go down and you can tell us what you been doing back in Exeter. Sarah'll want to know, she's been that restless since you sent her the shawl.'

Down in the kitchen, the cauldron of stew on the range was quickly pushed aside and the kettle moved over the poked up flame. Bella took off her hat and coat and went to the dresser to find mugs. A new warmth was spreading through her, as if being back here was enough to renew her strength and hope. As the tea brewed, they sat together on the settle, waiting for the broth to warm through. 'Sent Sarah to buy bread in the village; now, where's she put it?' Lizzie searched the room. 'A scatterbrain, she is, and getting worse. I got to find a situation for her – but will she last anywhere? Hampton's up at Radley Manor want a kitchen maid – I hope as how she'll be taken on there.'

Bella thought. 'She was here just now. So where ...?' She looked at Lizzie, saw resigned impatience on her face.

'Gone back to Verney's farm, I don't doubt. She can't leave Robert alone, but it won't get her nowhere – not him to marry a silly chit like her. Got his mind on bigger things, they say.' Lizzie rose and poured milk into the two mugs on the table and Bella watched, a chill running through her thoughts. Sarah and Robert Verney? Ridiculous, but—

'Who says?' Her voice was sharp and Lizzie looked at her.

'Gossip, that's who. Now he's back home, what's he gonna do with his bit of land? Not enough to earn a living, they say. Not even with his new Scotch cattle.' Lizzie poured the tea. 'And there's trouble about the newtake boundary walls. Need building up they do and Joel James forever going on at him for letting his beasts stray into Abworthy land. More trouble.' But she smiled, pushing a mug towards Bella and sitting again at her side. 'And so I want to hear your news – tell us something happy for a change.'

It was hard, settling back into this slow routine of remote country life, but Bella smiled and allowed her thoughts to return to Exeter. She spoke cheerfully about Jack, her solicitor friend, who was such a reliable person, and who she was probably going to marry.

But even as she spoke, she became aware of the room listening. Listening and waiting. But for what?

CHAPTER 14

The time passed, conversation quiet and easy, until Sarah
came in. As Lizzie was poking up the fire to heat up the
broth, she stared at Bella. 'You going to marry him?'

Bella stared. 'Who?'

'Robert, of course. Him carrying you in and taking trouble
to fetch and carry you when you come here – well....' Sarah's
face was one big scowl and Bella realized that the only way
to treat such a ridiculous suspicion was with humour. She
laughed, rose and went to Sarah's side, putting a hand on her
shoulder and smiling into the defiant eyes.

'What an imagination, Sarah! Of course I'm not marrying
Robert – Mr Verney – or anyone, for the present.' Jack's face
flashed through her mind, was quickly pushed aside. 'I'm
here to see how Uncle William is, and to try to help you and
your mother with everything.' And then, because the question nagged, 'Why on earth do you think I would marry Mr
Verney?'

Sarah's scowl grew ferocious. ''Cos he talks 'bout you. Made
me write and thank you for the shawl. And now he's fetched
you from the station again.'

Sharply, Lizzie interrupted. 'That's enough, Sarah. Cousin
Bella doesn't want to hear all that nonsense. But I been telling
her about you getting a place at the Hamptons.' She turned
to Bella, expression clearly asking for support. 'Tell her, will

you, that it'll be good for her. Teach her to earn her living, and maybe make her a bit more polite.'

'I agree. I think you'll soon get used to the situation, Sarah, and learn so much.' Bella's additional thoughts – 'and teach you some manners'– remained unsaid.

'Huh!' Sarah glared, and then yanked off the shawl wrapped around her shoulders, and threw it at her. 'I don't want yer old shawl – I don't want no more to do with you. You're making Robert stop thinking about me, which is why I'm going to the Hamptons.' She swished around, then almost ran to the door, opened it, slammed it behind her and was gone.

Bella stood, the shawl in her hands. Slowly she folded it before looking at Lizzie, standing unhappily by the fireside. 'I'm so sorry,' she said, very low. 'I hoped I was pleasing her with this – and now she's gone – where? And I don't understand what she meant about Robert Verney.'

Lizzie turned to the range and stirred the broth. Her voice was slow and hesitant. 'Never you mind, Cousin Bella. The maid's always been difficult. But now, well, see, she's got her eye on Robert, doesn't matter what her pa and me say about it. But he's well-to-do and double her age – so what she thinks he sees in her we don't know. It's good she's going to the Hamptons. Get away from here. From him, from us.'

She put down the wooden spoon, reached in her pocket, found a handkerchief and wiped her face. With two quick steps across the room, Bella put an arm on her cousin's turned away shoulder.

'Seems as if it's all my fault, Lizzie. Coming here, upsetting things.'

'No, don't think like that. Just that life's a bit funny these days.' Lizzie sighed, returned to the cauldron and said, more steadily, 'Get a couple of bowls, maid, and we'll have our meal. I 'specs she'll come back when she's hungry. Don't let's worry any more.'

Clearly, Bella thought, there was to be no more talk about poor Sarah. But, even as she helped slice bread, then went upstairs to see if Uncle William still slept – and he did – she decided to go out during the afternoon and look around. Keep an eye open for Sarah, perhaps. Even try and talk to her – be friendly. And then perhaps visit Mrs May.

The idea was invigorating, and once the dishes were washed and put away, and Lizzie had settled down next to the fire to iron the latest bundle of washing, Bella changed into her heavy boots, pinned her hat more firmly to her hair, buttoned her coat and said, 'I'll be back in time to take tea to Uncle William, Lizzie, and see how he is before I leave.'

Lizzie, spitting on the flat iron to check its heat, smiled. 'When'll that be? Shall I ask Joel to harness the trap before you come back, maid?'

Colour rose in Bella's cheeks as she said hastily, 'No need – Mr Verney is taking me to the station.'

Lizzie paused, and Bella thought her expression was one of surprise, perhaps even disapproval. Then she said flatly, 'I see. Good of him,' and bent her head to the ironing.

Outside the afternoon was grey and cold. Walking across the yard, Bella looked up at the tor, wondering where to go first. Look for Sarah? Then she saw a wisp of smoke spiralling out of nearby Mrs May's chimney, and at once headed that way. Mrs May would be sure to welcome her, would perhaps tell her a little more about the old days. Warmth and friendliness, just what she needed, thought Bella with a quick flash of irritation, remembering Sarah's unpleasant words. Yes, Sarah must wait.

The old lady greeted her with no surprise, just the familiar broad smile and an invitation. 'Come on in, maid. I been thinking of you and now here you be. Get up, Jessie, and leave that chair by the fire.'

Bella took off her coat, stroked the cat, which arched its

back and purred, and sat in the creaking chair. 'I'm only here for a few hours, Mrs May,' she said. 'It's difficult to leave Miss Carpenter, you see – but I had to come.' Her smile faded, remembering the way she had been somehow forced to think of Mrs May and what she was trying to say. Seeing the old woman smile, she added, 'I kept imagining you were trying to tell me something....'

Mrs May nodded, but said nothing. She reached out to the table at her side where the lamp stood, along with little pots of what looked like dead berries, dying leaves and some old bits of honeycomb, looking at Bella as she found and then started shuffling a pack of cards between her gnarled fingers.

'Take a card, maid. Any one. Don't look at it, give it here. That's right. Now, let's see what we got today.'

Eyes widening, Bella watched a few grubby cards being laid on the table standing between them. She felt excited, although self-control told her to banish the feeling; was this part of Mrs May's so-called witchcraft? Sarah's voice echoed. But whatever it was, she wanted to find out what would come from it.

'There you are, maid, queen of hearts right at the top, where you belong.' The old woman's voice was quiet and Bella felt a strong impulse to listen and learn. She looked at the queen's ornate headdress and smiling face. How could that be her?

Mrs May dealt more cards. 'And there he is, the black knave. Ah, but he's moved up a bit since last time. Getting nearer, maid.' She went on dealing cards. 'As for this one – well, he's still there, this old diamond jack, all bright and full of schemes and likely to make trouble soon. But you'll get the better of him, in the end you will.'

Bella searched for understanding. So she was the queen of hearts? Yes, she supposed she could accept that, outlandish as it seemed, but Mrs May's power had somehow opened a shutter in her conventionally closed mind, and it came to her that Robert, so dark, was the black knave. And – a shiver ran through her – of course she knew who the diamond jack was. Jack Courtney, smart, and full of schemes. She took a deep breath, looked at Mrs May and was at once caught by the gleam of light in those old, faded eyes, so narrowed beneath the wrinkled skin and yet so friendly. And wise? Held in this extraordinary atmosphere of what she now accepted must be the old woman's gift of second sight, at once she knew what to ask: 'And what do all these cards mean, Mrs May?'

'That you gotta live your life as they fall. It's fate, see.'

Bella sat very still, thinking about all that had happened since Lizzie's letter arrived, asking her to visit Uncle William. And then Uncle William's old, creaking voice sounded in her ears, *Family, land, inheritance. That's what matters. So you're to be my heir, maid. Abworthy'll come to you.*

For a moment the cottage sank into silence. Bella closed her eyes, waiting for the excitement behind them to settle. At last her mind was clearer, and she said, 'Mrs May, I can't agree with what you say – that the cards tell me how my life has to be lived. But then—' She stopped, remembering the story of how the Abworthy lands were half lost. 'So when Uncle William's father almost lost his estate and then recovered it on the turn of one card – for that's what I've heard – was that what had to happen? The card that upset everything in his life? Did he deserve to nearly lose, and then get it back?'

'Can't tell you that, maid. Didn't know the old man. But gossip says he was a hard drinker and neglected his farm, letting the gambling take his life over. Needed a lesson, maybe.'

She was silent for a moment, eyes searching Bella's face, her hands folded in her lap. Then she nodded, finding each word with care as she said slowly, 'But it wasn't just the Reeds who gambled; the Verney family did, too, in the end losing half their lands, see. Which is why the black knave, that Verney, is there in the cards. Close to you, and wanting to get you to give back something.'

Bella caught her breath. 'Give back – you mean land?' Her heart hammered. She had felt something powerful about Robert and had not understood, right from the first meeting. What could it all mean?

Mrs May nodded. 'Perhaps. But something more, something else from you. I dunno, maid, we just have to wait for it all to work out. And then, that diamond jack, he wants something from you, too. He's smart, he's trying hard.' She frowned, faded eyes almost disappearing between the wrinkles. 'Take care when you gets back to Exeter, maid.'

'Yes.' Bella tried to calm her fast breathing. She told herself, not finding any comfort in the thought, that this was all nonsense. Just a lot of old wives' tales. Certainly, Mrs May was an old wife. She managed a slight smile. But not a witch. Somehow, she knew that. She got up from the chair, smiled more happily at the old eyes watching her, and said, 'I'll think about all you say, Mrs May. And now I must go. I want to see Uncle William again before I leave. And already it's getting dark.' She did up her coat, made sure her hat was safely pinned, and walked to the door, instinctively turning before she slipped the latch.

'Did you bring me back to Abworthy? Was that what you were saying all the time when I thought I heard you?' It was a weird idea, yet she knew it must be the truth. For now she was sure that Mrs May was the wise woman Lizzie had described. Someone who knew more than ordinary folk, and who was willing to help if she could.

She saw amusement on Mrs May's face as she nodded, and then said, 'Yes, I called you. And you'll be back again soon, maid. I'm sure of it.'

'But—' Bella held open the door and paused, thoughts rushing through her mind.

'Yes, of course there's buts. But life must be lived as the cards fall. So don't be surprised by anything ... and I'll be here, all the time, thinking of you.'

'Thank you.' Instinctively Bella turned, went back to the old woman and kissed her on the cheek. 'Thank you,' she said again. A strange visit, but her steps as she left the cottage, closing the door and the homely warmth behind her, were firm and strong.

She walked rapidly down the track and back to Abworthy. She must see Uncle William before Robert came to fetch her. Robert, who wanted something from her....

Behind all these racing thoughts, Mrs May's words haunted her as she walked back along the track. *Life must be lived as the cards fall.* And slowly, seemingly with each step, she found herself rebelling against them. What nonsense! Life was to be lived as one ordered it.

And then, reaching the farm, and standing in the dung-heaped yard by the big black door, she heard again the memory of Sarah asking sourly, 'Going to marry him?' and discovered that, no matter what these new, strong and defiant thoughts said, she felt that all that Mrs May had told her was making sense in a fateful and rather frightening sort of way.

CHAPTER 15

Going back into the house a chill ran through her. A new stillness about the old room; a haunting emptiness, with no Lizzie busily working; the fire needing making up; there was no kettle cheerfully humming and bringing thoughts of shared mugs of tea around the long table. Throwing off her coat and hat, Bella went silently up the dark stairs and for a few seconds stood, indecisive, outside Uncle William's bed-chamber. No sound came from inside, not even his snuffly old wheezes. Sucking in a strengthening breath, she made herself open the door.

In the room Lizzie was standing by the window, hands to her mouth. Bella, with enormous relief, saw that the old man still breathed, unevenly but steadily. Very quietly she went up to Lizzie and put an arm around her shoulders.

'Shh!' she whispered. 'Don't let's wake him. Come downstairs, Lizzie – I'll make some tea. No, don't say anything, just come down.'

Lizzie's tear-stained face twisted and she stifled a sob, but then her dull eyes took on a brighter light and she nodded her head. 'Yes, all right, I'll come down.'

They sat on the settle by the reviving fire and drank mugs of strong tea, not speaking for a while. Bella waited for Lizzie to say something, but knew she must let her cousin regain her self-control. Meanwhile she was grateful to be still, to be here in this ancient room, which she sensed held so many secrets, perhaps even secrets affecting her. But for now it was enough to feel the promise of new strength flowing through her body. Was it possible, she wondered, if this was the result of listening to Mrs May's words? *Life must be lived as the cards fall.*

Difficult, thought Bella, but the dark thoughts cleared slightly as she saw Lizzie draining her mug, putting it back on the table, then turning to smile at her. 'You must think I'm a silly ole woman,' she said, half laughing. 'Don't usually let me feelings get so much on top of me, but today, what with Sarah playing up, and then the doctor saying yesterday that all we can do for Uncle is to ease his passing best we can, seemed like everything was going wrong.' Her voice broke, but a vestige of her cheery smile remained and she wiped her face with a steady hand. 'I got much to be thankful for. Even Dan getting up today and going to work ... seems Robert Verney offered him a few days' work building up his old walls.' She grinned then, adding wryly, 'And Joel James'll be that pleased if those boundary walls get mended, 'cos the Verney cattle keep rampaging through into our lands and that makes him real angry.'

Bella nodded, the words hanging in the air. She knew about the old conflict between Verney and Abworthy people. One more problem which, if she ever came here to live, she would have to deal with. Thinking this, she understood exactly how Lizzie must be feeling. She smiled back at her cousin, took her hand and pressed it, trying to think of something cheerful to say. Then it came to her. 'So tell me about Sarah's new position – when will she start?'

'On Friday, so Mrs Hampton said when I saw her last week.' Lizzie's smile returned. 'We'll be taking her there, Dan an' me.'

'That's good.' A sudden thought struck Bella, looking at the shawl, lying in a heap on the stool by the table. Her eyes met Lizzie's. 'Let's leave it there, shall we? Until Sarah herself comes back for it.' Perhaps the girl would eventually become more friendly. She hoped so.

Lizzie didn't answer, but nodded, poked up the fire and returned to the unfinished ironing.

As the afternoon darkened, Bella knew she must get ready to leave. Robert would soon be here to collect her. She washed the tea mugs and went upstairs for a last look in on Uncle William. Still he slept, and she was grateful for Mrs May's herbal mixture. She put a hand on the old man's forehead and found herself asking for a blessing – clearly there was no hope that he would last much longer, but she wished that his passing might be gentle and without more suffering. She bent, kissed his brow, a lump of overflowing emotion tightening her chest. Suppose she never saw him again? And suppose she decided to forget his notion of leaving the farm to her? No more thoughts of Uncle William, or this ancient stone house and its surrounding lands. Painfully, she accepted that this would leave a great emptiness in her life. Tears pricked behind her eyelids and she had to use all her resolve to push aside the racing thoughts. One last look at the old man, then she closed the door behind her and went downstairs to get ready for the drive to Bovey Station.

In the kitchen, warm and buttoning up her coat, smiling at Lizzie, Bella's thoughts began moving in a different direction. Mrs May's warning about the 'black knave' had her wondering what she would say to Robert when he arrived. She remembered him saying, 'I have to talk to you.' What about? A vague apprehension crept through her.

He arrived early, giving her no time for a last look around the yard, to notice whether Joel James was there or not. The trap turned around, wheels spluttering up mud and dirt as it did so, and he jumped down, came to her side, smiling. 'You're in good time. Looking forward to seeing me, I suppose.' The twinkle in his eyes took the cheekiness out of the words, and she couldn't help returning the smile as he helped her into the trap.

He said no more until they were out of the yard, rattling along, leaving Abworthy behind and then more smoothly moving down the road, heading for Bovey. And then, 'Bella, I need to talk to you. We'll have a cup of something at the tea rooms by the station. There's time before your train comes.'

She saw the determined jaw and angle of the turned away head, and felt something more than surprise, or even acceptance. It would be good to talk to him. Probably about something to do with Uncle William and her possible return to the farm, she guessed, but she found a tiny inner hope growing that it might also be more personal. And yet how could it be? They were almost strangers, and strangers kept their thoughts and wishes to themselves. But, even thinking this, she knew she was hoping for something more.

The tea rooms were almost empty, and they sat at a table away from the window, close to a paraffin stove that warmed even as it gave off slight fumes. Bella poured tea into the two cups, declined a piece of cream sponge cake, but watched how Robert devoured his slice in three mouthfuls, clearly enjoying it, and the thought struck her that he was a sensuous man, someone who knew desire and sought pleasure. But such unconventional thinking was foreign to her sheltered lifestyle, and although her cheeks grew warm, she kept her eyes away from him. Finally, he pushed his empty cup toward the teapot for a refill, and said, 'Bella, when are you coming to live at Abworthy?'

Her heart started to race. She said sharply, 'That's my business, and nothing to do with you.' Still she didn't meet his intent gaze.

'That's as maybe, but I'd like it to be my business.'

She looked up, meeting the fierce dark-blue stare. 'But ... why on earth would you want it to be your business if I come or not?' The refilled tea cup wobbled as she pushed it towards him, slopping onto the table, and she felt her control wobbling with it.

He took the napkin beside his plate and mopped up the spilled tea. 'Because William Reed is relying on you to keep the old place going.'

She searched for suitable words, and found them. Then hesitantly, 'But – Abworthy is – is no concern of yours. Why should you worry about its future?'

Robert spooned sugar into his cup and stirred it slowly, holding her gaze. 'It's not just Abworthy I'm thinking of, Bella – it's you, too.'

She caught her breath. 'And why should you be thinking of me?'

'Because I like you. No, admire would be the better word. For what you're trying to do for that dying old man. The time you've spent with him, despite the disapproval of your esteemed employer in Exeter. You see –' he drank his tea, folded the napkin and leaned across the table to look more closely into her wide, surprised eyes, '– you see, if you were at Abworthy from now on, we might become friends. Good friends. What would you think about that, Bella?'

She was silenced by the mounting thrill of her thoughts. And then, huskily, 'Robert, I thank you for saying that, but I don't think ... you see, my home is in Exeter.'

He sat back in his chair, his force making the legs grate on the floor. 'With that foolish old woman and your so-called reliable and charming solicitor friend.' She heard scorn in the words, but when next he spoke, the low voice was warmer, more persuasive. 'Now look, what advice did they give you? Anything really helpful? Only that the situation must be legalized. No warmth or understanding of your problem there. So why should you bother with them?' His voice dropped and she saw the dark eyes dilate. 'Come to Abworthy, Bella. You'll have Lizzie Wharton there, perhaps Sarah, once she's learned a few lessons, and even though Joel James and I are daggers drawn about the damned newtake walls, he's a good worker, faithful to Abworthy, and he'll help you with the farm.' Leaning forward, he slid his hand across the table, palm upwards, as if asking her for a reward. Amusement crept into the quietly resonant voice. 'And you'll have me, as your friend. Your advisor, if need be. There's so much I could do to help you.'

She stared at the upturned hand, understood its strength, recalled his kiss on her own palm and knew a terrible desire to touch him. But in her dull life women were always passive; all she could say weakly, and with a tremor in her voice, was, 'I don't know. I don't know....'

Robert's face grew taut. His hand dropping from the table, he stared at her with what she thought was an impatient flicker of a frown, and then surprised her even further by allowing himself to smile again, as he said casually, and in a lighter tone, 'I bought a nice little mare at Moreton last week. Well mannered, she is, just right for a lady rider. Bella, I could teach you to ride. I've got my mother's saddle somewhere – we could ride out over the moor. Remember I said I'd take you over Hameldon? And so many other places.' His smile was persuasive. 'I know the moor has already got a hold on you – well, doesn't that idea make you want to come back?'

Of course it did. Her mind immediately threw up pictures of her enjoyment in the few days she had been at Abworthy. The view from the tor; the green valley with its scattered farms. And with Robert to teach her to ride, to inform her, to tell her about the moor.... She stared at him, recalling what he'd said about the new mare and words came without thinking. 'Did you buy it 'specially for me?'

One eyebrow, dark and well shaped, lifted. 'Of course. What would I want with a tame little mare? My rough cob, Justice, is more my mount.' He sat back in his chair, looking across at her and she thought she had never really seen him before. But now the near blackness of his thick hair with its untidy curls almost hiding his ears, the deep blue of those intent eyes, and perhaps something quite new to her – the set of his straight mouth with its full lower lip – forced another impression on her whirling her mind. One that pleased her and which she knew she would keep a secret, even if she never came back to Abworthy, as he was trying so hard to persuade her.

But she sighed, let the extraordinary thoughts fade, found her watch, and said dully, 'The train will here in a minute. I must go.' He stood up, paid the bill, escorted her back to the trap and then to the station. They said nothing as she showed her ticket and then walked onto the platform, knowing he was a step behind her. Only as she stopped, half turned to look at him, did she realize just what she was leaving – a friend who had said he would help her when she moved back to the old farm – and wondered anew at the strength that idea gave her. Mrs May's words came back, something about the black knave becoming closer. It seemed exactly so; Robert wanting her at Abworthy; Robert taking her around the moor; Robert looking at her now, with his penetrating sultry eyes, and suddenly his hand on her shoulder.

'Bella, think about it. Don't let the Exeter lot influence you. You have a right to be here, you know you have. Remember that old William will die happy if he knows you're ready to take over his estate. And think what Lizzie will do if you don't come – who will help her to sort out everything when he dies? Imagine the state the house will get into with no one in charge.' He nodded and his hand slipped down to her waist, drawing her closer. He looked deep into her eyes, and said, very quietly, so that his words hummed in her ears and she knew she would always remember this moment. 'Think, Bella, and remember the moor is calling you.'

They looked at each other for a moment and then he bent his head, kissed her forehead, a brotherly kiss, she thought, disappointed, closing her eyes as he said, 'Remember, you'll have me to help you. I'll always be here. Dartmoor is waiting, Bella – and so am I.'

The train drew in, steam filling the station, and suddenly all she could see was Robert, walking away from her, quickly disappearing from view; here one moment and then gone. But he had said he would always be here. Such indecision. What was she to think about Robert, a man who had said that he, like Abworthy, was waiting? Could she believe him? She knew that she desperately wanted to do so.

Sitting in the train, Bella's thoughts stayed with Dartmoor. Was it true that Abworthy was to be left to her? The persuasive dreams returned: learning to ride on the well-mannered mare that Robert had bought, just for her; going on explorations into the ever-changing vistas of the landscape; the challenging wind on her face, playing with her hair; Robert beside her on his rough cob and the moor unfolding its wondrous beauty and haunting solitude as if rewarding her for finally accepting her inheritance.

But then, alighting at Exeter station with a smile on her face, waiting outside on the crowded pavement for a horse omnibus to complete her journey back to St Leonard's Road, she felt her face tense into a despondent frown as all those joyous, exciting pictures started to fade away. She was lonely, filled with a longing she had never known before.

And then, suddenly, with all her mind, all her heart, she decided to leave these grimy streets, filled with hurrying, unthinking humanity. And, stepping onto the omnibus, roughly pushed by the people behind her, an epiphany of surprise and gratitude filled her.

The decision was made. Of course she would be going to live at Abworthy.

CHAPTER 16

Robert drove very fast back to the moor, his mind full of thoughts of Bella. Suddenly uncomfortable, he took another look at himself; pursuing Bella and presenting himself as a suitor when he had no love for her. Abruptly, he saw how cruelly hypocritical this was. Until now he had always prided himself on his integrity, accepting the sort of man he was; someone who never thought much about anything save working hard to achieve a good living, while at the same time living amicably with the rest of the world, even doing what he could to help when required. But now....

Now Bella was a constant image in his head; he couldn't make her disappear. Her shining hair; the soft lips he had kissed as an additional persuasion to accept her Abworthy inheritance. Her firm body drawn close to his; her sweet breath, those wide, inquiring eyes and especially that melancholy expression, which too often marred the beauty of her face. Why wouldn't these images go away? He had no wish for them to persist; they emphasized the cruel intent of his plan and he wished they would leave him in peace.

Grimly he recalled that his plan had been to achieve a marriage that would bring him the land and ancient house he believed to be his by right, but which would offer her only a hard, physical and unfulfilling personal relationship. These thoughts circled and he felt a resulting anger spread through him. Anger at the way life so often turned in unwanted directions. Anger because the plan was proving unworkable. And what was the reason for that?

Turning into the track leading to his cottage within the Abworthy hamlet, Robert slowed down the cob and sought to understand. He had enjoyed feeling Bella's body, kissing those innocent lips, and watching pleasure fill her face. He'd had other women, of course he had; life on the other side of the world had been hard working and even harder playing. But Bella Reed ... he'd never met anyone like her before. So what was happening to him?

Rubbing the cob down in the stable before pulling hay from the tallat above, he was forced into one conclusion, one that he had no wish to accept. It dawned on him that he was starting to love her and he was damned if he was going to let it go any further. He must alter his plan; thoughts drove ahead of him and then settled in an unhappy confusion. What should he do next? But, just as he prepared to go into the cottage and think things out, he heard a shout. 'Verney,' and turned to see Joel James coming into the yard. He frowned. Something he didn't need at this moment; another problem.

Standing in the open doorway, he stared at the man approaching him.

Joel James was red-faced and slightly stooped. His hat sloped forward over narrowed eyes and his mouth was a threatening straight line. 'So what you doing 'bout they old broken-down walls, Verney? Said as you'd get them built up last week, but nothing's happened.' A footstep short of Robert, he glared at him. 'If I finds your beasts on our land again, I'll do something about it. There's rules, as you well know, and you can't just break them.'

Robert met the glare with his own taut stare, but didn't move. 'My cattle are on my land, James.' His voice remained low and steady. 'No rules broken. And I've told you the walls are being worked on, so don't waste my time coming around here and threatening me.'

It was good to release his anger. Pleasure rose in him, hot and satisfying at the expression of frustration on Joel James's florid face. Then he turned and went into the cottage, slamming the door and grinning to himself as he imagined what words were being thrown at him outside.

But the problem wasn't resolved. Had that idle Dan Wharton done any work at all? He was there this morning, even though he had complained about his stomach hurting. Was he still saying how ill he felt and breaking off before the day ended? Robert, making up his fire, determined to go and see the man first thing tomorrow. In the meantime, he had to decide what to do about Bella Reed. He slumped into the chair by the fire, stared at the mounting flames and tried to think about his future.

Bella sat in the comfortable drawing room in Exeter, embroidery on her lap, while the two elderly ladies, Hetty French and her younger sister, Elsie Carpenter, chatted on, slowly – boringly, thought Bella, impatiently – about trivialities that she no longer wished to hear. Eventually, Mrs French stopped bemoaning the behaviour of servants, and looked across the room at her.

'No, Bella, I'm not including you when I speak of insolence and lack of service.' Mrs French's smile was tight, her flesh-enclosed eyes penetrating. 'But I understand that even you have been rather demanding lately. Your absence, for instance, when you went off to Dartmoor for the day.' Her voice rose, clucking disapprovingly, as she added, 'But I understand that Mr Courtney will soon be able to put the extraordinary matter, which you insisted necessitated your visit to Dartmoor, completely at rest. Isn't that so, Elsie?'

'Yes, sister. And I think Bella must now accept that a very

unpleasant joke was being played on her, for Mr Courtney told me that his inquiries, plus information gathered from the copy of your birth certificate, Bella, entirely preclude any sort of inheritance whatsoever.'

Bella's breath caught and she leaned forward urgently. 'He told you this?' Disbelief raised her voice. 'He has obtained my birth certificate? Made inquiries? Where? And—' She stopped, shock and disappointment filling her with dismay. It couldn't be true. Just when she had finally decided to take up her birthright and move to Abworthy; when she was lying awake at night, trying to plan how she would break the news to her employer. And now Jack was going to tell her it was all a mistake. No truth in Uncle William's words. Indeed, who was Uncle William? No family after all, no inheritance? Just a terrible, wicked joke?

Colour drained from her cheeks and she fought to quieten her rapid breathing. 'Miss Carpenter, when did Jack tell you this? Why hasn't he told me himself?' Her voice was high, the words jerky. She stood up, muddled. Should she storm out of the room, shouting at these two silly women that they didn't understand, that Jack might be hiding the truth? And then – yes, she must go straight away and find Jack to learn for herself what it was he had discovered and was so dilatory in telling her. For the first time she wondered if, after all, Jack was the truthful, reliable man she had initially and happily thought him. She would go and talk to him – at once.

Rapidly, she said, 'Forgive me, but I have to go and see him, find out,' and left the room, hardly hearing the raised voices of astonishment following her.

'Mr Courtney is engaged,' said the receptionist at Langland, Morley and Courtney Solicitors, in the High Street. 'You can take a seat, if you wish to wait.'

'I can't wait.' Bella walked rapidly past the reception desk, pounded on the closed door ahead of her and then pushed it open. Inside the room was a large desk with a leather top, a big chair seating Jack who looked up at her with amazement, and a frail woman sitting opposite him, who opened her mouth and left it open.

'I have to talk to you, Jack.' Bella stood by the desk, then glanced at the woman staring up at her. 'I'm sorry to interrupt, but this is extremely important. Perhaps Mr Courtney could make another appointment with you?'

The woman nodded, wide-eyed, and fumbled her way out of the room. Now Jack was on his feet, standing beside her, eyes surprised and angry. 'What on earth are you doing, Bella? Didn't the girl tell you I was engaged?'

'Yes,' she said crisply. 'But I must talk to you. Please tell me what you have discovered about Abworthy – the inquiries you've made ... and about the copy of my birth certificate.'

Jack frowned, took a big breath, and then said slowly, 'I was coming to see you this evening. So Miss Carpenter has told you that I have news dismissing the ridiculous notion you had of inheriting that Dartmoor estate?'

'Yes, but why did you tell her before telling me?' Questions bubbled up. 'Jack, what did my birth certificate say about my parents?'

He smiled at her then, his expression becoming soothing. 'Calm down, my dear. You're over excited. Sit down, and I'll tell you all that I have discovered.'

Disconcerted, Bella sank into the vacant chair and watched him return to his own, with the desk between them. His smile broadened. 'Well, if you must know, Bella, I was deliberately waiting until you had settled down again after your last journey to the moor. Your birth certificate shows your parents were legally married, both names registered and witnessed – Marianne and Edmund, as you told me some time ago. So all is well there.'

But everything was far from well; her voice snapped out,

sharp and curt, 'Please let me see it.' She stared at him. 'I have to see for myself. Where is it? Please get it.' She held out her gloved right hand and tensed the waiting fingers. 'Jack, I must see it.'

She thought his eyes narrowed, grew darker. He fidgeted in his chair before getting to his feet again, then stood by the desk, frowning down at her. 'My dear Bella, please remember I am not just your friend, but also your solicitor – you must have faith in me. You sound as if you don't believe a word I am saying.'

She ignored that. 'And these inquiries you talked about? What inquiries? Where and about whom?'

He shrugged impatiently. 'I raised the matter of William Reed with our branch in Bovey Tracey and they had nothing, save dusty records that there is an old farmer they once had dealings with, oh, a couple of decades ago. You say this old man is near death, and yes, he is named Reed, but it's just coincidental that his name is the same as yours. No doubt the writer of the letter found your address in the current Exeter Directory.' He paused, his smile grew gentler. 'So I fear you must understand that the whole business is a fraud – probably a stupid endeavour to make money in some criminal way.'

She stared, her back straining with tension. William Reed, an old Dartmoor farmer about to die, so let's just forget him, let him go? Her mind raced. The name, a mere coincidence used by a crafty member of that particular Reed family – dear Lizzie, of course – to contact her and try to involve her in some terrible, wicked way?

She couldn't believe it. But Jack sounded so sure of himself; he had the law behind him, and she had nothing save an intuition that everything he said was wrong. She sat, stunned and muddled, staring at him, hardly seeing how his smile grew into the one she thought she knew so well. The loving, promising smile. Now he was putting his hand on her shoulder, saying quietly and reassuringly, 'I'll tell the girl to call a cab and you must go home, my dear. And I shall call this evening, by which time I'm sure you'll feel much calmer. And perhaps we can then discuss the idea I have of going to inspect the new building site down by the river. A little outing at the weekend, to give you some pleasure, Bella.'

But her mind was full of other voices, more positive thoughts, and then, like the remembered flash of sunlight on the high tor behind the old stone house, she heard Robert, saying with a wry note in his voice, *Bella, you have granite in your blood.*

So she smiled. Saw Jack standing beside her, his eyes expectant, but in her mind the whole business of Abworthy and her family was clamouring for her belief and trust. Uncle William was her uncle and she was to become his heir to Abworthy when he died. Of course Jack was playing a game with her; she understood now that he had no intention of letting her go and live in the depths of Dartmoor when he had a new house and a suitable marriage in view. But Jack must learn.

She rose, heard a new strength in her voice. 'Thank you for what you've told me. I know you think that all this is hearsay, and you might be right, Jack, but I believe quite the opposite. I won't fight you about it, but please understand that I intend to carry on seeing my relations at Abworthy.'

Their eyes met with a clash of wills. But she had never felt stronger. Rising, she said, 'I'm sorry I disrupted your routine, Jack. And, for now, goodbye.'

He had no time to open the door; she was outside, ignoring the furious stare of the receptionist and stepping out into the busy High Street, full of people, whom she hardly saw. For in her head was the memory of Abworthy, grey and old, and that glorious sun-touched tor rising above it. Abworthy, which, despite all Jack had said, she knew instinctively and beyond all doubt, was her rightful inheritance.

She walked to the Public Records Office at the top of the town, requested a sight of her birth certificate and, after a short wait, was shown the document. She looked at the names: Edmund Reed, Marianne Porter, Mother and Father. Address a house in Holloway Street. The date, August 23, 1871.

Sitting in the quiet room, she read and reread the paper until it was memorized. Then, returning it to the reception office, she left the building, walking slowly home to St Leonard's Road, her mind running wild with arguing thoughts. Of course, Jack was right; there was no evidence in her birth certificate that she had any connection with the Reeds living at Abworthy. It could be just a strange coincidence.

And yet. Deep down, hidden away, but fermenting like a fire searching for an escape route, she knew that she belonged to Abworthy. And she knew, too, that this longing to return to the old stone house, set in the mysterious and beautiful land that had taken such a grip on her heart, would never leave her. She reached the house with awareness of what Robert had said – Dartmoor granite was making her strong. And somehow, things would resolve themselves.

CHAPTER 17

By the time she reached home, her mind was made up. She was going to back to Abworthy.

Mrs French and Miss Carpenter looked down at their handiwork when she entered the drawing room and neither spoke, so Bella had to break the silence. It was challenging to try and find the words describing her argument with Jack Courtney, and even worse to tell them what she intended to do in the very near future.

Standing in the centre of the room, she cleared her throat, saw faded eyes suddenly flicker up at her, before turning down again to the work spread out on their laps. 'I am afraid I must tell you something that will upset you, Miss Carpenter. I apologize, but ...' she paused, realizing that only the truth would do. 'I have seen Jack Courtney who says he is convinced that my inheritance of Abworthy is fraudulent; I don't share his view and so....' She took a deep breath, bracing herself for what she knew must be unwelcome reactions.

'And so, Miss Carpenter, I fear I must offer you my resignation as I shall be moving to Abworthy quite soon.' A silence chilled the room, while two pairs of eyes stared at her. She added the final words. 'I shall be going there for good. It will be my new home,' and then waited unhappily for the response.

Miss Carpenter laid down her knitting, removed her spectacles and looked up at her. 'I am shocked, Bella, at your decision. After all Mr Courtney has done to free you from this unhappy affair, surely the least you can do is to thank him, forget it and then settle down once more here?' A moment's silence, and then the old voice wobbled slightly. 'And I have to say that you have disappointed me. After all your happy years here with me....' Miss Carpenter fumbled for a handkerchief and stared down at the carpet.

Guilt and dismay filled Bella, but even so, a hard core of determination forced her to say, 'I'm sorry, Miss Carpenter. But my family needs me. And in particular my old uncle, who is extremely ill.' She saw Mrs French straighten stooped shoulders and glance at her sister, before saying coldly, 'Well, Miss Reed, it's just as well that I have been trying to persuade my dear sister to move away from this damp old town and move somewhere brighter and healthier.' She nodded at Miss Carpenter, who sniffed but wiped her nose and then Bella saw a faint smile reappearing on the old face. She waited.

Mrs French continued, 'I am thinking of moving to Bournemouth – a nicer place than Exeter, with sea breezes and quite a busy social life. My sister is half inclined to accompany me and so, perhaps, now ... ' she turned and smiled very firmly at Miss Carpenter, who managed a small smile, and a half-determined nod.

'I see.' Bella's mind ran in circles. She was going to Abworthy, Miss Carpenter and her strong-willed sister were moving elsewhere, so if, by some unexpected chance she was unhappy at Abworthy and had to leave, there would be no more dull but safe home in St Leonard's Road to return to. Anxiety momentarily filled her.

But Mrs French's smug smile forced Bella to understand that she needed to let this autocratic woman understand that she had a new life of her own waiting for her. Then she smiled and found it easier than she had feared. 'I hope you will both be very happy in Bournemouth,' she said. 'I believe it's pleasant there. When will you be moving?'

'We shall be making plans quite soon,' Mrs French said shortly, and then looked down, stabbing at her embroidery with her needle.

Bella went to her usual chair, sat down and looked around the warm, comfortable room, contrasting it in her mind with the cold, shadowy kitchen at Abworthy. And suddenly, just sitting there, watching the two elderly ladies glancing at each other, exchanging looks before continuing with the knitting and the embroidery, she felt a different being.

She was a young woman about to start a new life. Someone with dreams of the mysterious, seductive moor; with plans of spending time with Uncle William in his last days; perhaps renovating the ancient house and making it more livable; and then, with his wry smile and dark blue eyes, came Robert. Smiling at her. Almost welcoming her, she thought, and she returned his smile without knowing she did so.

Joel James left his cottage, coat half on, striding through the yard, mouth tight and hard, huge red hands yanking his hat onto his balding head, while Lizzie Wharton stood in the doorway with Mrs James, watching him heading in the direction of the grazing grounds beyond the cottage. They stood there for a moment before turning back into the open doorway.

'Surely Verney's doing something about they old walls?' asked Lizzie. 'He got Dan up there, working on them ... but you saw the bullocks running wild, did you?'

Mrs James shut the door and went to the fireplace where a kettle steamed. 'Yesterday afternoon – and then they went back. But Joel, he gets angry; he don't have time for Verney. And they Scotch cattle got minds of their own, with those fearsome horns. Gotta watch out when they're running.'

She poured boiling water into a brown teapot. 'Stay for a cup, Lizzie?' She pushed a mug across the table. Lizzie looked at it, and half decided to sit down, but then shook her head. 'No, must get back to the old man. Worse this morning – that cough, and he so pale and thin. Well, the doctor did say—' She bit off the words, but met understanding eyes, and then walked to the door. 'I just hope he won't go when I'm not there. Poor old man.' They nodded at one another and then Lizzie went into the yard, hurrying back to Abworthy where the door stood half open. She went in, closed it and hurried upstairs to Uncle William's bedchamber. There she stopped, frowned, listened to his breathing and moved to the bedside.

He opened dark eyes and stared at her. Lizzie bent over, listening to the thin voice, and felt her sorrow grow. Surely he couldn't last much longer?

Robert Verney stared at Joel James marching into the yard of his cottage. 'All right,' he growled, 'I know what you're on about – well, I'm repairing the newtake walls. But it takes a while. And my cattle are grazing on *my* lands – you don't have cause to complain about them.'

Joel James scowled. 'They were through that wall yesterday – you think you've got all the rights in the world, Verney, well, you ain't. You think you can make us all do as you want. But I tell you you got to build those broken-down old walls real high to stop your beasts rampaging through into our grazing. I know Mr Reed be ill but I got the authority to stop you on his behalf.' He took a step nearer. 'I told you once, and yesterday they were doing it again. It's gotta stop, Verney, see?' His voice dropped to a snarl. 'Or else....'

Robert clenched his fist, lifted his arm, but let it fall it again. He wanted no violence. James was a rough man but he had right on his side. Those damned bullocks were all over the place. He must help Dan Wharton with the stones; get the man doing some proper work for once in his life.

Grudgingly, he nodded. 'All right, James. I'll see to it.' He managed half a grin, but it died, for he knew that James had no sense of humour. 'They're tamer than you think – no need to get yourself worked up.'

Joel James's eyes glinted, his mouth pursed, and he bit off an angry grunt, before swinging around and loping away, leaving Robert with a frown and a determination to stop any more trouble before the man's uncontrollable temper got the better of him. Saddling the cob, he rode out to the pastures where the troublesome animals were grazing. They'd come back from the Reed fields – all quiet here now – and Dan Wharton sitting down by the wall, eating his bait. For God's sake! Robert dismounted, anger growing. Damn this idle man. He had half a mind to put him off and do the work himself, but had a feeling he might soon be needed by Lizzie. Old man Reed must die before much longer, and then who would tell Bella the sad news? Who would be here to help bring her back to Abworthy?

He watched Dan get to his feet and guiltily turn once again to the pile of moorstone awaiting him. And suddenly, anger died, for all he could think of was Bella, and how hard it would be to tell her that her uncle had passed on and that Abworthy was waiting for her.

As Robert handed up stones and chipped away at awkward edges, in his mind he was searching for the kind, gentle words that would tell her; would bring her home to where he waited for her. He stopped, a boulder in his hands, staring at nothing but the grey, windswept sky; amazingly, he was thinking differently. No more selfish plans, just an attempt to make Bella smile. To make her happy.

In God's name, what was happening to him?

Jack took Bella to see the new building site. He had arrived early after tea, saying that the evening was still light; did she fancy a short walk? Feeling that she owed it to him to be pleasant after her earlier outburst, she agreed, and now they stood by the river, inspecting the foundations of the new housing estate that was being built here.

By now the whole extraordinary business of finding herself with an unexpected family, and an inheritance to come at any time, was settling in her mind. The problem at the moment was how to make Jack understand that, should he choose to propose, she must turn him down. She listened, slightly impatiently, to his description of the plans he had seen.

'Semi-detached villas, with three bedrooms, and the possibility of having electric light installed. Just think, Bella, no more smelly lamps and candles! You won't know yourself!'

His face tightened, and she realized that those last words had been tantamount to a proposal. But he looked around, adding quickly, 'I do believe we might be able to inspect the one house that is almost finished – over there.' Taking her arm, he led her up a rough path into the first house on the site. It was roofed, the windows in place, and the door stood ajar. Clearly, the invitation to explore was too great for him to deny. She went with him, wondering if this was likely to be the place for a proper proposal but feeling only amused and not anxious.

The house was newly painted and smelled strongly, but she looked around, imagining what sort of a home this might become, even comparing it in her mind with shabby, ancient Abworthy.

Jack led her into a large room overlooking fields beyond which the river flowed. He looked around, smiled, pointed out the fireplace already laid for an open fire, and again Bella thought of the hearth at Abworthy, with black pots and a rusty kettle simmering on it, and everybody clustering around its comforting warmth. Her mind was far away when, abruptly, Jack turned to her, removed his hat, took her hands to his chest, and said, 'This isn't the spot I had chosen, Bella – but

I seem to have said too much already to delay any more. So,'
– he smiled, lifting her hands to his lips, '– my dear Bella,
I am asking you to be my wife. To live here in one of these
handsome houses, and share my life. We could be happy here
– have a very good life ... so, yes, I'm proposing....'

There were no pangs of dismay, or anxiety as to how she
should reply. Her mind was quite clear: she couldn't marry
him. Very soon she would be moving to Abworthy and then
Jack would be forgotten. But what a difficult and hurtful thing
to have to say to anyone.

She saw a radiance in his face that she had never seen
before. But it made no difference. Slowly she drew her hands
out of his and said, with a calmness that surprised her, 'Thank
you, Jack, for the great honour of asking me to marry you. But
I cannot do so.'

For two seconds he was silent, his face registering shock.
Then, 'What? What are you saying?' The radiance had gone
and he seemed older and less attractive. His voice was strained.
'I don't understand. You and I have been friends—'

'Yes, friends – just friends, Jack.'

He grabbed her hands again, pulled her close to him and
stared, frowning into her eyes. His low voice held a challenge.
'More than that. You've always led me to believe that you and
I would one day marry. And now you're saying no? What has
happened to you?'

She stepped away. 'I have found my lost family. I'm a
different person now. I'm going to live on Dartmoor. I'm sorry,
Jack, but that's how it is.'

They stared at each other for what seemed a never-ending
moment until Jack clamped his lips together, put his hat on
and said frostily, 'It's those damned Reeds, isn't it? They've
poisoned your mind. You're behaving like a weak child, not
knowing what you're doing. Well, I refuse to let you go, Bella.
I shall find a way of keeping you here in Exeter; I shall marry

you – of course I will.'

A shiver ran down her back then. She had known this would be a terrible moment, but he was making it worse. Threatening her. And if he found a loophole in the law, could he really stop her moving to Abworthy? Could he truly force her to stay here, marry him, and live in this mundane little villa?

Suddenly she turned and ran, aware that he was running after her, and then she heard his voice, growing fainter and realized with relief that he was letting her go.

But the words remained in her head as she headed back to St Leonard's Road.

'I'll have you, Bella, somehow – no matter where you run, I shall find you....'

CHAPTER 18

The house was quiet and Bella sensed its new atmosphere of disapproval. Mrs French now walked past her without even a glance, and Miss Carpenter sighed, wiped her eyes and followed her sister, looking sideways at Bella with obvious unhappiness.

But Bella had a new feeling these days; she was trying to put Jack and his anger out of her mind, for suddenly her small world was expanding. She needed to go and see Uncle William before he died. Restlessly she started packing her few belongings into the valise, for she must be prepared. But then her thoughts swung wildly. How could she leave Miss Carpenter? How would Jack react? And then again she was back at Abworthy. Of course, she must also look at her clothes very keenly; her walking shoes would be no good on the moor. She must either buy new or get hers soled. And perhaps a thicker nightdress was necessary; she remembered the chill of the upstairs bedchamber. And then there were the few best dresses which, surely, she would never need at Abworthy? Perhaps Emmy might find a home for her one or two hardly worn smart dresses.

And then, folding and packing underclothes into the valise, she sat on the bed and daydreamed back to her first meeting with Robert Verney. 'You ride, of course,' he had said and she had felt a sort of shame because she didn't. He had also said he would teach her to ride. Remembering, she smiled, a glow bringing new vitality into her cheeks. They would ride out together, to all the places he knew so well, where he would take her....

But to ride meant wearing proper clothes. A riding habit, a neat hat. Her smile disappeared and she turned to her small hoard of savings of the last ten years. Well, she would just have to splash out and buy a riding habit. But then Sarah flashed into her mind – Sarah who bought second-hand clothes at Moreton market. Could she, Bella, not do the same? Surely, in Exeter market there would be old women who sold such worn clothes? She breathed more lightly. Another adventure, going and looking around the stalls, trying on what she found, wondering if she would look the part ... would look good enough for Robert to admire when he saw her on horseback. She felt her cheeks warming, and smiled again as she put a small amount of money into her purse. Tomorrow, when changing all the library books, she would hurry into the market and see what she could find.

It wasn't easy, making herself handle the old clothes hanging around the stall. They smelled and were dirty. But, turning away after the first few minutes and remembering how Sarah and Lizzie did this sort of thing without such fine feelings, she forced herself to concentrate and even to ask the old woman watching her for help. 'I'm hoping to find a riding habit. Do you have one?'

Mrs Lewis pulled her shawl tighter around her ample figure and came to her side. Smouldering dark eyes looked her up and down. 'Got some money, have ee, then?'

Bella flushed. 'Yes, I have. Please show me.'

The old woman handled heaps of skirts and dresses to one side, finally emerging with a dark blue pile of something, which she shook out, and then invitingly held over her arm, looking at Bella with assessing eyes. 'Fit you, this would.'

A lump formed in Bella's throat. Never had she thought she would be here, in the openness of Exeter market, buying second-hand clothes. That brought Jack to her mind, and at once she found herself smiling. Goodness! How shocked he would be! Finding it easier now, to make the next move, she asked, 'May I – er – try it on?' No good if it didn't fit. Of course she could make alterations; it needed airing and cleaning first of all, and even then ... she dithered, undecided, but Mrs Lewis had her by the arm, was pulling her into the shadows of the stall, away from the publicity of the market and she was being helped to put her arms into the sleeves of the jacket.

'Fits like it were made for you, it do.' Mrs Lewis chewed her mouth and suggested a price, which Bella thought was far in excess of the worth of the old clothes. A darn there, a patch on the bottom of the skirt. She caught her breath and offered less.

The old woman looked at her with disgust, then stretched out an arm and came up with a small, neat top hat from under a pile of shabby billycocks. 'Tell you what, my bird, put this in with it, for the same price.' Dark eyes glinted, Bella felt the skirt enclosing her body, tried on the hat, and knew at once that she was handsomely and appropriately dressed. Just right for those rides over the moor, with Robert.

'Thank you, I'll take them,' she said, smiled, and slipped off the long trailing skirt without any further thoughts. Now, hung out on the line, beaten, mended, pressed, the riding habit lay on her chair, filling her mind with dreams of the future and dispelling any dark thoughts.

It was the middle of the following week, an evening of grey mist and threatening rain, when Bella, passing through the hallway on her way to the drawing room, heard a knock at the door. She called down to Emmy, 'I'll get it, don't bother to come up,' and went to open it.

Against the hard backdrop of the oncoming night she saw

a tall man dressed in dark clothes standing there. Robert Verney.

His hat was in his hand and his handsome face brooding. 'Bella,' he said, in his low voice, 'I have bad news for you. Mr Reed died this morning.' There was no smile but she felt a sudden empathy, and was reassured.

She caught her breath and stood quite still, staring into his dark eyes. It had been expected, but this visit, to come now, out of the night, so abruptly.... He moved without seeming to, coming into the hall and shutting the door behind him.

'I've come to fetch you home, Bella.' Still no smile, just that quiet, deep voice holding all the solemnity of the occasion. 'We can catch the last train and James will meet us at the station. I've got a cab outside. Have you got your things ready?'

The question jolted her back into reality. 'Yes,' she said quickly. 'I'm all packed. I was just ... waiting.'

He nodded. 'Good. Then we can make a start. Go and get your coat. Tell me which room your bag is in and I'll fetch it while you go and say goodbye to Miss Carpenter.'

'Yes,' she said again, but faintly this time. It was all happening so quickly. Then she sucked in a big breath and nodded. 'Yes, Robert. My bag is in my room – I'll take you up there.' Confusion threatened but she pushed it away. 'I need my purse, my washing things, my nightdress....' She met his eyes, gentle now, she thought, and saw a look of under-standing on his face, usually so tight and sharp. He stood, waiting, watching her.

'And – yes – of course, then I must go and tell them I'm leaving.'

They went up the stairs together, with Emmy coming up from the kitchen, wide-eyed when she understood what was happening, but offering to help. 'I'll take your carpet bag, Miss, while the gennulman takes the valise.'

'Thank you.' Bella gathered all her belongings, took a last

look at the small room that had been her refuge for so long. She went down the stairs, watched Robert and Emmy take the bags out to the waiting cab, and then headed for the drawing room.

It took a moment of greater courage than she thought she possessed to enter the drawing room, but the sisters were sitting by the fire, embroidering, books open on tables by their chairs, coffee cups empty and suddenly she felt sure of herself. A swirl of self-importance swept her along. This was her new life; she must handle it as well as she could.

They looked up as she entered. Bella caught up her strength and smiled warmly at them. 'Miss Carpenter – Mrs French – I'm afraid I have to go. To leave you. You see, I've just had the news that my Uncle William died today. Mr Verney has come to collect me.'

'Collect you? *Now?* At *this* time of night?'

She knew she would never forget the rage and dismay of their old voices, as she broke the news, but with Robert waiting in the cab and Emmy holding the front door open she knew she had no other way to go.

'I'm sorry, so sorry. But ... goodbye.'

She left the house as an abrupt and disbelieving silence struck it, and was thankful when Robert's warm hand helped her into the cab at the gate.

'They'll get over it.' His deep voice held a wry note and then she was able to smile – weakly – indicating an emerging sense of humour that she was thankful for. Yes, there would be other companions for the old ladies. But only one Abworthy for her.

And indeed, only one Robert Verney.

The train rattled and shook and they sat opposite each other in the dark compartment, not speaking, but, Bella felt, at home with one another. When they reached Bovey, Robert got up, collected the bags and helped her onto the platform. It was dark and colder here than in Exeter and Bella shivered as the grey mist swirled around the gas lamp outside the station. Doubts waited here in the gloom, and suddenly thoughts grew dark.

'There's James.' Robert raised his arm and the trap came to their side. Joel said nothing, merely grunted when he met Bella's eyes, and threw her valise into the back. 'Sit by me,' he said roughly, then waited until Robert was in the back with the bags, finally trotting off out of the station and – Bella thought, so dark and frightening was the waiting night – into the mist and the unknown.

She longed for the warmth and reassurance of Robert's hand, but he was perched behind her and she could only wait until they reached Abworthy, when the trap halted and he jumped out to help her climb down. 'You'll warm up in a minute,' he told her as they went through the open doorway, up the cross passage and into the kitchen, the sudden light of the paraffin lamp making her stop and blink.

Emotion and uncertainty came like an inescapable wave, filling her, unsteadying her as she walked into the big room. What was she doing here? Should she have come?

They were all there. Wide-eyed, she looked around and saw, with surprise and even a touch of alarm, they were staring at her. Everybody, old and young, who lived in the Abworthy hamlet, here, in this shadowy room, with Uncle William dead in his bed upstairs. Looking around, from face to face, she could only wonder and try to banish the overriding emotions. Black-coated Mrs May by the fire; Sarah, watching with a frown; Mrs James glancing over to where Joel had shut the door behind him; Robert at her side and Lizzie putting warm arms around her, whispering soft words gently and lovingly, and making tears come to her eyes.

'You're here, now, lover. And wouldn't he just have been pleased to see you? Poor ole man, went off in his sleep. Best thing really, but oh my, I miss him already.'

The room, Bella thought, suddenly bereft of sense and only aware of her own feelings, was listening; was waiting for something important to happen before it slipped once more into the steady quietness of its long life. She caught her breath, looked at Lizzie, nodded and said, unsteadily, 'I came as soon as I could. Robert brought me. And now—' Tears threatened but she didn't know they were there. All she knew was that something was being waited for – what was it?

It was finally Sarah who stepped forward, coming to Lizzie's side, her young voice sharp and clear. ''S all right, Ma, I'll take Cousin Bella up to her room while you get a drink going for everyone. She doesn't want to wear her coat and hat no longer, does she? 'Cos I s'pose she's come for keeps now, hasn't she?'

Bella looked into Lizzie's moist eyes and saw the question there. It only needed her word. So she caught her breath, and then, from nowhere, it came. 'Yes,' she said firmly, 'I'm here to stay.'

Suddenly, and mercifully, it was as if a problem had been finally resolved, for at once there was movement and noise. People moving around the room, starting to talk to one another. Robert taking her valise, picking up a candle, saying, 'Sarah, bring the other bag, will you?' and heading up the stairs, looking back over his shoulder. 'Come with me, Bella. I'll take you up to your room,' and at once she did as he ordered, thankful to know that the decision had been made. She was at Abworthy, and they were, if not quite welcoming her, at least gathered to see her.

When Robert deposited her valise on the chair and told Sarah to put the carpet bag on the bed, before leaving the room again, she took off her coat and hat, smiled at him and said, quite steadily, without a hint of doubt, 'Thank you, Robert. I could never have managed without you.'

He paused at the open doorway for a long moment, looking

back at her, before saying, very low and almost inaudibly, 'And I hope you'll need me again, in the future. At any time, Bella – just ask me and I'll be here.'

She knew that Uncle William lay dead in the next chamber, but even so she felt warm and welcomed. He would be glad to have her here. Family ... the word rang in her head like a bell, proclaiming something she longed for, and suddenly the joyous thought was within her grasp – instinct told her that she had been right to return here. To come home. She went downstairs with lightness in her step and a warmth in her heart that had surely been waiting for life's extraordinary journeying to reach this moment: Uncle William's passing; Abworthy coming to her and an extraordinary hope that love was waiting for her, somewhere close at hand, if she chose to find it.

CHAPTER 19

When Bella awoke next morning it was with a shock at finding herself at Abworthy. She was here. Uncle was dead and today was his funeral. Knowledge flashed in a blinding light. So much to do, the house, the farm ... could she manage it all? And then a thought: Robert would help. He had said he would help if she needed him. She dressed quickly, glad she had thought to buy a thick black hat ready for Dartmoor storms and winds – and death. Now, she thought, it would give her extra confidence.

Lizzie was here – bless her foresight. Bella knew that the house would have been a haunted mausoleum without Lizzie staying the night, and now the carpenter had arrived and he and Joel James carried the coffin up the stairs, where Lizzie and Mrs May waited with Uncle William. The place was very quiet; Bella felt death hanging over it and had to force herself to think about household duties.

But there were people to think about, as well. Sarah had said, late last night, 'I can't come for the funeral. Mrs Hampton won't give me time off. Sorry,' and Bella thought she had looked peaky as if sickening for a cold or winter cough.

She had laid a hand on the girl's arm, smiled and said quietly, 'I hope you're getting on all right in your new situation, Sarah.'

She saw a fearful expression suddenly filling the girl's thin face and heard a note of something not right as Sarah twitched away her arm and snapped, sharply, 'Why not? It's a good place.'

Lizzie had raised eyebrows at Bella, who nodded and turned away. So Sarah was still a problem. Bella found her mind filled with new and cumbersome thoughts. Yes, she was at Abworthy and was glad to be; but perhaps she hadn't quite understood that there were many problems and burdens to be dealt with before she became truly mistress of this old house and its lands. The road ahead, she acknowledged heavily, was going to be a hard one.

But Mrs May smiled at her, whispering as she passed, 'We women'll follow the men when Mr Reed takes his last journey. We'll be with you, lover.'

And so they were. It was midday before Joel and Dan carried the coffin downstairs, and carefully set it in the cart waiting by the door. Bella, wearing her dark coat, new hat and freshly soled shoes, watched the few villagers who had come up to accompany William Reed to the churchyard and saw Robert as well following the horse and cart out of the yard, down the track and along the road towards the village church.

She and Lizzie, Mrs James and Mrs May followed, walking slowly, not speaking, but she knew their thoughts were all the same. Poor old William Reed, taken at last, and now going home. And then, as if the day knew and was trying to cheer up the proceedings, a faint sun shone through the heavy grey clouds and the small procession lifted its head and took firmer steps.

Back in Abworthy, they waited for Mr Langridge, the solicitor from Bovey, to read William's will. There was more money than Bella had imagined and gifts to his friends and workers. And the estate to her, Isabella Reed, with her address in Exeter. So William had thought about her for a long time –

Bella felt emotion filling her, remembering him.

Mr Langridge left after reading the will and Bella helped Lizzie prepare food for the wake. The little gathering warmed the room, the visitors relaxing slowly as they drank tea and ale and ate cold meats, telling each other anecdotes about the old man. How upright he had been, strong minded, careful with his animals and his money, but fair to work for.

'A good maister,' said Joel James with something passing for a smile over his usually scowling face, and fixing his gaze on Bella as he spoke. She knew what the look meant: What would the new mistress be like?

But doubt had left her. She was here, the work awaited her, and she would deal with it. Her eyes moved over the faces sitting around the fire to find Robert, discussing something with Dan Wharton. She saw how Robert brought a smile to Dan's gloomy face, and then saw him turn, looking around. Looking for her?

She moved across the room, trying not to make it obvious that she was doing so, but Mrs May's eyes followed, and Bella wondered if Lizzie, too, was watching. Yet it didn't matter. She was mistress of this house now; what she did was her own concern. And yes, she must speak to Robert, thank him for his help and remind him that he was going to teach her to ride.

The blue riding habit. The smart hat. The moor, in sunlight and no doubt a capricious wind; the turf beneath their hoofs green, the few late flowers and their colours ... her smile broadened, and she looked down to hide it. Not a smile suitable for a wake. But she knew as they eyes met, that he had seen and understood. She went to him, said quietly, for his ears alone, 'I must talk to you, Robert, when you can manage it.'

He smiled back, eyes amused, his deep voice answering just as quietly. 'I'll be around, Bella. When I can. You want advice about the stock, I suppose.'

She nodded, excitement flaring. 'Yes, please.'

Again his smile and her answering flicker of pleasure. Then, returning to the fire and the refilling of the teapot, she hoped no one was watching, for surely this feeling of excitement must remain a secret?

Robert left when the funeral tea was over. Darkness drew in and all the men, including him, had stock to see to. He had seen Bella speaking to Joel James, with Mrs James beside him, and had guessed that the Jameses, with William's legacy to come, were telling her what they planned to do with it. Would they move? If so, it would leave Bella without a cattleman and, with no experience of farming, that would be a disaster. But, walking back to his own cottage, he thought that in that probable circumstances, the sooner he moved into Abworthy the better. Doing the milking and shutting up the hens, he knew his plans were made.

Bella wanted to talk to him. Tomorrow morning, then. He went into the dark cottage, poked up the fire and sat down with a mug of cider. The old man's funeral procession had given him time to think about the past, about that game of nap played between Reed and Verney when the inheritance was thrown over the table as if it had no value. But in his mind William Reed was saying *Family, land, inheritance,* and he knew that Bella had heard him.

He lit his pipe, sitting by the dying embers, wondering what Abworthy meant to her; as much as it did to him? Abworthy was, to him, the inheritance that should have, by rights, been handed down to him by his family. He thought about marrying Bella, so becoming the owner of the house and land that way. Was there a problem? Surely not. He would make changes where necessary; give her what comforts she wanted. The land would make a good living. Knocking out his pipe, he got up and stretched. Those damned walls, needing rebuilding ... but suddenly he knew his plan was a sham. Bella was conventional; she would never accept him as her husband. She would want someone she loved, someone as straightforward and as honest as she was. He could almost hear her saying a very loud *No* to him if he proposed to her. And then into that nagging thought, came another; he couldn't do anything to hurt Bella Reed. She was someone who affected him in a new way; his affection for her was growing.

She was upright, strong, ready to take on the burden William Reed had left her, and he felt his admiration grow. The unexpected word *love* drifted into his mind before he slept. He had never thought to feel like this about any woman. What was he to do about it?

Bella was up early, aware that the house was empty and that life was making demands of many kinds. She knew nothing about farming. Joel cared for the cows and the sheep, and Steve, the stable boy, looked after the pigs, carthorse and the cob. Robert would tell her what she must do about her stock out in the fields; she expected to see him some time today. So get dressed, she thought. Be ready for him. What should she wear? Something serviceable; the old, almost worn out dark red woollen dress that was kept for physical labour back in Exeter would now be her daily uniform. She had purloined one of Emmy's long white aprons and this would tie around her waist, because, of course, she was cook as well as maid of all work. The heavy shoes would carry her around outside and she had the riding habit to wear when the lessons started. Halfway down the stairs, she stopped, smiling to herself. Riding out with Robert would be exciting and useful. Now that she lived here, she must get to know everything about Dartmoor. He would teach her.

It was difficult to push back the long black iron bar fastening the big door, but she managed it. Stepping outside, she was greeted by a flurry of hens and by the excited barking of the dog, loose now and ranging at Joel's side as he carried hay into the barn and shouted at the boy to get the horse ready for the cart. He looked her way, nodded and then ignored her, disappearing into another shed at the end of the yard.

The dog's barking increased as a man on a pony came down the rough track. 'Morning, Missis.' He fumbled in the sack hanging around his waist, found a letter and handed it down to her. Bella, trying to quell the advances of the dog, took the envelope, not believing it could be for her. Then Joel appeared again, saluted the postman, shouted at the dog and took it off with him.

Alone in the yard, Bella read her name and address on the envelope – Miss I. Reed, Abworthy Farm, Dartmoor – and recognized the handwriting. Her stomach suddenly knotted as she stared at it. Large, very black, leaning to one side and important-looking; it was in Jack Courtney's hand.

CHAPTER 20

She opened the letter and saw at once that it was, indeed, from Jack.

My dear Bella—

Anger flooded through her. She wasn't his. She was herself, alone, mistress of this farm and its lands. How dare he be so patronizing. Her fingers shook as she held the letter and continued to read.

> *I was shocked to hear of your disappearance. Miss Carpenter and her sister were most upset and needed comfort. I can't believe that you could so willingly disturb them like this. Indeed, I am more of the opinion that you have been persuaded by someone with a very charming manner and no scruples. And with this in mind I am planning to travel to Dartmoor and bring you home again to Exeter, where you belong. Had you forgotten utterly that we were planning a future together?*
> *My dear Bella, you really must rethink your foolish actions and see things from my point of view – and from your employer's. I know she will willingly forgive you for your desertion once you return and take up your familiar duties. And, of*

*course, I shall also resume my friendship with you
– a friendship which I hoped was growing into
something much fonder and more promising. And
so I plan to travel to Abworthy Farm very shortly –
on Friday, this week. No doubt I can engage a cab
from Bovey Station, and I shall hope very much
that you will be packed up and ready to return to
Exeter with me.
Until then, with very sincere friendship and hope
for our shared future,
I am fondly yours, Jack.*

She felt the wind tugging at her skirt, heard the dog barking
as it accompanied Joel, leading the horse and cart, loaded
with dung, out of the narrow gate at the far end of the yard,
into the fields beyond. She saw him look back at her, then
shout to the dog, and disappear from view, but still she stood
there. Jack's words rang through her head, and she couldn't
quite believe the startling arrogance of them. How had she
ever thought she was beginning to love him? And, indeed, how
could she possibly love a man who thought it his right to lay
down the law for her to follow? She folded the letter back into
the envelope and put it in her pocket. then she started to laugh
and found mirth was the best possible panacea for the hurtful
anger crowding her head. She laughed at the hens pecking
around her feet, smiled at the thin tabby cat slinking past into
the cowshed where Lizzie said a pan of milk was put out daily
for it. She thought of Daisy, the house cow, now grazing in the
field just beyond the yard; of the sheep which Joel had told
her were pastured on the far fields, those that bordered the
Verney land, so close to her own.

And she was still laughing when Robert appeared,
dismounted from his pony, and leading it towards her, smiled
as he asked, 'What's so funny? Don't tell me Joel James has
been joking ... I've never seen him smile, not ever. You must

have a magic touch, Miss Reed.'

She stood there, looking at him. Charm and a lack of scruples. That was what Jack thought of Robert Verney. Well, he certainly had charm, lots of it; she wasn't sure about the scruples, but so far he'd treated her well and had been helpful. And he had said he would be there to help with her farming problems, something even Jack couldn't attempt to do.

So she held out her hand to stroke the mare's nose, smiled at Robert and said, with laughter in her words, 'Shall I go and put on my riding habit? Have you come to give me my first lesson, Mr Verney?'

'No such niceties today, Miss Reed. Another day when I've got more time you can dress up. But if you want to get on Honey's back, then I'll put you there. Just pull your skirt around your legs and trust me.' He looked deep into her eyes. 'You do trust me, Bella, don't you?'

'Yes.' Her certainty was rewarded by the dark blue eyes gleaming back at her.

'Good. Then allow me.' His arms went around her and she let him pick her up, sitting her on the saddle with both legs sloping over the side. He grinned up at her. 'If you want to ride properly, Miss Reed, then I shall have to find that side saddle for you. No lady rides astride, you see ... except certain rough farmers' wives who can't be bothered to imitate the gentry.'

'Perhaps I'll be one of those. Oh, I'm slipping—'

But he was there, edging her back into position, putting the reins in her hands, showing her how to hold them. 'We'll walk around the yard, that'll be enough for now. And then I have to go and look at my cattle.'

'I'll come with you; I need to learn about cattle. And I've got very strong shoes.'

They laughed together and then he led Honey around the yard, his arm holding hers, until she was able to relax and enjoy the slow, rhythmic movement. 'You'll make a good horsewoman. Get into your riding habit tomorrow and I'll be around at the same time. You can have Honey and I'll ride Justice. We'll look at the cattle together. But now, off you get.'

'Do I just slip down?' She gathered her skirt into thick folds and prepared to move.

'I'll help you.'

And then he was there, gathering her in his arms. They stood looking at each other while the hens pecked around their feet, and the cockerel mounted the midden, to stand there crowing his invitation to his harem.

Bella felt Robert's invitation, too. In the strength of his arms, in his body's warmth pressing against hers; in the smile on his face, in his eyes, and in the huskiness of his voice, as he said, low and quiet, 'Miss Reed, forgive me, but I have to kiss you.'

'Please do, Mr Verney. I want you to....'

It was something she had never experienced before, so different from Jack's tepid peck. She could hardly believe the happiness that tingled through her mind and her body. His mouth was gentle and warm, his arms holding her careful and strong. It was like a wonderful dream and as she relaxed and pressed closer, the kiss deepened, became more urgent. And then suddenly, surprising her, leaving her breathless and lonely, he dropped his arms and stepped away. 'I'm sorry. I should never have—'

She stared into eyes that blazed, at the beautiful mouth now tightening, as if making amends for giving her so much pleasure, and heard him say, low-voiced and sharply, 'I think you should return to the kitchen. I'm sure you have a lot of work waiting ... and so do I. I must go and see about the walls, about the stock. Wharton will be there. And that troublemaker, James.' He turned, leading the pony to the end of the yard, mounted and then rode away.

It was over. She rocked on her heels in a moment of

unsteadiness, shame coming like a black cloud and obliterating all the pleasure she had felt. He had found her fast, easy, a woman who offered too much; perhaps too soon. And now it was too late. Why had she allowed him this freedom? Why, oh why, hadn't she thought before she said that fatal *Please do*?

For a long painful moment she stood quite still in the yard, blaming herself, trying to excuse the wanton pleasure she had felt, but finding it impossible. She would never forget. Then familiar farmyard sounds came to her aid. The pigs snorting in their shed, hens crowing, coming out of the henhouse, an egg laid, perhaps; something she must think about. She had to feed the stock, collect eggs, organize the mucking out of the stables and cowshed. She heard rooks shouting in the trees behind the farmhouse as they went about their own personal business. The wind soughing through sycamore branches was trying to tell her that life went on. No matter the pain, everyone had to get on with their own journey. She sucked in a great breath and found her strength was returning and with it a decision. She must never let Robert know she had found his embrace as exciting as it had been. Briefly, knowing she was wrong, she wondered if perhaps Dartmoor farmers were not as conventionally minded as town-dwellers. Perhaps a kiss indicated just a normal sealing of friendship. But she knew his kiss had meant more than that and she wondered how she would get over the need for more of Robert Verney's kisses.

But, turning towards the door behind her, and following on from Jack's abrasive letter, and that embrace, she discovered a new sort of strength. Yes, as he said, she had work to do. And she would apply herself with true diligence. Indeed, finding she could now actually call up a wry smile, she knew she was beginning to feel the reassurance of – what had Robert called it? – the emergence of the moor's power in her family background. As he had said, she had granite in her blood.

And then the stable boy, Steve, came towards her, cap in hand, looking anxious. 'You got orders for me, Missis? Mr James went off, said to ask you meself.' He looked nervous, and she understood that Joel James had played his first trick on her.

Well, here she was, mistress of Abworthy and about to give her first order. Her smile was real, strong and confident, her quiet voice in command of the situation. 'Yes, please, Steve. Fetch me two buckets of well water and put them in the larder, please. And then later this morning, you can show me the duck pond and tell me where the ducks usually lay.'

His lopsided smile and firmer answer assured her that her position was clear and he was willing to help. 'Yes, Missis – they do lay in the reeds, mostly ... I'll show you.'

They smiled at each other, then Steve put on his cap and loped towards the well at the far end of the yard, while Bella entered the house, looked around the cold, empty, lonely kitchen and prepared to start work. And she made a firm decision to have the old stone house, her inheritance, looking neat and tidy, warm and welcoming, when Jack arrived on Friday.

Robert cantered the pony towards the pasture, his mind seething with anger at his uncouth behaviour. He had been a fool, allowing himself to indulge Bella's willing friendliness and now it had got him into the situation where he knew he must not be alone with her again. But clearly she had enjoyed his kiss; had even drawn closer to him, which had been too much for his self-control. Bella Reed was a warm woman who could be loving, given half a chance. But this had not been in his scheme of things; marriage, yes, control of the farm and the house, of course; but not a true marriage of bodies and minds. He had never envisaged that. And yet, now....

He cantered on towards the pasture where he could see his Scotch cattle cropping the newly rained on grass. Dan Wharton was at the wall, half-heartedly heaving moorstone into likely spaces and making a hard job of it. And in the distance he saw Joel James, on Abworthy land, spade in hand throwing out dung. As he watched, he saw the man pause in his work, lean on the spade and look towards his own fields. Robert imagined the animosity that accompanied the long stare; he grinned grimly; more trouble. And coming on top of that mistaken embrace with Bella, he knew he could do without Joel James's rancour.

Turning to walk amongst his stock, he felt in his bones that there had to be a confrontation between them, sometime. And sometime soon, if things kept on this way. But a row with James would involve the new owner of Abworthy. Another thing that Bella might blame him for.

It was later in the afternoon, when, tired and hungry, he had returned from a day's newtake walling with Dan, a frustrating job as he had to do most of the hard work himself, that he found Steve, the stable boy at his door.

'Well?' he grunted, pushing the boy aside.

'Missis says you're not to come tomorrow morning after all. Says she's a visitor coming and needs to clean the place up. That's all. Oh, but says she'll maybe see you next week sometime.'

The boy stepped away from the door, eager to get back to his tea and his warm tallat. Everyone knew that Mr Verney was a gruff sort of man when not pleased. And he didn't look pleased now – tight-lipped and frowning. Gratefully, Steve hurried away.

Robert flung off his coat and hat, sank down into the chair by the dying fire and allowed his thoughts to flare out. All right, he deserved this. But not to see her, not until, what did she say – sometime next week? And a visitor coming? Now who, in God's name could this be? Slowly he got up, filled the kettle and pushed it over the fire, which he now wriggled and built up. And more and more he got the feeling that he must be there, at Abworthy, when Bella's visitor arrived.

CHAPTER 21

At Radley Manor Sarah was getting used to the work of kitchen maid and the teasing and rough comments of the staff working alongside her. It was even enjoyable being away from home – no moaning Dad always on and on, and Ma forever telling her off. In fact, she became happy at the Hamptons. Especially when Mr Henry, the son of the family, developed an eye for her.

She got into the habit of waiting in the shadows just outside the baize door that led into the kitchen. He found her there, whispered, with a gleam in his eye that she had skin like peaches, whatever they were; that she should be kissed all day ... and that he'd like to put his advice into practice. Of course, she knew he would never marry her, but she could dream, couldn't she? And dreams filled her sleep until the night Mr Henry came creaking up the narrow wooden stairs, pushed open her attic door, fell on her bed and breathed drunken fumes into her startled face. But he had the sense to whisper hoarsely, 'Not a sound ... keep quiet ... ' as he pulled off the coverlet, ripped her nightshift and pushed her legs apart.

When he left, Sarah found her dreams had turned to a nightmare. She was angry, ready to tell the world about this wicked man, but sense came slowly as she worked on during the following days. No one would believe her, for this is what happened to foolish young maids. Well, she'd certainly learned a lesson. No more handsome, smooth-voiced gentlemen in future. From now on she would look out for someone of her own kind – a farmer's boy, like Steve at Abworthy, or someone in the village.

But then, just after Uncle William's death, she found she was in real trouble. Mr Henry went off for a tour of Europe, never even looking at her before he left, and that day she discovered that her monthly bleeding wasn't happening. Anger burned, and suddenly there was only one thought in her mind – tell Madam, tell her how her son had been cruel and wicked and she, Sarah, needed help.

But Madam, sitting in her boudoir, frowned as Sarah entered, having sneaked upstairs when Mary the housemaid was busy with the beds and Cook talking to the butcher in the kitchen. Madam asked coldly, 'What do you want, Wharton? I don't expect to see you above stairs.'

'Mr Henry – he come to my room and, and … did what he wanted. And now I'm not having my bleeding. You gotta help me, Madam.'

Mrs Hampton's smooth cheeks tightened and her grey eyes narrowed. 'What nonsense! I never heard such a rigmarole. How dare you say such things! Go back to your work, Wharton, and don't let me see you up here again.'

'No! It's true! You gotta help me, Madam!'

Full lips pursed and the aristocratic voice hardened. 'The only help I can offer is to put you off. I don't need staff who make up tales. Go and pack your things, Wharton, and ask Cook to see me before you leave. We shall have to engage a new kitchen maid. So annoying....'

Sarah was overwhelmed. 'But … but—'

'Just go,' ordered the exasperated voice, 'and don't let me hear that wretched tale of yours again.' Madam turned back to her desk and picked up her pen.

Sarah stared, hands trembling. 'But – my wages?'

'Cook will see to them. Now go.'

And that was the end of it. Sarah crept from the room, anger mixing with wretchedness. Put off? Without a reference? And Mr Henry getting away with it? She went back to the kitchen, her mind seared with hatred and distress and wondering where she would go.

Ma would be angry and shocked, the neighbours laughing behind their hands; Mrs May would offer potions; ah, was that the way to go? No, she wouldn't ask that old witch for help. And that Robert Verney would say she was a little fool who deserved what she got. And Cousin Bella – whatever would she say?

As Sarah walked slowly away from Radley Manor, bundle in her hand, her mind worked feverishly. She couldn't live on the moor; she had to have somewhere else to go – but where?

Bella worked hard, ordering herself to forget Robert, who had just walked off like that. She had been weak and foolish, allowing him to awaken in her the feelings and hopes that now she knew she must abandon. He had said he was a rough man, without manners. And this proved it. She hoped he would keep away.

And strangely she found that sweeping and then washing the kitchen floor, dusting down cobwebs, cleaning windows, and bringing in armfuls of peat to keep the fire going was just the way to help blank him out of her mind. There was a comfort in being busy; in seeing the ancient room responding to her actions. It was almost as if Abworthy were opening itself up to her ministrations. There was simple pleasure in working like this, seeing neglected mahogany shining to a new liquid polish, picking the rugs clean of dirt and fluff. She opened windows, feeling she was airing away the ghosts of yesterday, perhaps welcoming in today's new arrivals. Sitting down in the settle at mid-morning, sipping a mug of tea, she wondered at the wide range of thoughts and emotions suddenly arriving in her mind.

And when Lizzie Wharton came, eyes wide, looking around at the new cleanliness and comfort, Bella felt that she had achieved something worthwhile. She had found her place in life and already all the problems that had threatened only yesterday were lessening. Here, at Abworthy, there was an air of new lightness; of warmth and welcome. She laughed at Lizzie's startled expression, and said, 'I knew you'd be surprised, but doesn't it all look bright and nice? Mind you, I don't know if I can keep up all this activity; I'm exhausted already!'

Lizzie took off her coat and accepted a mug of tea. She sat down beside Bella and said firmly, 'You'll need another pair of hands, lover. Pity our Sarah's gone off to the Hamptons – she could help you. But I'm here today, so tell me what to do.'

Bella thought. Still so much not yet cleared up. Uncle's room. The unused guest room; the smaller one where she was sleeping. Passages, stairways, all forgotten over the past months when Lizzie had been busy nursing the old man. But now, slowly, everything could be tidied and cleaned. It would keep her busy. Here her expression grew less bright as she recalled Robert. She must keep busy, keep such thoughts at bay. And then – suddenly something else flashed into her mind. A visitor was coming tomorrow. *Jack*. One more day. More cleaning, washing, cooking. But still a sneaking thought at the back of her mind – what had she told Robert? That she would see him sometime, probably next week. Pain hit her then, pain that she knew she would take a long time to get over. If ever. But that was nonsense.

Jumping up, she pushed another cauldron of water onto the fire, and said brightly to Lizzie, 'I thought I'd scrub out the dairy. Can you tell me what all the equipment in there is for? I'd like to be able to make cream like all the farm wives do.'

'Need another cow or two for that, maid. And it's hard work – but you could sell butter and cream in the market – get you out, meeting folk. And bring in a few extra pennies. Ask Robert Verney about buying another cow – he knows all about that sort of thing.'

Bella had no answer. Everything, it seemed to her, came back to Robert. Even the business of buying another cow. Was she quite unable to manage without him?

Sarah shivered as the damp mist soaked through her clothes. Her shoes squelched when she floundered into a bog, not seeing it, and now despair took hold of her. Where could she go? Who would help? Ma, of course – weakly she longed to be back at home, with the fire and Ma's cooking waiting for her. Her own bedroom in the eaves, where she had lived all her life until this terrible time at Radley Manor. But, even cold, wet and miserable, she knew she couldn't run home to Ma and put it all on her loving shoulders, no matter how broad they were. It wouldn't be right. So, where could she go?

Mrs May's name flew into her mind. Mrs May who would help with her remedies and charms to get rid of the baby – to take her back into her old life, with no worries and no fears. But … Mrs May was a witch. Wasn't she? The question wouldn't go away, and as darkness folded into the thickening mist, slowing her steps even further, Sarah grudgingly knew that Mrs May was her only refuge. She floundered on, hoping she was on the right track to the Abworthy hamlet, her stomach empty and her whole body a-shiver, and hardly knowing what she was doing.

And then she started remembering old tales of her childhood. They had been light-hearted then, but now, here, in the loneliness of the wild moor, she found herself bringing life to them. The small folk, the pixies who led you astray. Could she be pixie-led and lost for ever? And then the whisht hounds, baying and howling over the wasteland along with their master, the Devil, in search of poor lost souls – like her.

She walked faster, trying to stop the images from overwhelming her. And then there was a sound behind her. Gasping, she turned and looked into the mist-spangled face of a snorting pony with a man leading it. Robert Verney! Too weak and startled to say anything, she just stood still and waited for what would happen next.

'Sarah? What're you doing out here?'

At the sound of his deep voice – no whisht hound, no Devil, but a human voice, a man and a strong one, who would probably tell her what a fool she was, but never mind, she felt tears bursting out with relief. Robert Verney! Of all people, he would know what to do. He would help her. She could only shake her head and let the tears flow. He put an arm around her, pulled her into the shelter of a nearby hawthorn tree and said, quietly and, she heard gratefully, without blame, 'Never mind, maid, just come along with me. I'll take you home and dry you out. You feel like a bit of washing waiting for the mangle.' She could only nod, allow him to help her onto the pony's warm back. Legs dangling, she felt relief surging through her as they headed for home. And then it was easy to tell him about Mr Henry. Her silly dreams. Being put off and not wanting to shame the family. And now, the nightmare, and being lost out here – but wanting to go to Mrs May, who would put everything right.

Robert made no reply to all these gasped, broken sentences, but when she got to the bit about Mrs May, he halted the pony, and looked up at her. 'What do you mean, Sarah? Not what I think, I hope.'

She saw an expression on his face that alarmed her. Her voice rose, then, hands gripping the pony's mane with a fiercer hold as she realized that he might refuse to take her to Mrs May. She knew him as a man of strong thoughts and actions.

But it wouldn't be him having the baby, would it? It would be her, young, foolish, unready for dealing with birth and new life.

She shouted. 'I gotta go to Mrs May. Here, let me down, I'll find me own way.'

His hand, rough, big, too strong for her to deny, found hers – it was warm and reassuring. 'Stop screaming, you silly maid. We'll think of something. But first I want to get you dried out, put some food in your belly. Then we'll talk it out. Now, come on, hold on, I'll get Justice trotting.'

They reached his cottage and she was bundled inside, to sit by the revived fire and shiver until he produced a huge shirt and told her to take off her wet things and put it on. 'I won't look, don't worry. I've got to get that damn kettle boiling if we want some tea.'

An hour later she was half asleep in the chair by the hearth, warm, dry and with a full belly, watching the fire with its glowing heart and wishing she could stay here for ever, when his deep voice roused her. 'Up you get, Sarah. Time to go. Can't have you spending the night here – imagine what they would all say. No, keep that old shirt, you're not going anywhere special. Not tonight, anyway.'

She got to her feet and looked into his dark eyes, saw the glow in them and realized that she trusted him. Whatever he suggested next, she knew it would be the right thing to do.

'Were're we going, then?'

He held the door open for her, and put an arm around her shoulder. 'I'm taking you along to Mrs May.'

CHAPTER 22

'Trouble, Mrs May,' Robert said shortly as he pushed Sarah through the cottage doorway. 'I'm going to leave her with you. She'll tell you about it and then you must do what you can.'

He gestured back towards the door, and after Mrs May had propelled Sarah into the cane chair by the fire, she went towards him. He pulled her into the doorway, saying, very low, 'She wants to get rid of it. Silly girl, someone must drive some sense into her. You'll do what you can, won't you?' Mrs May nodded, and Robert added, with a twist to his mouth, 'And not what she wants. Maybe Bella Reed'll take her in tomorrow. I'll go and tell Lizzie Wharton before I go home now. All right, Mrs May?'

'All right, boy. Leave her to me.' Mrs May looked at Sarah, shivering and frightened. Another poor maid with the same old trouble. She shut the door behind Robert and turned back to the hearth, meeting wide, anxious eyes.

'We'll have a hot drink, maid, then you can tell me, and don't worry, I won't tell no one. I'm a good one for keeping secrets. Now – let Jessie sit on your lap, and then we'll be cosy and pleasant, like, won't we?'

As the evening went on, something strange happened to Sarah. She calmed down, felt an inner warmth soothing her frightening thoughts, and listened to what Mrs May was saying. 'Everyone makes mistakes when they're young. No need for blame, just make sure you learn the lesson. And now, why not sit there for a bit before going upstairs to the little bed that's always ready? And listen to what I haves to say, maid.'

Perhaps it was something that Mrs May had slipped into the hot drink, or perhaps Jessie's smooth purring, Sarah could never be sure when she thought about it afterwards, but some sort of miracle took place: she felt the glow of warmth, comfort, and loving kindness, and that creaky old voice muttering strange words and producing even stranger thoughts.

So, no terrible remedies to get rid of the baby; not even, now, the need to do so. Instead a warm knowledge that her child would be safely born, be loved and live happily. Could it have been a charm that Mrs May murmured as she rocked in the chair on the other side of the fireplace, her old eyes fixed on the dead berries in her lap?

Sarah, half asleep and content, only heard a few words and couldn't make any sense of them.

In and out of breath
To and fro of blood
Safe deliverance, love and life

And a bowing of the grey head, the dead berries carefully put into the fire as if they were something special and the flickering flames, and Mrs May sitting there, smiling.

Then, drowsy, Sarah was helped up the narrow stairs and into the waiting bed. Free of problems, she slept. While downstairs again, Mrs May returned to her chair, sighed, and sat very still, dark eyes watching the patterns in the glowing fire. And there she saw something that took a very great and abiding weight off her stiffening old body – the knowledge that with Sarah's child would come the young man to whom she could offer her gift of power.

The days of life were running short, as William Reed had known, and as Mrs May also knew, and arrangements had to be made about important matters. Now she could rest easy when her passing came, for the great gift of the natural power that could be used helpfully by its owner would be safe in the hands of the newborn child. To be passed only between the sexes, it was a blessing that Sarah's child would be a boy and so could inherit it.

No purrs from Jessie, just the gentle movements of sleep, and Mrs May, too, slouched in her chair, lost in dreams of a better land where she had, so far, only tiptoed during odd, betranced times. But now she knew she would tread there more firmly when the time came.

Bella was up early, ready to open the door. There she met Lizzie Wharton and Sarah, saw at once from their faces that something had happened, invited them into the kitchen, and said, 'What is it? And can I do anything to help?'

Lizzie sat down heavily, told her the sad story, and looked at her daughter, standing by the far chair. 'Mrs May's saved the baby, she says. And Sarah's wanting to have it. We wondered—' She stopped short and Bella read the message in her anxious eyes.

Her thoughts circled. Sarah to help her with the work. A girl with a happier expression on her face; another child at Abworthy, the generations continuing. She caught her breath.

Uncle William passing, but a birth to come. Her smile grew radiant. 'Of course she can come here! You said only yesterday that it was a pity she wasn't around ... another pair of hands, you said.' Quickly she walked across the room to Sarah. 'Please come. I shall love having you – and the baby when it's born. We'll make a real home for us all. Sarah,' she looked into the girl's eyes and saw a new shy softness, 'perhaps we can be friends now.'

Sarah nodded, looked around the room, then moved towards the chest at the far end, by the scullery door. The scarf Bella had given her lay there, neatly folded, waiting, as Bella had so hoped, for it to be taken up again, enjoyed and used. Now Sarah unfolded and wrapped it around her shoulders. She smiled. 'I'll work hard as I can. Reckon I'll be happy here. And this is warm and lovely. I'll wrap the baby in it. Thank you, Cousin Bella.'

They met in the centre of the room, beside the table, hesitant, not knowing what to say next. But Bella knew that enough had been said, no more was needed. So she smiled at Lizzie, watching so keenly, and said, 'Time for a cup before we start work, then?' and at once the old kitchen settled back into its usual workplace.

Lizzie went home, her face creased in a brighter smile. 'Dan'll be pleased,' she said, as she left, pulling her coat close against the wind. 'Maybe it'll make him think of something else but his stomach. A grandchild – my soul!' and Bella watched her stomp off towards her own small cottage, at the far edge of the hamlet.

She went back into the kitchen, to see Sarah, already on her knees, cleaning the hearth stones. The girl looked up, hesitated, as if she needed to say something, but Bella spoke first. 'You've had a terrible time, Sarah, but now you must forget it, and enjoy living here.'

Sarah sat back on her heels, determination filling her face. 'It was Robert Verney, who helped,' she said. 'He found me when I was lost, took me back, then to Mrs May. I'll always be grateful to him.' She and Bella looked at each other for a long moment, and then she added, 'He was good to me. Didn't want me to get rid of it, said I must think again. I never knew he was so good – and kind. I'll always remember.'

Something inside Bella abruptly unknotted. It was like a

pain that had stopped hurting, even although the pain was so hidden and so continual that she had learned to ignore it, but Sarah's words had released it. No more pain. Instead she felt a quiet sort of joy as she told herself that of course Robert was good. He had always been kind to her, so why had she thought him any different? She watched Sarah again bending over the hearth, scrubbing the stones, and knew that she and Robert must meet soon, and talk. They needed to be together to discover all the secret things that people normally hid away. Secrets that only emerged as love grew. With the thought, so a new happiness grew. She returned to the table to start cooking the meal ready for Jack, thinking all the time that she had not understood Robert's rapid departure after that blissful embrace the other day. But of course there had been a reason for it. Next time they met she would discover that reason.

Rolling pin in hand, arms floured to the elbow, she decided that she must go and find him. But there was little time. He would be out with his cattle now. It was already Thursday; there was still work to do to make the house presentable, and this meal to prepare ready for Jack.

She had told Robert she would see him sometime next week. Could she wait that long time? Rolling out the piecrust she decided. At teatime she would call on him. He would be back from the fields then. Perhaps he would be glad to see her, and she could tell him how grateful she was for his help with Sarah.

She smiled as she brushed out the burned furze from the bread oven; she had seen Lizzie do this; then she tested its heat and pushed in the finished pie. Things were going to work out – she was sure of it.

Robert's cottage was empty when she reached it, knocking on the door and then wishing she hadn't come. She had been so certain he would be home by now. What to do next? She couldn't wait for him here; that would only raise gossip. Already she knew the neighbours must have seen her walking towards his cottage. Voices would be busy and minds even busier.

And then the sun, setting in a clear sky in the west, magnified its strength and reached the tor above the Abworthy farmhouse. The granite stones responded with a radiant beam of light that shone on the chimney of Robert's cottage, and also entered Bella's heart. She would climb up the tor and sit there for a few minutes, looking around at the vast landscape and allowing the beauty and mystery of the moor to fill her mind. She made her way up the narrow path and then stepped into the heather and furze, up, up, surprising the small herd of ponies as she came upon them, and then climbing even higher. Now the tor was in sight, her breath was faster and she was pleased she had come.

But she wasn't alone. A dark figure leant against the rocks, rising as she approached. 'Bella—' The deep voice, the surprise, the ... pleasure?

She stopped abruptly, not knowing what to say. He came to her side, keen eyes looking through the growing dusk. 'I didn't expect to see you here. Thought you'd be warm and busy at Abworthy.' The familiar note of amusement was there, helping her find an easy answer.

'That's where I've been all day, working, cleaning, turning out, cooking, getting ready for my visitor tomorrow. I needed a rest.'

He led her back to the rocks and found a flat one. 'Sit here. I have to talk to you.'

He was big, strong, he had a sense of humour that always came to the rescue when things got too difficult. Yes, they needed to talk. And then he would take her home before it got quite dark, and she would keep remembering this unexpected meeting. She looked at him, settling beside her. What would they talk about? Her cattle? Her pigs? The farm accounts? Their embrace, which had come to such a sad ending? Quietly, she said, 'Go on, then.'

Silently, for a moment, he just sat there, staring at the fiery, but paling sunset and then slowly, turning his head again and looking into her eyes. 'I came up here because I needed time to be alone and think. You don't know me, Bella. You think I'm just a rough farmer, back from the other side of the world, and trying to make a living from my meagre lands and awkward stock. You have no idea of what goes on in my head.'

Something shifted in her. A vague chill made her pull her coat closer. Mrs May had said he wanted something from her. 'Well?' she asked and heard her voice sharpen.

'I'm not all you think. I have good manners, I can be charming – so I'm told – or I can be rough and throw my weight about. Ask Joel James what he thinks of me and you'll be surprised what you'll hear. He sees me as the enemy farmer who allows his cattle to invade the holy Reed lands. But that's still not all.' He reached across and took Bella's hand in his.

Warm, strong, what she needed to feel. Bella allowed her taut shoulders to drop and looked for the fascinating gleam in his dark eyes which, until now, had been her undoing. But now she knew that there would be no kisses up here in the dimpsey of the dying day. Robert had things to tell her. Things to which she must listen, and upon which she must act. She felt something tighten inside her and knew intuitively that whatever he now told her would be very important. It might even affect her whole life to come. But she loved him. Of course, she had always loved him, but only now did it shout joyously through her mind. So, whatever happened, of course she must listen. And then decide what to do.

'Bella,' he said, slowly, and with a resonance in his voice that rolled through her, 'I love you. But that wasn't my plan.

Not at first. You see....'

She let the words continue but she wasn't listening. Now she knew the glorious truth, what could ever matter again?

CHAPTER 23

Robert had no words. She was looking at him with such radiance in her eyes – how could he tell her the truth, that he had planned to manipulate her into a marriage which would give him back the ancestry he craved? Slowly he took her hands, drew her nearer to him and discovered he was saying very low, very quietly, all that was in his heart. 'You're a wonderful girl, Bella Reed, and I don't want to spoil this minute when we're together and close. I can't believe you might love me as I love you. I have nothing to offer you, but – please tell me how you feel.'

Even when he left her, as he must, at least he would know her feelings; the memory of her love would be a sop to the wretched bitterness he knew he would feel once he had ended it all. Of course there was only one thing he could do to absolve his conscience. Now his guilt rode high and hard; he must leave her, leave Dartmoor and find a new life somewhere far away. He stared into her wide eyes and waited. What would she say?

'Of course I love you, Robert. Don't doubt it. Surely you must know?'

Her hand reached out, went around his neck, and her face tilted towards his. Her mouth was half open, her eyes closing.

But he knew what he must do. Carefully, pain wracking him, he released her hand, put a finger on her lips, and said,

'Thank you. I shall never forget what you've said. But you see, Bella, I'm not the right man for you. You need someone of your own kind and upbringing – not a rough farmer living a life with no comforts. The Reeds were always higher stock than the Verneys. You must marry a man who can offer you a better life, a more comfortable home than a neglected cottage. Do you understand me?'

Suddenly her face paled, peachy colour draining with every word he said. The radiance had gone from her eyes, and he felt tension mounting in her body as he held her hand. Silently, she looked at him with disbelief. And then, 'But if we married, we would live at Abworthy.' Her voice was pleading. 'And it's not going to stay neglected. I'm cleaning it, making it comfortable – when you come, Robert, you'll see the changes I've made already. And now Sarah is living with me – she'll help.'

He nodded. 'Yes, I know all that. It's us I'm thinking of, Bella, you and me. You at Abworthy with all its work; I feel I should help but my conscience won't let me stay. I've treated you wretchedly and so I have to make amends. I'm going to leave you in the hope that you'll find someone who's more worthy of you than I am. No – don't argue....' He thought for a moment. 'So tell me about Sarah?'

'Mrs May has persuaded her to have the baby. She's a Reed, and it's right that they should live at Abworthy. And Robert, I must thank you for what you did for her. She's a changed girl now.'

He drew in a great breath, felt the dampness of the air striking him, a salve to the pain that had struck him as he imagined being married to Bella and sharing the old house with her. But it could never be. Dropping her hand he stepped backwards. Turf beneath his feet, a granite edge cutting into his back, rain demanding a descent to cottage and house – and his life ending. But he was strong, he knew what had to be done. So, putting a smile on his face, he took her elbow and led her down the slope. Talk, talk. Don't let either of them feel the misery which he knew was stalking them.

He raised his voice cheerfully and said, 'So you have a visitor tomorrow. Good company for you.'

'No, it isn't.' She was sharp. He looked over his shoulder and saw her vivid face set in an expression of determination. Something forced him to ask, 'Why not? You don't seem very pleased to see whoever it is.'

She met his eyes. 'I'm not. It's Jack Courtney, Miss Carpenter's solicitor. He's coming to ... to—' Abruptly she stopped, and stared at him. 'Can you believe it? To take me back to Exeter, he says. It will be a horrible meeting.'

Robert saw the expression on her face change from that wonderful radiance to something filling him with a chill. 'So why are you allowing him to come?'

'Because I think he may need proof that I am truly a member of the Reed family – for, once he has that, he may well decide to leave me alone. But if he doesn't ... he will go on worrying me, on and on.' She stopped, words dying.

Robert saw her eyes begging him to understand, to help, and felt anger surge through him.

'He wants to marry me,' she whispered. 'But I shan't agree to it.'

'No,' he growled. 'Of course you won't.'

They stared at each other and now he knew that he must help her with this unpleasant meeting. It would be the last thing he could do here on Dartmoor, for, bitterly, he knew what his future held. His voice was firm, distress forced away. 'Shall I be with you tomorrow?'

'Yes!' Her smile, like a shaft of spring sunshine, beamed out and his heart warmed.

He nodded, managed a smile. 'I'll be there, and don't be afraid – we'll see Jack Courtney to the door. He won't worry you any more – and he certainly won't marry you ... I'll see to that.'

She nodded, kept the smile on her face, and held out her hand. 'Thank you. Sarah told me how good you were – and kind – but I always knew it.'

'Did you?' Hard to believe, and yet her words dulled the pain that filled him. Did it mean she would remember him, once he had gone? Yet that was the last thing he wanted – once he had left Dartmoor and England, Bella Reed must get on with her life and he prayed that it would be a happy one.

'Of course. You've always been kind, Robert. And now you're proving it – by being with me when Jack comes.'

'Very well. I'll drive to the station and meet the usual train – he's not likely to come earlier than that.' He smiled tightly. 'With Sarah and me beside you surely the visit won't be all that bad. And when everything's settled I'll drive him back to the station.' *And then I shall know the bastard has gone.*

The weather had worsened; heavy rain now came down in stinging shafts. He grabbed her hand. 'Come, we must run.' It was a jolting, breathtaking journey back to Abworthy. He left her at the door, having seen her entering the cross passage, looking back over her shoulder and smiling as she called, 'Thank you, Robert. I shall see you tomorrow, then.'

Robert returned to his own cottage where the fire had almost died. He sat in the shadows, not lighting a candle or poking up the crumbling peat, his mind too busy to care about his discomfort. Damp clothes began to dry on him and all he could think of was Bella being happy in the old stone house once he had gone.

She had good friends: Sarah, apparently now reformed, Mrs May forever on the watch, and good-hearted Lizzie Wharton. He wouldn't be missed. Yes, there would be the empty cottage and ungrazed lands, but maybe Sarah would marry a man who could take on all that. And in Australia, in that sunlit, adventurous land, he would soon settle again – wouldn't he? He forced his thoughts towards more positive horizons. Why, he might even find a willing mate. Here he smiled wryly, bending to remove wet boots, telling himself he only needed Bella. There would never be anyone else, and although at first he would be thinking only of the moor and the old stone house and its mistress, he knew that time would help resolve the painful problem. But forget her? Never.

Eventually he roused, changed his clothes, saw to the fire, thought about a meal and spent the evening smoking his pipe, drinking a mug of cider, and imagining just what might happen tomorrow, when that wretched Jack Courtney arrived.

He was at the station as the train drew in, waiting for the few passengers to alight: some local villagers, and then a well-dressed man wearing a tweed suit and carrying a rolled umbrella. As the man drew close to the trap he called out, 'Mr Courtney?' and was rewarded with a frown.

'Yes?' A sharp voice and unfriendly expression.

Robert felt enjoyment warming him. He knew what to expect from this Courtney. Politely he said, 'Miss Reed asked me to meet you. Robert Verney. Get in, will you?'

Obviously unused to riding on the bench seat of a slightly dilapidated trap, his passenger didn't look too pleased, but he sat there, beside Robert, umbrella clasped tightly between gloved hands, looking about him with that same frowning expression.

Robert drove back to Abworthy, mischievously allowing Justice to canter. The trap rattled and Courtney edged about in his seat, one hand gripping the side of the bench. 'Not very far now,' Robert said cheerily. 'Do you know the moor at all?'

'No.' The response came out between gritted teeth as several potholes made the rattling trap almost leave the road. 'Once a day trip to Widecombe when a child, but otherwise, no. My business is in the city. I have no time – or inclination – to come here.'

Robert slid his glance sideways and smiled wryly. 'But I'm sure you'll be glad to know that Miss Reed is settling in here very well. Developing quite a passion for the moor. Wants to get to know it better – I shall be teaching her to ride.'

'You?' The word was barked out and Jack Courtney's frown deepened.

'Me.' Robert reined in Justice now that the track was leading towards the hamlet. 'I farm nearby. We've become friends since her return here, which is why she asked me to meet you. And to bring you to Abworthy for the meeting you have requested.'

Jack Courtney gave a snort. 'I think you have misunderstood, Mr – Verney, was it? This is no meeting; I have come to collect Miss Reed and take her back to her home, in Exeter.'

Robert drove the trap into the yard, where the dog began barking, Steve stood, staring. Hens flew up around Justice's hoofs, and the huge black door of the farmhouse opened to reveal Bella, and Sarah, standing there. For a long moment a cold finger touched his heart. Bella's home – if only it could be his, as well. But Jack Courtney was fidgeting beside him, gingerly putting one trousered leg down onto the filthy surface of the yard, and Robert knew he must forget his wretchedness and fulfill his part in this unwanted encounter.

'Good morning, Jack. Robert. Please come in.'

Robert heard a new note in Bella's voice and saw from the expression on her face that she had prepared well for this meeting. She was dressed in a plain, dark red dress, a white apron covering most of it. Her hair was tied back and he saw the clear contours of her face; the high cheekbones, serene eyes with well-drawn brows matching the rich colour of her hair, and that generous mouth, now, he noticed, set in a firm line that belied how warmly she had offered it to him only yesterday. But there was something else about her today; following the visitor into the kitchen, Robert noticed a new strength in her straight back. And when she turned, indicating the settle to Jack, there was determination written all over her lovely face.

'Do sit down. Jack, will you have a cup of tea, or some cider? It's early for dinner, and we have some talking to do. Sarah, please get the mugs out.'

Robert preferred to keep his distance from the visitor, so leant against the panelling at the back of the room, watching, and enjoying this feeling of matriarchal dominance that Bella was showing. How she had changed, from the quiet, nervous girl in Exeter.

Jack's clipped voice cut into his thoughts. 'Nothing to drink, thank you. So this is the farmhouse you think you have inherited, is it, Bella? Not exactly beautiful. Or even comfortable.' He shifted on the hard wooden seat, and smiled sardonically at her as she sat down on the chair opposite him on the other side of the hearth. 'How thankful you will be to return to the comfort of Miss Carpenter's house in Exeter. I hope you're packed up and ready to accompany me later today?'

Robert watched Bella return his smile, and saw something on her face that pleased him. She was sure of herself. He knew then that Jack Courtney would be gone and out of mind before the afternoon was through.

'I'm not coming with you, Jack.' Her voice was calm but firm, and echoed faintly through the old room. He thought it had the tone of victory about it and then saw her glancing up at Sarah, bringing plates to the table, and looking down at her questioningly.

'Sarah, please show Mr Courtney what you found upstairs in Uncle William's room.'

All eyes focused on the girl, taking a piece of crumpled paper from her apron pocket, smoothing it out and then laying it on the table. There was a sudden tightening of the atmosphere and Robert knew more trouble was on the way.

CHAPTER 24

There was a taut silence in the room. Jack leaned forward, picked up the paper with an expression of distaste. 'What is this?' His frown grew.

Bella waited a few seconds and Robert watched her face registering great pleasure. Then she said, quietly, and without any sense of drama, 'It's a letter my mother wrote to Uncle William. It's crumpled and faded, so let me read it to you.'

She paused, smoothed out the wrinkled paper and, voice a little uneven, began.

> *My darling William,*
> *Just a note to tell you that our child, little Bella, is well and growing fast. If only I could bring her to see you. But I daren't run the risk of Ned finding out the truth. I just pray that one day you might be able somehow to meet her. I'll write again when I can.*
> *My love, as always,*
> *Your Marianne.*

The room was silent, the atmosphere oppressive. Bella put down the letter and said, in a steadier voice, 'Sarah found a heap of old family papers under his bed when she cleaned out the room this morning. This was among them.'

She stared at Jack. 'I think you must now accept that I am

William's daughter. And not, as I thought and as he told me, his niece.' She repeated, almost under her breath, 'His daughter. William was my father, not Ned. He loved my mother, cared for her, but I never knew.'

Sarah pulled out a stool and sat down, and Robert watched her pulling the scarf Bella had given her around her shoulders. Today even Sarah looked different, he thought; the sullen expression had gone and she was clearly interested in this family drama. No longer did she send him longing glances as she had done before she went to the Hamptons. Mrs May had worked one of her small miracles on the girl, and he was glad of it. She would be useful, living here at Abworthy, when he had gone, and Bella needed help with all the work and advice.

But then his thoughts were disrupted. Jack Courtney was on his feet, the letter snatched up and being waved about, an expression of rage spreading over his face. 'I don't believe it!' he shouted. 'The birth certificate I examined was proof of Edmund's marriage to Marianne.'

'But it concealed the truth, Jack – that I am *William's* child.'

Bella was in control of herself, remaining seated, watching Jack as he started to pace the floor. His voice rose. 'You can't possibly believe this; no decent woman would carry on an illicit affair like this.'

'Yes, she would – a woman who loved so deeply would do anything to keep that love going, even hiding her love child from her husband. I know now that William truly loved my mother, and was kind to her when my father became drunk on their wedding night. They must have shared their love that night but kept their meetings over the years secret from him because Ned was such an aggressive man and would have made terrible trouble if he knew the truth.' Bella sounded calm, but in her mind pictures and voices abounded. Uncle William – her true father – saying, *Marianne. And the little one....* with that smile on his old, pale face. It all made sense now and she was becoming aware of a new, inner joy spreading within her. Abworthy was, indeed, her home and she was here, safe and happy. But she must get rid of Jack.

She turned in her chair, watched him pacing up and down, then got up and went to his side. 'Jack, please understand that I am so thankful to have found out the truth, and, of course, I won't blame you any longer. I know you thought you were doing it all for my own good.'

He stared at her with furious eyes. 'For *our* good, Bella. Do you not remember that we had become good friends, indeed, more than just friends? Have you forgotten that I proposed to you? That I was preparing to take the huge financial step of buying a house for us? For you and me, Bella – you can't just ignore all that and pretend it never happened.'

Bella was silent. He was right, of course. She was treating him badly. But what else could she do? She had never loved him – not as she knew that she loved Robert. Not as her mother had loved William. And then, suddenly, she saw Robert leaning against the panelling at the back of the room and saw his expression. He was alert, ready for anything – he was watching her with those dark eyes wide and full of something which she knew to be an offer of the help she needed.

'Robert—' Just the one, pleading word, and he moved.

He strode across the room, coming between her and Jack Courtney, saying in a rapid undertone, 'Get away, Bella,' and then looking at Jack Courtney's flushed face and set mouth, 'You've said enough, Courtney. Miss Reed is within her rights to live here and to forget you if she wants to. I think we should leave now. No point in keeping on arguing. I'll take you to the station and you can wait for the next train.'

Bella felt the room vibrating as Jack's right arm lashed out and caught Robert on the chin. *Violence*, she thought, shocked. *Something that has happened here before, working itself out again. Ned and William, always at odds, Mrs May said. And then the gun out there in the yard, all those years ago....*

She moved fast, intent on separating the two men, but already Robert was hitting back. A blow landed on Jack's shoulder, pushing him off balance for a moment, but then he was steady again. His face was livid, and as he aimed blow after blow at Robert, words came out in furious grunts. 'And who the hell are you, eh? Her bit of rough, is that it? Do you imagine that she might fancy you? You, a dirty, unkempt rogue with no manners and no education! I'll teach you to look at my Bella.'

Appalled, Bella watched them struggling. She had no idea that Jack was so quick to anger – now his temper in his chambers that day when she went to claim her birth certificate came to mind, and she realized that she had never known him well enough. Reliable, kind and responsible, she had thought. But not this man with flailing arms and harsh voice throwing insults as he tried to floor Robert. She moved closer, only to feel Robert's arm pushing her away. 'Keep out of this, Bella,' he ordered, and she found herself being pulled away by Sarah.

'Leave them alone,' Sarah cried passionately. 'Don't never try and part fighting men. Let them sort it out themselves.'

Which they did. Jack suddenly slipped and fell to the floor, with Robert standing over him, breathing heavily, holding a hand to his nose, which spouted blood. He pulled Jack up and shoved him, half standing, against the closed cross passage door. 'Don't ever come here again, Courtney.' His voice was harsh, breathless 'If you do, you know what to expect ... and you can forget Miss Reed 'cos she isn't for you. She may not be for me, either, but at least I don't insult her as you did. Now, on your feet and we'll go.' He pushed open the door, held Jack's arm as he overbalanced and nearly fell on the cobbles of the cross passage.

Anxiously Bella followed them into the yard, and then Sarah came running, brandishing the rolled umbrella that Jack had put down when he arrived. 'We don't want his things left here, do we. Take these, Robert and put them on the train with him.'

Bella looked at her cousin, saw the smile on her face, and suddenly knew that it was all over. Reassurance and safety enveloped her. Jack Courtney would never trouble her again.

But Robert had a bloody nose. She ran up to him, offered her kerchief and said, as he wiped his face, 'Thank you. I didn't want you to fight, but ... but—'

'Sometimes fighting is the only way to resolve things. I'll come and see you once I've got this troublemaker out of the way.' He turned to Jack, who was mopping his brow as he leaned against the trap. 'Up you get – come on, I'm in a hurry.' His voice was curt, but the smile he sent Bella as the cob drew the trap across the cobbles and towards the track was warm and amused. Clearly, she thought, watching them drive away, Robert had done her a good turn, and he was pleased with himself. She would thank him properly when he came back.

She and Sarah returned to the kitchen, closed the door, looked at each other and then went and sat by the fire. Sarah fidgeted and cleared her throat. Bella looked at her inquiringly.

'Don't 'specs you know about thanking a wise woman, do you?'

'You mean Mrs May? No. Why?'

'Well, you don't give any money, 'cos that'd make her lose the gift. So it's eggs, or a loaf, or rabbit, or something small like that, just left on the doorstep.'

Bella understood. 'And that's what you want to do? Because she has helped you?'

Sarah nodded and picked at the fringe of her scarf. 'But I ain't got anything to give.'

Bella's mind widened. What had Steve said about ducks laying eggs in the reeds? It could be one of Sarah's jobs to collect them, and she could give a few in return for her healing. 'When we've finished today,' she said, smiling, 'get Steve to take you to the brook and collect some duck eggs. Then you could leave them on Mrs May's doorstep. I'll give them to you as part of your wages here, and then they would belong to you, and be a true gift from you to her.'

She watched Sarah's face lift, saw the smile that emphasized her prettiness and her new liveliness. 'Thank you. Yes, I'll do that.' Sarah got up, intent on the next job and then paused in the doorway. 'You're good to me, Cousin Bella. You and Robert. I'm glad that nasty old Jack's gone. Robert'll be back soon, won't he?' Her smile became a saucy grin. 'I'll stay upstairs 'cos I 'specs you've got things you two wants to say.'

Bella sat in silence, thinking. Yes, she had so much to say to Robert when he came back. She would invite him to share the mutton pie and then perhaps they would talk about the farm and the advice she needed from him, of her love for him, and his for her.

It was perhaps an hour later that Robert knocked on the door and then came into the kitchen. 'That's got rid of him,' he said, looking across at Bella, busy with a pan of vegetables.

'Were you badly hurt?' She was worried that the nosebleed was worse than they had thought.

'No. Nothing. But –' he paused, looked at her with penetrating eyes, and said quietly, '– I have worries, Bella. Things I must share with you.'

She stopped stirring. 'What things, Robert?'

His voice was tense; she waited for him to unburden himself, but he came to the table, looked at the cutlery and plates and then the familiar note of wry amusement returned. 'Three places laid – does that mean I'm to have Mr Courtney's piece of pie? I'm honoured.'

Reassured, Bella returned to her cooking. The pie smelled good, and it was time for the shared meal in this old room, which would, she felt, create another loving bond between

Robert and herself.

His voice made her look up. 'Why don't we ride out this afternoon? Your first lesson. It's time, you know. And already today I've neglected my stock – they'll have to do without me for a bit longer. I'll fetch Honey and that'll give you time to climb into all your finery.' He gave her his warm smile as if nothing awful had happened.

Bella's heart quickened. 'I was beginning to think we'd never do it,' she said, smiling back as she leaned down to open the bread oven.

With Robert sitting on the settle in Uncle William – Father's – place, Bella felt something wonderful happening deep within her. It felt as if they were already together, married, sharing a meal, talking about the farm, and bringing a new happiness to old Abworthy.

Later, the dishes washed, and Robert vanishing to go and tack up the mare, Bella went up to her bedroom and put on the riding skirt, bodice and hat, which had been waiting for this longed-for event. Then she went down, found Robert with the pony in the yard, looked askance at the side saddle he had found from somewhere and then allowed him to lift her onto Honey's back.

A new life, starting today, she told herself, and smiled as slowly, Robert, on Justice, led the mare out of the yard, down the track and then into a green lane leading to the expanse of moor that surrounded them. She had so much to be thankful for.

CHAPTER 25

She looked beautiful, Robert thought, as she sat on his mother's old side saddle, smart little hat securely fastened to her thick chestnut hair. And the riding habit, made of dark blue wool that, he noticed had clearly seen better days, but which suited her slim figure, presented an elegant silhouette on the gentle little mare. Her gloved hands held the reins quite naturally and he saw no fear in those smiling eyes. Bella would soon become an efficient horsewoman.

He led Honey down the lane leading away from the hamlet and into fields belonging to his family. He would combine this trip with a visit to see how his cattle were getting on, hopefully not pushing through the newtake walls still needing repair. Dan Wharton was still working for him, but was inclined to take time off, and too often was found sitting, bait or a bottle of ale at his side. Robert knew that Joel James was always on the watch for straying animals; indeed, he wondered if the man wasn't almost wanting them to wander, to fuel his bad temper and vicious tongue. Slowly leading the pony with its precious rider, watchful for potholes, he kept an eye open for Joel's possible presence out here.

But as the landscape opened up and he saw Bella relaxing on the pony and looking around her, he thought he should allow Dartmoor and its beauty to fill their eyes and their minds. Talking could come later, when he must tell her what he planned to do, and the reason for doing it. He dreaded telling her about the selfish future he had originally envisaged, and that now it was impossible to go ahead with that plan, but knew it must be done. But not today.

The cattle grazed peacefully, Dan Wharton was working on the broken wall and doffed his hat as they rode slowly past. Robert pointed out the immense bulk of Bowerman's Nose ahead of them. 'You can have a good look at the old man as we pass, before we climb up onto Hameldon. I expect Sarah will be able to tell you a few stories about the rock.' He smiled broadly. 'And on Hameldon you'll see some of the old barrows where ancient chieftains were buried. Are you comfortable, Bella?'

'Yes.' Her smile was radiant, her eyes met his with such obvious joy that he couldn't help but ask:

'And are you happy?'

'Of course I am. Here, with you, on the moor, knowing that the trouble with Jack is finished, and that Abworthy is my home. Of course I'm happy!' She looked at him for a long moment wondering whether she should demonstrate her joy, and then said quietly, 'And you, Robert? Are you happy, here, with me?' He was silent and her radiance dimmed. She shouldn't have shown her need, her longing. But he had said he loved her.... She watched how his face slid from easy, comfortable amiability into something darker and tighter as he gazed around at the scrubby moorland and the rising tors. Her body stiffened.

Then he looked at her, breathed deeply, and nodded. 'Being with you is all I want. But I have things to tell you which will alter our feelings for each other. Not now, though.' Smiling again, he drew nearer on Justice, until they were side by side. He reached out and touched her hand. 'Don't let's think about the future, let's just enjoy this moment of being together here, on the moor.' And before Bella could ask any of the questions raging inside her, the old note of amusement returned to his voice, as he added, 'Remember to ask Sarah to tell you the old folk tales. They'll give you something to think about on a dark night.'

She smiled. 'All right. I'd like to know more about the moor and its past.' But she felt a prickle of wonder. Old tales? And could they possibly be true? She shivered; Dartmoor was certainly a haunted place.

By now they were riding down a path towards the distant village, and Robert told her they would take the church path up the slope of Hameldon and that she would have an amazing view to look at. He was right. Reining in their ponies after the steep climb, she saw Dartmoor spread out beneath her. Distant tors, green valleys, small patches of woodland and everywhere those remote farmhouses with cattle in the home fields, and sheep grazing up the slopes of the enclosing hillsides. The wind blew sharply, the clouds drifted over the granite tors, changing shapes and colours, and she was glad of the wool of the riding habit. Robert helped her dismount and they walked around a big turf-covered barrow where he said a warrior chieftain of ages past was buried.

'So people have lived here on the moor for a long time?' She was experiencing something quite new – a sense of history, which she was part of. When Robert answered that prehistoric tribes had lived here, survived and left their dead along the hilltops, she thought of her father – William Reed – buried in the churchyard far below them, and knew that Abworthy's own history was continuing. But she had the sense not to say anything to Robert. She agreed with him about enjoying the moment, and put aside the knowledge that sometime soon he would tell her whatever it was that was plainly bothering him.

The wind buffeted them as they turned their back on the barrow and Robert, taking her in his arms to help her remount, held her for a moment, her body close to his, and his dark eyes so deep and dark with longing that it was all she could do to restrain her own need to pull his head down and kiss him. But instinct said the moment was wrong. In his own time Robert would tell her his problems and then they would truly be together.

On the way back to Abworthy, they headed for Robert's fields and were close to the boundary walls when they heard a gunshot. The ponies were spooked and Bella was almost thrown, but Robert's hand caught her before she fell.

'What on earth? Someone's shooting on my land....' His voice grated and he kneed Justice into a trot, saying over his shoulder, 'Stay there, Bella. I'll see what's happening.'

She remained mounted, thoughts running back into memory; Mrs May saying how Ned Reed had shot his brother William there in the yard at Abworthy. And now someone shooting on Verney land. A niggle of apprehension rose through her body and she stared in the direction that Robert had taken. She heard rough voices and knew she must go and join them. Honey carried her quietly over the scrubby turf, around a half-broken wall and then Bella drew rein, her breath quickening, hands tightening into fists as she watched the unpleasant scene being acted out before her.

Joel James held a gun and had several dead rabbits swinging from the belt of his coat. He looked up at Robert, still mounted, who stared down and said, voice harsh and angry, 'You're shooting on my land, James. What the hell do you think you're doing? Haven't you got enough rabbits on your own fields? You say that my beasts invade your lands, but here you are with your gun and your rabbits on mine. Explain yourself, man.'

Joel's face was tight and Bella felt her stomach knot at the sound of his raised voice. 'I was chasing the last one, thought I'd got it but then he raced off round the wall so I come over and got it with my last shot. No need for you to be so uppity,

Verney – no harm done.'

Robert said nothing and she watched as both men stared at each other, faces furious and unwilling to give way. Then Joel stepped back, fiddled with his belt and his hanging victims, got one free and threw it up at Robert. 'All right, take your bloody rabbit, and I'll keep mine. An' Verney, one of your wild beasts nearly horned me this morning, pushed me against the wall, and if I hadn't jumped clear would have got me. I'm telling you, wild they be, and dangerous. If you don't get those walls up proper soon I'll do something about it.'

Robert had laid the dead rabbit over Justice's neck and Bella tensed, feeling danger in the air. She called out, 'Robert, let's go home.' Was James's gun still loaded? She feared that uncontrolled anger might force him into using it again.

Abworthy yard, the two men, the smoking gun and the wounded arm ... it was all happening again in her mind. She raised her voice. 'Robert – let's go,' and without waiting for his response, turned Honey and rode towards the track leading back to the hamlet.

Robert caught her up, his face still grim, but when he spoke, it was the low, musical sound that she loved. 'Are you all right, Bella? There was no point in our staying any longer with that madman. And looks like you'll be cooking rabbit stew tonight!' She was thankful that the dangerous moment was over. But deep inside, intuition insisted that it could not be forgotten.

In the yard, Robert helped her dismount. Steve came running from the stable to take the pony and Sarah appeared at his side, making Bella wonder if a friendship had struck up between them. Robert led her into the house, and she found that being back in the ancient kitchen was salve on a raw wound. Abworthy, she sensed, was settling into happier ways. And yet she felt that something still hovered here. Something that still needed dealing with.

It came unexpectedly, knotting her stomach, halfway down

the stairs after changing out of the blue habit: what Robert had said to Jack, something she had chosen to forget because it was unbelievable and yet now was returning, searing her with disbelief.

You can forget Miss Reed 'cos she isn't for you.

Yes, yes, but it was the next sentence that Robert had flung at Jack that was now ruining her happiness. *She may not be for me, either....*

What had he meant? Was this the something he said he must tell her? Impossible. He loved her as she loved him – they had both declared it. Bella flew down the stairs and then stopped. Robert was walking down the cross passage, on his way into the yard. He turned, saw her, and smiled. 'I'll tell Steve to stable Honey and look after her and then I must take Justice home....' The words died as he looked into her desperate eyes. 'What's wrong, Bella?'

'You said I might not be for you, you didn't mean it, did you? Tell me.'

CHAPTER 26

Robert sought the right words. He should have told her long before this, before their love had grown, bringing them so close. Now it would hurt her, which was the last thing in the world he wanted, and inevitably, it must part them.

Pain seared but he pulled the threads of his strength tight. Say it. Get it done. Finish the matter for good; except that no good could come of it for either of them. He would try and make a life in Australia while Bella would grow old at Abworthy, learning how to housekeep and run a farm. Perhaps she would marry. And have a family....

He saw her watching him with dismay written all over her lovely face, and then words came out, just telling her as it was. 'When I knew you were the old man's heir I decided to marry you and so get back Abworthy and the lands, which I still thought of as Verney property. I didn't think of love or anything except what I considered to be my own cheated inheritance. I tried to be your friend, to make sure you would say yes when I proposed marriage. Love didn't come into it. Just the longing to get Abworthy for myself.' He watched her pale face tighten, lose its colour, saw those glorious eyes widen and fill with disbelief. He knew this was the worst thing he had ever done in his life and he hated himself with deep disgust.

'But you said you loved me.' Her voice was so soft he had to bend his head to hear it. She was looking up at him, her hands pressed to her breast, breathing faster with every word.

He couldn't drag his eyes away from the pain on her face. 'Yes,' he said roughly. 'I did. I do. But still I kept on with the plan of marrying you and becoming the owner of Abworthy. It was only as I got to know you, saw you dealing with your problems, being kind to Sarah, grateful to Lizzie and Mrs May, that I realized your lovely character was too much for me. I just – well – loved you, wanted you for my own; wanted to forget the dreadful plan about Abworthy. But I've been putting off telling you because I know how your love for me must inevitably turn to dislike, and you'd lose your trust in me, wouldn't want me around any more.'

He watched her, saw emotions moving across her face. He knew he had done all this and that she must think him a cheat, a rogue, someone even more hateful than Jack Courtney. God, he thought, why should he and Courtney have treated her so badly? A beautiful girl, both in looks and personality, with a new demanding life ahead of her, but having to endure all their dreadful plans and desires.

Brokenly, he said, 'All I can say is that I'm sorry, Bella. Of course I love you, but it's too late now that you know the sort of wretched man I am. I shall sell my stock, leave the cottage and go back to Australia. But you have so much to do here, and I'm leaving you alone.'

Her expression said she couldn't believe him. But she must. She must get over the lost love; she had Sarah and Lizzie and Mrs May. And Joel James might even curb his temper and help. Steve, the stable boy, could learn and be useful. 'I shall be going as soon as I can,' he said shortly. 'You don't want me hanging around any longer but I'll tell Joel and Steve what they've got to do to help you.'

He waited, breath held, for her to speak, but she was silent, just stared at him, and wretchedly he read her thoughts. She might not, at this moment, believe what he had told her, but she had the intelligence to know, eventually, that he was doing the right thing. And then her loss would break through. He waited for her to say something that would scourge him, emphasize how his actions, his roguery had hurt her ... and he would accept it, because it would be true.

And then, quietly, she said. 'But Robert, I love you. It doesn't matter what you did, what you thought, I understand all that. The other day you told me you love me and I believed you. And you know, don't you, how deeply I love you?'

He nodded, emotion tight in his chest, hands fisted, wanting only to take her in his arms, kiss away the misery and the bleak knowledge of his actions. But that would only make matters worse. He must go. Now. He tightened his mouth. 'I'll come and see you again before I leave. But one thing that's important – forget me. Pretend I was never here, never did such miserable things, never—' He stopped abruptly because she was smiling.

'Pretend we never kissed? Never loved each other?' She took in a long breath. 'Never wanted to love properly? Oh, Robert, you can't possibly ask that of me. But yes, come and see me when you've had time to think things over. When you'll realize that all I want is to be with you, and that Abworthy can still be yours – when we marry.'

He could stand no more. He looked long and lovingly at her through the raked shadows of the darkening cross passage, letting her image imprint itself on his memory, and then he turned and left. Out into the yard and the dimpsey, mounting Justice and riding back to his cottage, telling himself he had done the only good thing he could be proud of. But at what cost? Bella's unhappiness, and the feeling that his own life had come to a miserable and self-created end.

The cold, damp cottage held no comfort and he sank into the one chair in a state of anguish and self-hatred, which lasted until finally he plodded upstairs and fell into his bed. Sleep might help.

Bella returned to the kitchen, thankful for the fire and for Sarah's smiles and offer of tea. But her unhappiness was plain, and the girl said quietly, 'What's happened? Not fell off the pony, did you? Why, we all do that first time . . .' and then stopped suddenly. 'Something about Robert? Oh, men's always trouble – but he'll be back again, don't you worry.'

Bella sighed, accepted a mug of tea, and then thought back over all that had happened that afternoon. She couldn't talk about it – not right to burden Sarah with her own problems. But she would never forget today. The revelation of her birth, the trouble with Jack and now Robert saying things that threatened to break her heart. But, bravely, she managed to pass the next half hour making plans for tomorrow and the rest of the life that stretched ahead of her. Abworthy was her home and she must cherish it, even alone and unloved, without Robert.

But sleep, even restless and dream-filled, helped ease her unhappy thoughts by the time she awoke next morning. The day held a sense of freshness and perhaps even hope. She got up at once, needing to go out and climb the tor behind the house where surely the old moor would work its ancient magic on her sadness. For there were other things in life than a broken heart.

She climbed with surprising energy, and had been right – the view from the granite rocks, already touched with gleaming golden light, persuaded her to sit down and look around. A small herd of ponies came around the corner of the tor, halting when they saw her, but then grazed peacefully. She remembered yesterday, being on Honey's back, and knew that she would be riding often in future. Even when Robert had gone, his careful teaching would stay in her mind, a loving gift she would hold to herself for ever.

Sunlight grew and the view became even more beautiful. Dartmoor might be haunted by past violence and disasters, as history told her, but still it was inspiring. She looked down at the Abworthy fields, and then into the far reaches of moorland, and felt a sense of eternity enclosing her. Slowly she accepted that, living here in all weathers, waiting, as now, for the blue of wide skies to break through mountainous grey and white clouds to drift across the land, was a blessing, to be grateful for and enjoyed.

She was mistress of her estate, just as William Reed, her father, had longed for her to be. It was a calling she valued and she began to think of everything awaiting her. Scanty crops, according to the year's weather; cattle pastured on the moor in the summer; time spent preparing peat for fuel; the care of the house and the overall necessary landlord's watchfulness of the estate cottages scattered around Abworthy. Hard labour.

But with the growing sunlight her mind expanded. Now she knew what owning an estate meant, and it brought a pride with it that warmed her. And yet ... she would be alone. No Robert to love and share her life with. The warmth of the sun slowly diminished as her thoughts spread ahead of her, suggesting that, hard as it was, there was a choice to make and only she could make it. Her mind flared with imagination.

A final choice....

Her breathing slowed. She watched the ponies ramble off, heard the farm dog barking and slowly made her way down the hill, seeing a pony trap driving ahead of her, leaving the track and then trotting down the road to Bovey. Robert, she thought, dismayed; no doubt going to make arrangements about selling his cattle. Her mind darkened. So he really was leaving.

She hurried back into the stone house – so much to be done to keep things going, both here and on the farm – but as she worked on her resolve grew stronger; when Robert came again to Abworthy, she knew exactly what she had to say to him.

*

Late afternoon and a knock at the door brought Mrs May into the kitchen. Lizzie, who had called around, sat by the fire knitting something white and small and she and Sarah chatted as they worked. They looked up, struck by the expression on the old woman's face.

'Whatever—?' began Lizzie, but Mrs May broke in before she could finish.

'Joel James,' she said. 'One of Verney's beasts stuck him in the shoulder, got him against the wall, so he said. He come to me 'cos it's bleeding fast. I sat him down and said the charm, gave him a drink, waited 'til it stopped a bit, and now he's gone home. But he's proper angry. And I come to say watch out, Bella, 'cos when Joel's angry there's trouble.' She nodded, and then accepted Lizzie's gesture to join her on the settle.

Bella looked at the two women, dismayed by the anxiety on their faces. Sarah, scraping vegetables at the sink in the scullery, said, 'Even Mrs James can't stop him when he's angry. I'll find Steve, tell him to look out for trouble.' Drying her hands, she went out into the yard.

Lizzie looked at Bella. 'Men,' she said grimly. 'No stopping them. Well, Cousin Bella, we'll all watch out for you.' She paused. 'All right on your own, are you?'

Bella pushed away her anxiety. 'Sarah's here,' she said, then, managing a stiff smile, 'And Robert's only a short distance away.'

Lizzie nodded, and then exchanged a quick, secret glance with Mrs May, who clumsily got to her feet, crossed the kitchen to Bella's side and said, almost beneath her breath, 'Take care, lover. Cards showing things going badly for that black knave, for Robert. But keep your sweet mind on what's good and right, an' mebbe it won't happen.'

Bella caught her breath. 'What might not happen?'

'Can't tell. Just got to wait and see. But I'll be round in case.'

'In case of what? Mrs May, tell me, please.' Bella's heart was racing, but there was no answer as the old woman shook her head, opened the door and then disappeared.

Bella looked back at Lizzie who packed away her knitting, and also headed for the door. 'I'll go find Sarah, and may be have a word with Mrs James.' Seeing the expression on Bella's face, she smiled and added, as she left, 'Let's hope that wise old woman's a bit too wise for once, eh? No, nothing's going to happen – cheer up maid. I'll go and see what I can do with they Jameses. Goodnight for now.'

Alone in the kitchen, stirring the pot on the range, then going into the scullery to find the unfinished vegetables, Bella was thankful she had plenty to do. She told herself firmly that Mrs May, for all her wisdom, was also a real old wife, full of tales and some of them were sure to be nonsense.

Going into the yard to call Sarah, she saw the girl talking to Steve, standing by the stable door. They were smiling together and she felt a happy sense of something going right for a change; was it possible that Sarah, already showing signs of her pregnancy, had found a man who would undertake the serious role of husband and step-father?

Her smile was hopeful as she walked across to them. Sarah, Steve and the baby sharing Abworthy? But then the enormous decision she had made earlier that morning rushed through her mind, and her smile faded. She knew that she had a choice, but, perhaps, like Mrs May had just said, one could only wait and see what life brought with it.

CHAPTER 27

Something was wrong. Dog barking in the yard. Justice whickering in the shed. A smell. Robert leaped out of bed, grabbing trousers, coat and pushing feet into boots. Down the stairs he ran with uneasy knowledge gnawing inside him.

FIRE....

In the yard he stared at the thatched roof, glowing and smoking with pockets of flames thrusting up into the night sky. He unchained the howling Nip, took a panic-stricken Justice from the shed and led him into the safety of the orchard at the end of the yard. Grabbing a bucket, he raced back to the well, filled it and then returned to the cottage. Pausing on the door-step, ready to fling the first slosh of water into the smoke, he caught his breath, remembering. The gift that he was giving Bella as a parting present was inside, beside the chair. He had been admiring it before he went to bed, wondering sombrely if it would make her remember him after he had gone. It mustn't go up in the flames; it was all he could give her. He must rescue it.

Grabbing the kerchief from his pocket, dipping it into the water then tying it around his nose and mouth, he shoul-dered his way inside, throwing the water ahead of him as he went. The fire reached for the beams but he forced himself on through smoke and flames.

Hold your breath. Think of Bella, how you love her ... that nothing else matters.

Mrs May was in the yard; she had been uneasy all the evening seeing disaster in the fresh spread of cards, and was now alert to the danger threatening the entire hamlet with its many thatched roofs. She took one look at Robert's smoking cottage and ran – something she didn't know she could do these days – to Abworthy, where she pounded on the big door and shouted for Bella to come down. Standing, waiting, looking towards the well and wondering where buckets were kept, she berated herself. She'd had this feeling, she'd known, hadn't she? It had been clearly imprinted on Joel James's livid face that he had something terrible in mind. And so this was his revenge on the wound caused by Verney's rampaging beast.

She hobbled across the yard to the stables, where the mare and the cob were thundering about and snorting with fear as they smelled the fire; she shouted for Steve. Then off again, away from the stone house, out of the yard, up the track towards the Wharton cottage. 'Lizzie, Dan! Fire, fire!' Her voice was shaky, losing its strength now, but she blundered back into the yard, found a half-dressed Steve piling buckets around the well, and took her turn in filling each one and then traipsing with it back to the burning cottage.

Bella looked out of her bedroom window, gasped, then, shouting for Sarah, threw clothes on and ran down the stairs into the yard, joining the group busily bucketing water from the well. She joined the chain of fire fighters, moving from the well to the cottage, back again, and then, more buckets, once more rushing to throw water onto crackling flames that seemed to reach out ever higher.

It took a minute or two for her mind to settle, before fully understanding that everybody from Abworthy was here; Mrs May, Dan Wharton and Lizzie, Sarah and Steve, no sign of Joel James and – suddenly her stomach jolted. No Robert. Racing down to the head of the group of bucket carriers, she clawed at

Mrs May's arm. 'Where's Robert? It's his cottage that's on fire, isn't it? Where is he? Have you seen him?'

Dan Wharton, turning with an empty bucket hanging from his right hand, said baldly, 'He's inside. Saw him go in. We gotta get him out.'

Bella struggled with chilling fear. She trembled but denied the weakness, forcing herself to be sensible and to help. He was in there. In that flaming pit of death – her Robert. She must find him, save him. She ran forward, pushing back Mrs May, who tried to stop her, finding her breath taken short as smoky fumes came out of the doorway. 'Robert,' she shouted, 'Robert – where are you?'

Arms wrenched her back away from the flames, and then she saw him, a crouched figure almost crawling out of the burning doorway. He held something in one hand and he fell as he came into the yard. On her knees beside him, half turning, she shouted for the help that immediately came to her. 'Mrs May, do something, help him.'

Long before dawn lightened the sky, they all sat, exhausted, in Abworthy kitchen, faces sombre in the shadowy candle light, hands wrinkled with scorched flesh, looking at Bella on the settle, with Robert beside her.

Slowly and painfully they had got him here, feet dragging, blistered hands loose at his side, and had sat him on the old settle, a bolster from upstairs cushioning his head and back, feet raised onto a stool so that Mrs May could use her remedies on burned fingers and arms. Robert had said little, but they had all seen the way he looked at Bella, dark eyes deeply set among seared flesh, yet alive with a light that overwhelmed all the horror and terror of the night.

And Bella, beside him, holding his hands, rubbing one of Mrs May's herbal salves into them, had the same look in her eyes. They smiled at each other, and Dan Wharton was moved to say slowly, 'You were lucky, Robert, so lucky ... and thank goodness for it, I say.'

Very carefully, Robert turned his head and looked at them all. He nodded, face registering pain, but said, with a determined ring in his voice that cheered them, 'No, Dan, thank goodness for all of you, for saving me. I'll always be grateful.'

The atmosphere in the room lightened slightly, enough for Lizzie to get up, helping Sarah to pour tea, and handing out the filled mugs, before saying, 'How did it start, Robert? Do you know? A spark, p'raps? But the misty days lately have kept the thatch wet....'

Robert shifted his position, and looked at Bella, so close beside him, now holding the mug of tea Lizzie offered. She lifted it to his mouth and he sipped, smiled at her, before looking back at Lizzie. 'No, I doused a fire – not a spark. I don't know how.'

Mrs May looked up and met his eyes. 'It was that Joel James. Getting his revenge, 'cos one of your beasts horned him early in the day. He came to me for help, and then I saw in his face he was going do something.' She stopped, shook her head. 'But I never thought it would be this. Threw a burning rag, did he? Or just a slab of red-hot peat.'

Suddenly Steve got to his feet. 'Never did anything 'bout Mr James not being there, did we? I'll go and see if he's about.'

Bella watched Sarah go with him to the door and disappear. Into her mind flashed a picture of the girl and Steve together and she knew a moment's gladness, but then she was back beside Robert and the old haunting problem returned. Would he really leave? Especially now that his cottage was ruined and he had no home, he would have to go somewhere. But he must recover first. Perhaps in the days to come she could talk to him, tell him her new thoughts. But for now, all that mattered was that he was alive, that his burns were superficial and would react quickly to Mrs May's remedies. And that he was looking at her with that gleam in his eyes that spoke without words.

Lizzie broke into her thoughts. 'If you're able to walk, Robert, me an' Dan'll help you back home to our place. There's a bed where Sarah used to sleep – you're welcome to that 'til you know what to do next.'

Robert nodded his head. 'Kind of you, Lizzie, yes, I'd like to do that. You're right, I don't know what to do next. With the cottage gone....' His eyes met Bella's, then looked away again and she knew what was on his mind: leaving Dartmoor, returning to Australia and a new life. But not yet, she prayed silently. *Don't leave yet, my love. I must talk to you.*

Steve and Sarah returned, saying that the James cottage was empty. 'And the old handcart's gone, too,' Steve said. 'Reckon they loaded their bits and pieces and got out before we could get there.' He stopped, looked around the room. 'I'd like to get him,' he added forcefully. 'Wicked, what he did. But he and Mr Verney were always at odds; we're better off without him now.'

A silence in the room, heads nodding and then the slow decision made to move and go home. Lizzie came to Robert and looked at him with questioning eyes. He nodded and then began the painful business of standing up. Bella stood in the doorway of the stone house with the lantern in her hand, watching the small procession moving across the yard. They walked slowly and carefully, Lizzie and Dan with Robert between them, his charred hands loose and the weight of his arms and body taken by their stout shoulders.

Robert had said just one word, as he tried to hide his pain and discomfort before starting the slow journey. His voice low and deep but full of meaning; it was enough.

'Tomorrow.'

Bella nodded, smiled and watched until the threesome, with Steve following in case he was needed, disappeared out of the yard, and knew that Robert was in good, loving hands. She could only wait, and give thanks for his survival.

As she closed the big door, she saw a new day dawning, the eastern sky already illuminated with a pearly glow, which helped her go up to her bed and, exhausted, both physically and emotionally, sleep deeply until cock crow.

She awoke jerkily, with the night's terrors instantly darkening her mind. But she was strong; she must think positively. Robert was alive. He would be coming to see her today and until then she had work to do. Joel James was gone, so no one to milk the cow. Would Sarah know how to do it and teach her? Also, pigs and hens to feed, sheep and cattle to manage and thank goodness for Steve, who would deal with the horses. And then the house, the cleaning, the washing, the meals ... could she possibly do all this? Alone, and without the help Robert had promised her?

But she dressed with determination growing inside her. She was a farmer, so had no time for lazing about, or even wondering if she could do all that was needed. Of course she could. But she would have to find another farm manager, arrange something about the empty cottage, help Robert deal with the loss of his home.

Out in the passage, she called for Sarah. 'Come down quickly, we have a lot to do and no one to help us.' Then she ran down the stairs and started the routine business of building a new fire on the still warm ashes of last night so that, at least, a boiled kettle would give them both a strengthening cup of tea.

And the kitchen, she thought as she bent to the hearth with newspaper and furze and sticks, had a new feel to it. Gone was the gloom she had always felt pressing down on her. Gone, too, was the sense of people of the past watching and criticizing, waiting for the next thing to happen. And even if they still watched, she sensed that it was with hope instead of sadness and blame.

She fetched milk from the dairy, listened to the cheerful

crackle of the new fire, and pushed the kettle closer to the leaping flames, thinking hard as she did so. For now she knew without doubt that this new life was making her into a true moorland farmer and the years ahead of hard labour, even probably on her own, still held a cheering hope of satisfaction and contentment. A steely feeling of new purpose spread through her.

How right Father had been to bring her back to Abworthy. How pleased he would be – must be? She looked at the empty settle and had a glimpse of him sitting there when she had first arrived – to know that all was well with his daughter. His 'little one' as he had called her. He and Marianne, loving and yet never finding what they longed for. But their love had lasted and, she felt instinctively, was still surrounding her. Of course she would bring new life and prosperity to Abworthy. And yet, without Robert....

Bella paused, as if in a dream, thinking about the past, wondering about the future, until Sarah came clumping down the stairs, saying, 'Daisy's lowing. Who's going to milk her?' And then the day spread ahead, perhaps dark in places, but with a faint light shining through it. For, above all else, Robert was alive, and who knew what the future might bring, after all?

CHAPTER 28

Robert was up at first light, never mind Lizzie saying he must rest. Dan mumbled that he would be out there with the cattle, so there was no need to worry.

With an enormous effort somehow he got into his coat and breeches – boots also presenting great difficulty – but even with charred fingers and swollen wrists he managed. Then down and outside, the cold early morning air clearing his head, bringing a sting of rebuke; don't be sorry for yourself, just be thankful you're alive.

Out in the yard behind the cottage he found an ash staff and with its help began the short walk through the hamlet, back to his own home. He heard life stirring as he slowly and painfully went down the track; the farm dogs barking, cows lowing, pigs snorting and noisy cockerels shouting to their cackling wives from each dung heap.

As he walked the short distance, he understood something new about his life. He had been saved from a terrible death and now he had to get on and start again. Not easy. Nearing the stone house, he thought of Bella, seeing her pale face in the candle-lit kitchen last night, hearing her voice, longing to have her in his arms, his lips on hers. But that was just a dream now, rapidly fading. Surely she could never love him again, knowing the shameful truth about his false courtship of her and the cruel plan that he'd devised Now he was even more aware of the need to leave Dartmoor.

He trudged on, passing Mrs May's cottage and smiling as he recalled her incantations and remedies and, indeed, said a few silent words of thanks for her undoubted wisdom and help. He passed the James's cottage, deserted, without curtains, even, at the staring windows. He wondered how Joel James must feel, remembering what he had done. Thoughts moved on; no one to help Bella with the farm work. How would she manage, alone? Remembering his offer of help his shame grew and his footsteps lengthened.

And then, there was the stone house itself, grey and gaunt in the shadowy morning light, no signs of life behind the shuttered window and the firmly shut black door. Fly, the yard dog, barked as he passed and he heard the ponies whickering in the stables. There was Honey, who would give Bella safe and enjoyable rides during the years to come, but no Bella. Pulling together his wretchedness, he walked on, not looking back, not allowing himself to think of the temptation to give in and return to Abworthy.

He reached the wreck of his cottage, now just charred thatch, broken chimney stones and fallen cob and plaster. No longer his home. A sense of loneliness swept through him, but then Nip ran out from wherever he had been hiding, giving yelps of joy at finding his master again. Robert stroked the dog and gritted his teeth. No good remembering.

His few personal things in the cottage had been destroyed and he would need to renew them. But the one thing that really mattered – the gift for Bella, which he had risked his life to save last night, where was that? He stood still, looking carefully about him, poking at the debris, thinking dismally that it must have been caught by the ashes and bits of burning beam. And then – there it was, the costly riding whip he had bought for her. He felt a surge of new hope. Painfully he bent, picked it up with sore hands, eyes searching every inch of it, enjoying the smoothness of its length, the still-shining silver top. Anxiously he looked for irreparable damage, but amazingly it had survived the flames. He smiled, with a new strength of purpose running through him; he would give it to Bella, with his love, and his last goodbye.

Bella was up and outside long before the sun rose. With so much to do, the kettle was left to boil for Sarah to make the tea. First, she knew she had to be in the yard looking about her, planning her jobs for the day. And then, dim in the hazy early morning light, she saw, in the near distance, a figure walking slowly and unevenly as if each step was a great and painful decision to make.

Robert. Impulsively she longed to call his name, run down to him, bring him inside, out of the cold and the shadows, for tea and the talk that she yearned for. But sense said, wait. Robert was his own man. He must make his own decisions. He had said he would come today – and she knew he would. When he was ready. So until then she must get on with her own life. The busy life that she had accepted and which now awaited her with all its hardship and problems – ah, the problems; but, if she could be strong enough to tell him, there was a choice to be made.

Resolutely she turned her back on the slow-walking figure and went into the granary to find corn for the hens, scraps and cake for the pigs and then into the cowshed, where a thin cat waited for the empty bowl to be filled, and the house cow mooed reprovingly, as if milking time had long gone. Bella breathed deeply. Abworthy at the beginning of a new day, and she had to manage it all. Alone.

Robert walked slowly back to Abworthy. The door was open; leaving the staff in the porch, he knocked before entering. The cross passage was cold and shadowy as usual, but the kitchen a different place all together. Cleanliness. The floor swept, furniture shining, beams free of cobwebs and windows allowing the rising sun to filter through the panes. He felt something new, too, for now there was a friendly warmth in the old room. Remembering the antipathy between himself and old man Reed, he was thankful that the atmosphere had lightened.

For a moment he stood still, before walking across to the table and laying the riding whip down on it. He glanced around; the settle was empty now, but he recalled William Reed sitting there, gasping, coughing, and yet so clearly the master of his estate. Sucking in a deep breath, his thoughts turned from the past to the future, and then back to the present. He must find Bella, give her what advice he could about replacing Joel James, and then make his farewell.

He left the house and was at once stopped by Steve, coming out of the stable. 'Your cob, Mr Verney, where is he? Bring him in, shall I? There's a free stall here.'

Guiltily, Robert knew he had forgotten poor Justice. 'Thank you, that would be very helpful. And he could do with a feed.'

The young face looking at him, brightened and smiled, and it seemed to Robert that Steve had grown older since last night. Perhaps the challenge of fighting the fire had matured him. Would it be possible that Bella could mould the boy into a useful farm manager?

And then, as Steve walked away, Robert heard peals of laughter coming from the cowshed. Telling Nip to stay, he went towards the happy sounds and then paused in the doorway, relishing what he saw and heard.

Bella was sitting on the milking stool, a huge apron tied around her, covered head pressed against the cow's flank. Sarah positioned the bucket while Bella's small fingers strove to produce milk from Daisy's teats. They were laughing, and their mirth sent a feeling of relief through him.

He stood there for a moment, unseen, until Bella turned, saw him, moved too fast and kicked out the bucket with its small offering of milk. Sarah gasped, bent to retrieve what she could and Bella got to her feet and came to him, looking at him with wondering eyes, but saying nothing.

'I reckon you need a few lessons before you get the knack, Miss Reed. Let me finish the job and you can watch and learn.' He brushed past her very carefully, their shoulders touching as she turned.

'But your hands—' Her voice was too high, the words too rapid and he knew instantly all she was feeling. Her love for him was still there and he felt his heart respond, a rush of emotion that struck at his resolve to leave her. He sat on the stool, spoke softly to Daisy, let his shoulder sink into her warm flank and started milking. And then, slowly, as the milk spurted out, filling the bucket, he said, 'My hands are better already for being used. Are you watching me, Bella? See how my fingers work? It's easy.' He glanced back at her, met her eyes, and saw from her rich smile that despite the disturbances of living and loving, she still thought of him with a lasting and enduring love. He returned to the milking, reminding himself grimly of the parting that was to come, and said, in a low, rougher voice, 'How about some breakfast? You and Sarah go back and I'll come when I've finished.'

'Yes. I'll go and get it ready.' She turned away, but gave him a last radiant smile, and he felt a warm strike of hope spreading slowly through him. Sarah bent down to him. 'You were so lucky, Robert. And Cousin Bella's been so worried 'bout you this morning. We're both glad you're here.' She nodded, gave him a grin and left the cowshed. He heard her calling Steve as she ran down the yard, and wondered again if, perhaps, the empty James cottage might not provide a new home for the young couple, should marriage be their plan.

With the bucket filled and the cat purring as it sipped at the usual dish of milk, he walked back into the house. He stood at the open door, saw Bella standing at the fire, tending a sizzling pan; saw plates and knives on the table beside the riding whip. As Bella carried the milk into the dairy, he glanced back at her. She must be wondering what on earth....

Back in the kitchen he sank heavily onto the settle, thankful to ease his pain. Bella pushed the pan to one side, looked intently at him, then came to sit beside him. She carefully reached for his hand, looking into his eyes as she did so. 'Robert, I have something important to say to you.'

He didn't want to talk about anything. Simply needed to say he was going to Australia and then – *Goodbye*. But his gift must still be given. He reached out, and offered it to her. 'Bella, this comes with my love and regret about all that has happened between us.' He cleared his throat, said more firmly, 'But one good thing is that I have taught you to ride, and soon you will be a good horsewoman. This little whip is to reward you – it's also my way of saying goodbye.'

She caressed the whip with both hands, stroking the silver top and he saw the gleam of tears in her eyes, but then she looked up, straightened her back against the settle, and said, 'Thank you. I shall always prize it, love it.' A pause. And then, 'But now you must let me say something important.'

'Well?' His voice was gruff, his body tense, wanting simply to go. He fidgeted on the settle; sitting so close to her was torture. He stood up and she stood beside him. 'Well?' he said again, more harshly.

She caught her breath. This was the moment of decision; could she truly offer to give up all that Abworthy had brought into her life? Was her love for him strong enough?

She looked at him; his weather-beaten face with hard, reddened skin from last night's flames; an unshaven dark stubble emphasizing the strong, square jaw and the deepest, hooded eyes – blue, such a deep sea blue – staring at her in wonder and expectation.

Could she do this? Did she love him enough?

Yes.

With that one word came a strange feeling; an intuition that the old kitchen was thankful for their love. All the past years of lovelessness, of lack of hope, of brooding hatred and the threat of violence, now gone. Instead, a new warmth and a new purpose. Her strength grew, even though her voice was unsteady.

'I can't let you go. If you won't come here to be with me, then I shall go with you to Australia. But please –' she had half turned, was looking into his eyes, her face soft and pleading and he thought, beautiful as never before, '– please, my love, don't force me to chose.'

Choose?

The truth was shattering, hitting him hard. She loved him in spite of everything. She was offering to give up her family, her land, her inheritance and be with him. As this amazing fact overcame his doubts and his guilt, relief surged through him.

'No choice,' he said simply, and opened his arms.

She flew into them, a bird to the nest, and they kissed.

And kissed. And kissed....

They rode out that afternoon, Bella in her blue habit, silver-topped whip proudly held in her right hand. Robert, at ease on Justice's back, held the reins carefully and thanked fate for something he could still hardly believe.

The typical moorland day was all around them. A keen easterly wind pulled at manes and skirt, billowing among trees, scrub and bending grasses. Above, grey clouds moved as in a race, with here and there sudden shafts of vivid light breaking through them and lighting up the wide landscape. Looking about, Bella saw tors, valleys, plains of desolate waste, glimpses of shining water telling of rivers and bots, and all around them the haunting mystery of ancient lives spent here long ago; and, she felt gladly and with great hope, the destiny of people still here, trying to make a living in this hard place.

Turning back, they rode towards Abworthy. Entering the yard, they saw it illuminated in a sudden gleam of sunlight, falling from the radiant tor above, shafting down through the racing clouds like a blessing, bringing the promise of new life.

Bella reined in and looked at Robert beside her. 'Home,' she said softly. Returning her smile, he nodded, reached out and took her free hand. 'Home,' he echoed, and together they rode on towards the stone house.

The cards of fate had fallen happily, after all.